— The Tombstone Epitaph

BA...

W9-CGV-202

"Was it you who followed me?"

"It was," Mad Dog admitted.

"Why?"

"I was out for some fresh air."

Boyd started to move closer but caught himself. "They have nothin' to do with any of this. You should leave Sam Wilson be."

Mad Dog smiled. "Oh, it's him you're worried about, is it? Not that gal I saw you with in the parlor?"

Boyd swore he could feel the blood draining from his face. "What about her?"

"Like that gal, do you? I'd be worried as hell if I were you," Mad Dog said. "Two of us are dead and we don't take kindly to that."

"What does Calloway have in mind?"

"It's not just him," Mad Dog said. "It's all of us. We aim to show the whole territory what happens when they stand up to us."

"Show them how?" Boyd persisted.

"By goin' on a killin' spree," Mad Dog said, and grinned.

Ralph Compton

THE LAW AND THE LAWLESS

A Ralph Compton Novel
by David Robbins

A SIGNET BOOK

SIGNET
Published by New American Library,
an imprint of Penguin Random House LLC
375 Hudson Street, New York, New York 10014

This book is an original publication of New American Library.

First Printing, August 2015

For more information about Penguin Random House, visit penguinrandom house.com.

ISBN 978-0-451-47318-9

Printed in the United States of America
10 9 8 7 6 5 4 3 2 1

Penguin
Random
House

THE IMMORTAL COWBOY

This is respectfully dedicated to the "American Cowboy." His was the saga sparked by the turmoil that followed the Civil War, and the passing of more than a century has by no means diminished the flame.

True, the old days and the old ways are but treasured memories, and the old trails have grown dim with the ravages of time, but the spirit of the cowboy lives on.

In my travels—to Texas, Oklahoma, Kansas, Nebraska, Colorado, Wyoming, New Mexico, and Arizona—I always find something that reminds me of the Old West. While I am walking these plains and mountains for the first time, there is this feeling that a part of me is eternal, that I have known these old trails before. I believe it is the undying spirit of the frontier calling me, through the mind's eye, to step back into time. What is the appeal of the Old West of the American frontier?

It has been epitomized by some as the dark and bloody period in American history. Its heroes—Crockett, Bowie, Hickok, Earp—have been reviled and criticized. Yet the Old West lives on, larger than life.

It has become a symbol of freedom, when there was always another mountain to climb and another river to cross; when a dispute between two men was settled not with expensive lawyers, but with fists, knives, or guns. Barbaric? Maybe. But some things never change. When the cowboy rode into the pages of American history, he left behind a legacy that lives within the hearts of us all.

—*Ralph Compton*

Chapter 1

Cestus Calloway sauntered into the Alpine Bank and Trust Company as if he owned it. Which was remarkable, the people in the bank would later tell a journalist for the *True Fissure*, since he was there to rob it.

Calloway wore his usual wide-brimmed, low-crowned hat, tilted up on the back of his head so that his brown curls spilled from under it. One lady would tell the newspaperman that it gave Calloway the look of the Greek Adonis. His handsome face was split in a wide smile and his blue eyes danced with amusement as he drew both of his Merwin Hulbert Army revolvers and held them out for all to see. "Ladies and gentlemen," he boomed in that grand way he had, "we're here to make a withdrawal."

By "we," Cestus meant the seven members of his wild bunch. Five of them strode in after him, spreading out as they came so that they blocked the windows and the doors. It was plain they had rehearsed what to do. As one bank customer would say to the reporter, "They moved like clockwork."

The *True Fissure* would able to identify the five by the descriptions witnesses gave. They were Mad Dog Hanks, Bert Varrow, Ira Toomis, a man who was only ever known as Cockeye, and the Attica Kid.

The bank's patrons and the pair of tellers all froze. Mrs. Mabel Periwinkle blurted, "My word!" and then blushed as if embarrassed.

Behind the rail at his desk, the bank's president, Arthur Hunnecut, was the first to get over his surprise. Rising, he moved to the rail. "What is the meaning of this?" he demanded.

Calloway chuckled and ambled over, saying, "You're a mite slow between the ears, Art."

"I don't believe I've made your acquaintance, sir," Hunnecut said stuffily. "And I'll thank you to stop waving pistols around in my bank."

Gesturing at the customers, Calloway laughed and said, "Do you hear him, folks? I bet if we look in his earhole we'll find a turtle in there."

Mrs. Periwinkle snorted and turned red again.

"Let me gun him," Mad Dog Hanks growled. He'd acquired his handle because he looked exactly like a mad mongrel about to take a bite out of someone. It didn't help his appearance any that he had large tufts of hair growing out of his ears.

Calloway glanced at him sharply. "What's the rule?"

Mad Dog scowled and said, "Well, damn."

"No swearing in my establishment," Arthur Hunnecut snapped. "Not with ladies present."

Calloway hooked the gate with the barrel of a six-shooter and opened it. "You're a marvel, Art, and that's no lie. Step out here while me and my boys clean your bank out."

"I'll be damned if I will," Hunnecut said.

The Attica Kid came over, his spurs jingling, and just like that, his Colt Lightning was in his hand. The youngest of the outlaws, he always wore black, including a black vest. His eyes, as one person would describe them, were "cold green gems." Cocking the Lightning, he said, "You'll be dead if you don't."

"I'd listen to him, were I you," Calloway said.

Arthur Hunnecut blanched.

Over by the wall, Mad Dog Hanks grumbled, "Oh, sure. Me, I have to behave. But you let the Kid do whatever he wants."

Calloway shot him another sharp glance.

"Step out here, moneyman," the Attica Kid said, "or your missus will be wailin' over your grave."

Hunnecut stepped out.

"That's better," Calloway said, and clapped the banker on the back with a revolver. "Now let's get to it." He nodded at Bert Varrow and Ira Toomis, and the pair went to the tellers and held out burlap sacks.

"Tell your people, Art, to empty the drawers and the safe," Calloway commanded, "and be quick about it."

Arthur Hunnecut looked into the muzzle of the Attica Kid's Lightning and became whiter still. "You heard him."

Showing his teeth in a dazzling smile, Calloway moved to the middle of the room. "I'm truly sorry for inconveniencin' you folks. This won't take but a few minutes."

"Are you fixing to rob us too?" a man in a suit and bowler asked.

"Rob you good folks?" Calloway said as if the notion horrified him. "May the Good Lord strike me dead if I ever took from the likes of you."

"What do you know of the Lord?" Hunnecut said archly.

"I know he's not fond of money changers," Calloway said. To the man in the bowler he said, "You must be new in these parts or you'd know I only rob those who deserve it."

"What did I do to deserve this?" Hunnecut said.

"Do you mean besides the high interest you charge those who borrow from you? And besides those you've driven from their homes when they couldn't pay their mortgage?"

"Now, see here," Hunnecut said. "That's a normal part of doing business. A bank isn't a charity, after all."

Calloway winked and smiled. "I am."

At the front window Cockeye stirred and called out, "There's a tin star comin' up the street toward McGivern and Larner."

"Who?" Hunnecut said.

"Pards of ours," Calloway replied, moving toward the window. "Watchin' our horses while we conduct our business."

"Is that what you call it?"

The Attica Kid pressed the muzzle of his Lightning against the banker's bulbous nose. "I'm tired of your sass. Give me cause and I'll splatter your brains."

"If he don't, I will," Mad Dog Hanks said.

Cestus Calloway looked out the front window, careful to hold his revolvers behind his back. "It's that new deputy they got. Mitchell, I think his name is. He's supposed to be out of town with the marshal."

"That's what I was told by that barkeep when I scouted out the town last night," Bert Varrow said. He was the only one of the outlaws who wore city clothes, and a derby, to boot. His Colt Pocket pistol had pearl grips, and he wore a diamond stickpin.

"Either Deputy Mitchell didn't go or he came back early," Calloway guessed. Quickly moving to the front door, he poked his head out and said, "Send him in here, boys." He stepped to one side, his back to the wall, and waited. It wasn't half a minute that a shadow filled the doorway and in walked Deputy Mitchell.

The deputy wasn't any older than the Attica Kid, and had red hair and freckles. "Mr. Hunnecut," he said, "a man outside said you wanted to see—" Belatedly he stopped and stiffened. "What in the world?"

Calloway stepped up from behind him and tapped a Merwin Hulbert on Deputy Mitchell's arm. "Turtles all over the place."

"What?" Mitchell said, gaping at the Attica Kid and then at Mad Dog Hanks as if he couldn't believe his eyes.

"Undo your gun belt," Calloway said, "if you'd be so kind."

"What?" Deputy Mitchell said again.

"You need to catch up," Calloway said. "The bank is bein' robbed."

"Some lawman you are, Mitch" Arthur Hunnecut said. "I told the marshal you were too young for the job, but would he listen? No."

Deputy Mitchell's features hardened and he started to lower his right hand to his holster. "Now, see here—"

"Don't be stupid, boy," Calloway said, jamming his revolver into the deputy's ribs. "We can blow you to hell and back without half tryin'."

For a few moments it appeared that Mitchell would draw anyway, but then he frowned and deflated, remarking, "I'm not hankerin' to die."

"No one has to if I can help it," Calloway said good-naturedly. "And I usually can."

Deputy Mitchell's eyes widened. "Why, you're him, aren't you?" he said as he pried at his buckle.

"President Hayes?"

"No. You're Cestus Calloway. The one everyone talks about. The Robin Hood of the Rockies, they call you." The deputy let his gun belt fall to the floor.

"I should thank that scribbler from the newspaper," Calloway said. "What was that book he talked about? *Ivanhoe*?"

"You are him, though?" Deputy Mitchell said in awe.

Calloway gave a mock bow. "Yes, 'tis I."

"Why, aren't you somethin'?" Mitchell said.

Arthur Hunnecut muttered under his breath.

The tellers were hurriedly stuffing money from the drawers into the burlap sacks under the watchful eyes, and leveled six-shooters, of Bert Varrow and Ira Toomis. Toomis, the oldest of the gang, had a cropped salt-and-pepper beard and a wad of tobacco bulging out his cheek. Thrusting his revolver at them, he barked, "Hurry it up, you peckerwoods. We don't have all week."

"And get the money from the safe," Bert Varrow said.

"It's shut," a skinny teller replied nervously, "and only Mr. Hunnecut has the combination."

"Is that a fact?" Cestus Calloway said. He bobbed his chin at the banker. "You know what you have to do."

"Never," Hunnecut said.

"We're takin' it all, Art."

"I refuse. Do you hear me?" Hunnecut said. "The people of this community have put their trust in me and I won't disappoint them."

"Kid," Calloway said.

The Attica Kid's smile was as icy as a mountain glacier. "How's Martha? Should I go call on her now or wait until tonight when you're off with your friends at that club?"

"What?"

"Or maybe I should have a talk with Cornelia. I hear she likes to wear her hair in pigtails."

A tremor rippled through Arthur Hunnecut's entire body, and he had to try twice to speak. "How is it you know my wife's and daughter's names?"

"We do our homework, as Cestus likes to say," the Attica Kid said. Suddenly leaning in close, he said so only the banker heard, "Now open that damn safe, or so help me, I'll pay your missus and your girl a visit sometime when you're not around. And you don't want that."

"You wouldn't," Hunnecut gasped.

The Attica Kid stepped back. "When I was little, I used to drown kittens in a bucket for the fun of it. I broke the neck of a puppy just for somethin' to do. And when I was twelve, there was this boy who used to pick on me and tease me because I was smaller than him and he reckoned he could get away with it. One day he was doin' it and I took a rock and put out his eye and broke most of his teeth besides. Later there was this gent who—"

Hunnecut help up a hand. "Enough. You've made your point abundantly clear. You're a hideous killer of women and children, and if I don't do as your lord and master wants, my wife and daughter will be added to your string."

"I couldn't have put it better my own self," the Attica Kid complimented him.

His brow dotted with beads of sweat, Arthur Hunnecut went through the gate and over to the Diebold safe. Bending, he quickly worked the combination and turned the handle. There was a loud click, and he pulled the door wide open. "Happy now, you scoundrels?"

The Attica Kid glanced at Cestus Calloway, and grinned and winked.

"The puppy was a nice touch," Calloway said.

In short order the safe was emptied and the tellers handed the bulging burlap sacks to Bert Varrow and Ira Toomis. Varrow hefted his sack and whistled. "This will be some haul."

"Bring it here," Calloway said, shoving his revolvers into their double-loop holsters.

"Must you?" Varrow replied as he carried the sack over.

"You know the rule."

"Cestus and his damn rules," Mad Dog said.

Backing toward the door, Calloway beamed at the banker and his patrons. "We're obliged for your cooperation. Remember to tell everybody how decent we treated you, and that no one was hurt." He paused and flicked a finger at the deputy's gun belt on the floor. "Mad Dog, bring that with you. We don't want Deputy Mitchell gettin' ideas."

The outlaws filed out. Last to leave was the Attica Kid. Standing in the doorway, he twirled his Colt forward and backward and then into his holster, and patted it. "Do I need to tell you what happens if you poke your heads out?"

"When the marshal hears of this, we'll be after you," Deputy Mitchell said.

"You do that," the Attica Kid said. "And be sure to tell

the marshal that Ben Larner can drop a buffalo at a thousand yards with that Sharps of his." Spurs jangling, he backed out.

By then Calloway was in the saddle and reining away from the hitch rail. Some of the people on Main Street had noticed the flurry of activity and stopped to stare. "Folks, this is your lucky day!" Calloway hollered. "The bank is givin' away money for free." Laughing, he reached into the sack, pulled out a fistful of bills, and cast them into the air.

The astonished onlookers gaped.

"Get it while you can!" Calloway yelled and, gigging his mount, he made off down the street. He threw another handful of money at several women who had come out of a millinery and more bills at a group of boys who were playing with a hoop. Then he let out a yip, and with a thunder of hooves, whopping and hollering, the outlaws galloped off.

No one tried to stop them. No one fired a shot. It was, as the *True Fissure* would later report, "as slick as could be."

Chapter 2

Marshal Boyd Cooper loved to fish. He loved it more than just about anything. Which was why he had snuck away to the pond on Sam Wilson's farm. It was a sunny day, the temperature in the eighties, perfect fishing weather. Not that Boyd cared so much about catching fish as he did about being able to relax and forget the cares of his office.

Boyd knew that his jaunts to the pond were the worst-kept secret in Alpine, but no one complained. He worked hard at his job, and Alpine was as orderly and peaceful as a town could be. No one begrudged him a few hours of indulging in his favorite pastime, especially not at his age. A man in his fifties was entitled to treat himself now and then.

Only a few people knew Boyd's other secret, namely that the fish weren't the only reason he came to the Wilson place. He could fish in any of the nearby creeks or the Rio Grande or Alpine Lake. The pond had another attraction.

A farmhouse stood less than a hundred yards away, and Boyd had barely cast his line and made himself comfortable when the screen door creaked and out came the other attraction. Today she wore a grass-green dress and had done her graying hair up in a bun. Her hands clasped behind her back, she meandered toward the pond by way of the pump and a cherry tree, making it seem as if she were only out for a stroll.

Boyd smiled. He liked that about her. She wasn't one of those pushy gals, the kind who threw themselves at men and practically demanded they catch her.

Some might think she was being coy, but that wasn't it. She wasn't sure of him yet; she was taking her time and taking his measure.

Boyd pretended not to notice her until she was almost to the bank. Looking up, he greeted her with "Why, Miss Wilson, this is a surprise. What brings you out and about on this fine day?"

"How many times have I asked you to call me Cecelia?" she replied in that throaty voice of hers.

Boyd felt a tingle run down his spine. "Couldn't be more than ten or twelve," he said, and smiled.

Cecelia Wilson returned it. She was Sam's sister and had the same pointed chin, but that was the only trait they shared. The years had been kind to her, and her complexion was smooth except for the crinkle of crow's-feet around her eyes. She had a full figure and an ample bosom and always hid them beneath dresses that ran from her ankles to her neck. "A body would think you would have learned by now," she said, then frowned and added, "Although, by rights, it should be Mrs. Zeigler and not Miss Wilson."

"Your husband died, what, ten years ago?" Boyd said. "Usin' miss and your maiden name is perfectly proper."

"Eleven years next month," Cecelia said. "Hard to believe."

What Boyd found hard to believe was that she had remained a widow for so long. It wasn't like in the old days when men outnumbered women by three to one, but there were plenty of older men—like him, for instance—who would delight in having her say I do. "You're welcome to join me," he offered.

"Gracious of you," Cecelia said. Tucking at the knees,

she sank gracefully down and clasped her fingers in her lap. "I was hoping you would come today."

Boyd swore that his chest fluttered. "You were?"

"This has been going on for over a year now, off and on."

"You mean me fishin'?" Boyd said.

"You know perfectly well what I mean. Forgive me for being so forward, but when are you planning to muster the courage to ask me out?"

Boyd shammed shock and said, "Why, Cecelia, you hussy, you."

They both laughed, and Boyd was on the verge of doing what she wanted when Cecelia gazed past him and a puzzled expression came over her.

"Goodness, your deputy is in an awful hurry."

Boyd looked over his shoulder. Sure enough, Hugo Mitchell was running toward the pond as if his britches were on fire. He'd taken his hat off and was holding it, and his limbs were flapping like an ungainly turkey trying to take flight. "What in the world?"

"Maybe there's a calamity," Cecelia joked.

Boyd hoped not. On weekends a besotted cowhand or miner or townsman might act up, and there had been a couple of stabbings and one shooting since he took office, but that was all. He'd been fortunate in that regard, seeing as how Alpine had twenty-three saloons and a reputation for being on the raw side. "Dang. I wanted to spend some time with you."

"Oh, did you, now?" Cecelia teased.

The deputy excitedly waved his arms. "Coop! Coop! We've got trouble!" he bawled.

"Uh-oh," Cecelia said.

Boyd refused to move just yet. His deputy was green and tended to exaggerate things. "Calm down, Mitch," he said as the younger man came to a stop and doubled over, wheezing and puffing. "What's so all-fired important?"

"The bank," Mitch panted.

"Which one? We have three."

"The Alpine," Mitch got out. "It was robbed."

Pushing to his feet, Boyd gripped Mitch by the shoulder. "How long ago? Did anyone see who did it?"

"I did. I was right there. He disarmed me in front of everybody and made me look the fool."

"Who did?"

"Why, Cestus Calloway, of course. Who else goes around robbin' banks in these parts?"

"Oh my," Cecelia said.

Boyd felt another flutter but this time of anger. "Calloway," he said bitterly. "Did they hurt anybody?"

"Not a soul," Mitch said. "You know how he is. He rode out of town laughin' and throwin' money at folks. Who's goin' to shoot somebody who's throwin' money at them?"

Boyd realized he was still holding his fishing pole and held it out to Cecelia. "Would you hold on to this for me? And my basket? I have to hurry back."

"Naturally," she said. "Do what you must."

Wheeling on a bootheel, Boyd strode off. He'd left his horse in a shaded stand of trees that bordered the road and come to the pond on foot.

Mitch quickly caught up. "You should have seen them. As brazen as you please. They made poor Mr. Hunnecut open the safe and cleaned him out. They're a scary outfit."

"So I've heard."

"The scariest is that Attica Kid. You should have seen him. Mean as a snake, and he can twirl that pistol of his like nobody I ever saw."

"How many others took part besides those two?"

"All of them," Mitch said. "It was the whole bunch that the newspaper says ride with Calloway. They headed west. Mr. Hunnecut wanted me to go right after them, but I figured I should come fetch you."

"You did right."

"Why do you reckon Calloway picked one of our banks this time? He's fought shy of Alpine until now."

Boyd pondered on that. Cestus Calloway had been robbing banks and stagecoaches for the better part of two years. The first anyone heard of Calloway, he and his men struck the Cloverleaf Bank and made off with seven thousand dollars. Not six months later, they relieved the Red Cliff Bank of twelve thousand. Two stages were stopped earlier in the year, and now this.

"Folks say it's because he's afraid of you," Mitch mentioned. "On account of your reputation."

In a rush of memories, Boyd relived his early days, his years as a deputy in Missouri and then his stint as a marshal in Kansas. Once, and only once, he'd shot a man, a drunk who had stabbed two other drunks and was waving a bloody knife around in the middle of the street. Boyd told him to drop the knife and surrender, but the jackass came at him slashing with the knife as if it were a sword, and Boyd had no choice but to put lead in him. Boyd shot to wound, but the shoulder became infected and the man died.

Boyd wouldn't have thought a small thing like that would mark a man for life, but it followed him everywhere. He was a man-killer, they whispered, which was ridiculous. He hadn't had to shoot another human being in fifteen years, and God willing, he never would again.

"I told Harve to start roundin' up a posse," Mitch said.

Boyd grunted. Harvey Dale worked part-time as a deputy, and the rest of the time swept out the stable. Dale was in his sixties and had been a buffalo hunter and a scout for the army at one time.

"How many should we take with us? Twenty or thirty?" Mitch asked.

"Why not fifty while you're at it?" Boyd scoffed.

Mitch took him seriously. "Thirty should be enough. There's only seven outlaws, so it's more than enough if they put up a fight."

"I was joshin'," Boyd said to set him straight. "Half a dozen will do."

"We're talkin' Cestus Calloway and the Attica Kid," Mitch said. "The Kid alone is a tiger. They say he's bucked out twenty men or better."

"Not likely," Boyd said. Going by his own experience, he added, "It would surprise me considerably if it's more than four or five."

Mitch had tied his roan next to Boyd's chestnut. Mounting, they reined out of the trees and headed north toward town at a trot. It was only half a mile, and when they got there, Main Street swarmed with two-legged bees buzzing about the robbery.

Boyd threaded through to the hitch rail in front of the Alpine Bank and Trust Company. He wasn't out of the saddle when the door was flung open and Arthur Hunnecut strode toward him like a rooster on the peck.

"*There* you are!" the banker exclaimed. "Where in heaven's name have you been? It's been forty-five minutes since my bank was cleaned out."

"I was out of town," Boyd said, and let it go at that. Looping his reins, he stepped around the rail. "Suppose you tell me how much they took and anything else that might help."

"We're still tallying the figures," Hunnecut said, "but I expect the total will be over fifteen thousand dollars. I had at least that much in the safe and they emptied the drawers as well."

Mitch whistled. "Lord Almighty. I doubt I'll see that much money my whole life long."

"Go see how Harve is doin'," Boyd said. "Get grub from Tom at the general store, and ammunition for whoever needs it. We might be out all night, so have them bring bedrolls."

"Will do," Mitch said, and gigged the roan.

"You'll have to hurry if you're to have any hope of overtaking those outlaws by nightfall," Hunnecut urged.

"There's no rush," Boyd said.

"I beg your pardon? They've stolen the town's money. If that's not reason enough, I don't know what is."

"We push too hard, we'll wear out our horses, and if they have relay mounts waitin', we'll lose them for good," Boyd explained. "So long as it doesn't rain, we'll catch them—eventually. Harvey Dale can track like an Apache."

Hunnecut regarded the cloudless sky. "I guess you know what you're doing," he remarked, but it was plain he was skeptical. "Just make sure you *do* catch them. The good people of Alpine won't like having their savings stolen from under your very nose."

"That's hardly fair."

"Be that as it may, you wear your badge at the discretion of the town council. We appointed you and we can appoint someone to replace you if you can't do your job."

Boyd bristled but held his temper in check. "I don't take kindly to threats."

"I was only saying," Hunnecut said, with a barely concealed smirk.

Were he thirty years younger, Boyd might have hit him. He'd never liked the man. The conceited so-and-so thought he was God's gift to creation just because he owned a bank. "Let me hear what happened. Don't leave anything out."

Hunnecut's account was short and to the point. He ended with "I'm surprised you didn't expect something like this and take steps to prevent it. After Cloverleaf and Red Cliff, it was inevitable that Calloway would strike here."

"I can only do so much with one deputy and a part-timer," Boyd said, "and that's all the council had money for." He paused. "If you were so worried, why didn't you hire a guard out of your own pocket?"

"I was as careless as you."

Boyd looked away so the banker wouldn't see the flash of anger on his face. As luck would have it, just then a boy of twelve or so hustled up and extended a handful of bills. "What's this, son?"

"Some of the money from the robbery. My ma says I'm to give it back."

"I should say you are," Hunnecut said, and snatched the bills before Boyd could. "Thank her for me. It's nice to know there's at least one honest soul in this town."

"Ma told me that you might give me a reward," the boy said hopefully.

"For doing what's right? That would hardly be ethical." Hunnecut wagged his fingers. "Now shoo. We adults have matters to discuss."

The boy slumped in disappointment and walked off.

"Proud of yourself?" Boyd said.

"I certainly am," Hunnecut said. "I've taught him an invaluable lesson. Never rely on the cup of human kindness, because there's no such thing."

"I don't believe that."

"Those outlaws do. You'd do well to remember that when they have you in their gun sights."

Chapter 3

Cestus Calloway liked it when things ran smoothly. He worked hard to ensure that they did. Some folks wouldn't call robbing banks and stages work, but they didn't realize how much planning it took to carry out a robbery and get away with your hide intact.

Take the Alpine Bank and Trust Company, for instance. Cestus had spent weeks preparing. He'd sent some of his men into town—those less likely to be recognized—to scout things out. Bert Varrow was the best at it. A gambler before he took to the owl-hoot trail, Varrow had a good memory for details, as well as cards. Butch McGivern was a natural at ferreting information out too. A former cowboy, he used his friendly disposition to fool folks into gabbing.

From them, and from other tidbits he'd picked up, Cestus had learned that of the three banks, the Alpine Bank and Trust Company kept the most money on hand. The bank's president, Hunnecut, liked to brag as much. That made picking the target easy.

Cestus had also learned that the town's law dog liked to go fishing now and then, which was right accommodating of him. Occasionally he took his deputy along. By timing the robbery just right, Cestus had hoped to get in and out before they returned. As luck would have it, this time the deputy hadn't gone, but he was so green he'd posed no threat at all.

Yes, sir, Cestus congratulated himself as the eight of them descended a pine-covered slope toward Alpine Lake, things had gone well. Now all that remained was to shake the inevitable posse and make it to their hideout unseen.

Cestus never would have imagined he'd be so good at being so bad. When he was a boy growing up in Ohio, there was nothing about him to show that one day he'd be the scourge of Colorado. Or the scourge of anything, for that matter.

Cestus had been as ordinary as dishwater, a boy who liked to roam the woods and hunt and wrestle other kids and do all the other things kids did. Then his father took it into his head to go West and they moved to the Plains. But farming in Nebraska wasn't the same as farming in Ohio. The climate was harsher. In the summer the temperature could climb to a hundred and ten or more. In the winter, arctic winds drifted the snow feet deep. There was less rain, and without irrigation, their crops wouldn't thrive.

The family was always struggling.

Cestus thought he'd help out by taking a job sweeping out a saloon and cleaning the spittoons. The gamblers and doves and two-legged wolves fascinated him. It was his first taste of vice, and he drank deep.

By his sixteenth year he was sick of farm life. He said good-bye to his folks and struck out on his own. He took up with those on the shady side of the law, and liked the life they lived. The excitement of it. The drinking and the card-playing and the willing ladies in their tight dresses.

Cestus made the rounds of all the Kansas cow towns, living life to the fullest but always short on the money he needed. Then one day in a small farming town called Newberg, when he was half-drunk, he had a brainstorm on how to get that money. He and some pards robbed the Newberg Bank.

It had been ridiculously easy. So much so that, when he ran out of the money from Newberg, he robbed another bank to see if it would be as easy as the first. It was. He had found his calling.

And now, years later, he was still robbing for a living, still taking each day as if there was no tomorrow, and loving the hell out of life.

The pines thinned and the lake appeared. Fed by runoff from a glacier, Alpine Lake had the bluest water anywhere. It was so far from Alpine—over ten miles—that few folks ever visited it except for occasional fishermen and hunters.

Cestus slowed his mount to a walk and started around the shore toward the far end. That was where their fresh mounts were tied.

Hooves clomped, and the Attica Kid came alongside Cestus's bay. "I'll be damn glad when we reach the cave."

Cestus looked at him, and grinned. "Gettin' grumpy in your young age, are you?"

"I'm tired of the dirty looks Mad Dog keeps givin' me," the Kid said. "He keeps it up, you'll need to find somebody to take his place."

"He's jealous, is all," Cestus said. "He thinks I treat you special. Likes to call you my favorite."

"That's no excuse. I won't be looked down on. Not by him or anybody."

"Do you ever regret leavin' Texas?"

The Kid glanced over. "Where did that come from?"

"I was thinkin' of the old days," Cestus said. "About how I got my start. A man can learn a lot from his past."

"Learn all you want. I never look back. What's done is done. So no, I don't have any regrets. Except maybe that you brought Mad Dog into the outfit."

Cestus laughed. "I'd be obliged if you rein in that temper of yours and don't gun him. He has his uses."

"Since when is gripin' a use?"

Cestus laughed louder. "That's another thing I like about you, Kid. Your sense of humor is almost as good as mine."

"I wasn't bein' funny. He's a pain in the ass."

More hooves drummed, and now it was grizzled Ira Toomis who came up on Cestus's other side. "No sign of anyone after us yet."

"They will be," Cestus said.

"What makes you so sure?" Toomis asked.

"Marshal Boyd Cooper. He takes his law-doggin' serious," Cestus said. "He won't like us robbin' his town."

Toomis snorted. "Just another nobody with a badge."

"That's where you're wrong, Ira. He's killed his man."

"Hell, who hasn't?" Toomis replied. "Bein' a man-killer is as common as fleas these days."

"Why are you arguin' with me?" Cestus asked.

"I just don't see him as anyone to sweat about."

"You should. I heard of him over to Kansas. He's not famous like Wyatt Earp, or like Wild Bill was. He's no gun hand, but he does what he has to to get the job done."

"I'm more worried about Harvey Dale," Toomis said.

"How so?"

"I got to talkin' to him one day a while back when I put my horse up at the stable. He used to scout for the army. Did a lot of trackin'. Told me he tangled with the Sioux and some other tribes. And now he's a part-time deputy."

Cestus drew rein and the others followed suit. Shifting in the saddle, he glared at Toomis. "You're just now tellin' me this?"

"Huh?"

"I knew Dale does a little deputy work, but I didn't know the rest," Cestus said. "I sure as hell didn't know he used to be a scout. How did it never occur to you to tell me?"

Toomis sheepishly shrugged. "I'm sorry, Cestus. It was over a year ago that I was there. After we'd robbed the Cloverleaf Bank and you had us split up to throw the Cloverleaf posse off our scent."

"Damn," Cestus said. "A tracker."

"He's an old codger, like me," Toomis said. "Likely as not, he's not near as good as he was in his younger days."

"Don't treat me like I'm dumb," Cestus said. "A minute ago you were worried about him, and now I am too. This changes things." He brought his weary horse to a trot.

Cestus didn't put all the blame on Toomis. He should have had Varrow or McGivern nose around in Alpine when he first heard about the old man at the stable who helped out the marshal from time to time. It was an oversight, and mistakes like that could prove fatal.

They arrived at the north end of the lake. Their horses were right where they'd picketed them. Ranks of spruce bordered the shore, and higher up, aspens shimmered in the sunlight. Out on the water, ducks swam and geese honked.

A fish leaped with a loud splash.

Normally Cestus liked to appreciate Nature in all her glory, but now he was all business as he had his men switch to their new horses. He transferred the burlap sacks to a sorrel and went over to Ben Larner, who was adjusting the cinch on a grulla.

Larner was the second oldest, after Toomis. In his younger days he had hunted buffalo and still had the Sharps he'd used, converted from percussion to cartridge by a St. Louis gunsmith. He was cradling the buffalo gun as he tugged on the cinch. He had gray eyes and skin like old leather, and was the only one of them who wore buckskins. He wore a bandoleer across his chest and a bowie knife on his left hip.

"Ben, we have a problem," Cestus said.

Larner looked up. "Oh?"

"Could be a tracker is on our heels."

"The real article?" Larner said in his gravelly way.

"Old army scout."

"Then he's for real all right and not one of those blowhards who say they can track but couldn't find their own ass in the dark without a lantern."

Cestus chuckled.

"What is it you want me to do?"

"I'd like to discourage the tracker and the rest of the posse," Cestus said. Turning, he surveyed the blue expanse of Alpine Lake and the wide shorelines on either side. "You could wait in the spruce there, and when they come, shoot the scout's horse and maybe one or two others besides."

"Why not shoot the tracker?"

"You know why," Cestus said. "I keep tellin' all of you. We don't kill unless we have to. There's nothin' that stirs folks up more than a killin'. They send out bigger posses and hardly ever give up, and we don't want that."

"It's hard not to kill when killin' is so easy," Larner said.

"I know. But it's not smart, and smart is what keeps us alive. So long as all we do is rob and give away money, people don't get riled. We're harmless. They like us, and laugh at the law behind their backs. We want that. We want them on our side, not scourin' the countryside to string us up."

"The horses it will be," Larner said.

"I'll leave one of the others to lend a hand and the rest of us will push on. Join us at the cave when you're done."

"I don't need no nursemaid."

"Just to keep you company," Cestus said. "Toomis, maybe? The two of you get along."

"He's always spittin' tobacco juice. My pa used to do it. I couldn't stand it then and I can't stand it now."

"Cockeye, then. He doesn't use chaw and hardly ever talks."

"That eye of his makes my skin crawl, the way it looks off one way when his other eye is lookin' right at you."

"Well, ain't you fussy?" Cestus said.

"I'll be fine by my lonesome. I'll shoot a few horses and fan the breeze and be with you by sunset."

Cestus gave in. "All right." He trusted Larner to get the job done. The old buffalo hunter was one of the most dependable of the bunch. "But don't take chances, you hear? Use that Sharps of yours to its best advantage and drop their horses a ways off. Don't let them get close."

"Yes, Ma," Larner said.

Laughing, Cestus turned and climbed on the sorrel. The others were already mounted and waiting. He led them into the spruce and up a steep slope to a ridge thick with firs. A switchback brought them to the aspen belt, and from there it was a short climb to a narrow pass and a sweeping vista of the surrounding mountains and valleys.

To the west was the Divide, the backbone of the continent, the miles-high peaks capped by snow much of the year. Far to the south, smoke rose from the Tilden Smelting and Sampling Works, one of the three large mines that accounted for Alpine's prosperity. To the east the mountains sloped away toward Alamosa.

Once through the pass, Cestus descended to the tree line and followed it north to an imposing series of cliffs. Midway along, a dark maw yawned. It wasn't visible from above. Nor could it be seen from below, thanks to the heavy forest. Cestus had learned about it over a card game in Denver from an old trapper deep in his cups. Finding it had proven difficult but worth the effort.

"Home, sweet home," Bert Varrow joked as they drew rein at the cave entrance.

"It keeps the rain off us," Mad Dog said. "That's all I care about. I don't like bein' wet."

Bert sniffed a few times and grinned. "We know."

Butch McGivern laughed. He had taken off his hat and was swatting dust from his sleeves and his britches. "I try not to breathe when Hanks is upwind of me. It about kills my nose."

"Go to hell," Mad Dog said. "I don't stink that bad."

"Says you," Butch McGivern replied.

"Enough," Cestus said. Dismounting, he stretched and arched his back. It had been a long ride and he was a little stiff.

"Are you tellin' us when to talk now?" Mad Dog asked.

"Don't start," Cestus said. "I'm still annoyed with you for how you acted at the bank."

"What did I do?"

"You were mouthy," Cestus said. "You complain too much, Mad Dog, and it gets on my nerves."

The Attica Kid had climbed down and was flexing the fingers of his gun hand. "Gets on my nerves too. And you don't want to do that."

Mad Dog opened his mouth to say something but apparently thought better of it and didn't.

"That's what I like about us," Bert Varrow said. "We're one big happy family."

"Like hell we are," Mad Dog said. "We're robbers and killers and we'll all come to a bad end."

"Not if I can help it," Cestus said.

Chapter 4

Marshal Boyd Cooper had to hand it to Harvey Dale. The old scout was a marvel.

Dale had found where the outlaws left the road and cut north into heavy timber, and from then on had stuck to their trail like a hound dog to a raccoon's scent. For his age he was remarkably spry, and stopped often to spring down and examine the ground. With his buckskin shirt and old cavalry hat and patched army pants, he might as well be leading a patrol deep into Indian country as guiding a posse after outlaws.

In addition to Boyd, Mitch, and Dale, their posse consisted of two cowboys from the Circle T who happened to be in town, a blacksmith who did a lot of hunting, the owner of the stable where Dale worked, who was a superb rider, plus Sam Wilson, who had shown up as the posse was set to ride out and said he needed to talk to Boyd so he might as well tag along.

Boyd didn't know what that was about, but he did know he was pleased with his posse. Mitch had picked well. The two cowpokes, Sherm Bonner and Lefty, spent most of their lives in the saddle, and Sherm was reputed to be more than a fair hand with his six-shooter. The blacksmith, Vogel, had muscle enough for three men, and spent all his free time off

in the woods after big game. Vogel's favorite rifle was a Maynard .50 caliber. With it he could drop a bull elk at five hundred yards. The stable owner, Clell Parsons, had brought a
Spencer, but by his own admission he'd hardly ever used it.

Now, riding hard, they came to a shelf and started up the
steep slopes on the other side.

Boyd slowed to spare their animals. He was keeping an
eye on Dale, who was well out in the lead, bent low from his
saddle.

"They were still movin' fast," he called back. "Too fast, if
you ask me."

Sam Wilson happened to be riding beside Boyd and
cleared his throat. "What does Dale mean by that?"

"They keep goin' like they are," Boyd said, "they'll ride
their horses into the ground."

"Awful dumb of them," Sam said.

"That's just it," Boyd said. "One thing Cestus Calloway
isn't is dumb. I suspect he has horses waitin' somewhere so
they can switch and leave us eatin' their dust."

"You don't say," Sam said, as if it were a stroke of bril-
liance and not mere common sense. "Well, you should know
about these things. You're the lawman. All I do is milk cows
and raise chickens."

"There's more to farmin' than that," Boyd said, wondering why his friend was acting sort of peculiar. Reining
around an oak in their path, he said, "What did you want to
talk about anyhow?"

Sam brought his animal so close their stirrups almost
touched. Lowering his voice, he said, "My sis."

"Cecelia?"

"You know of any other sisters I have that I don't?"

Boyd chuckled.

"I shouldn't be doin' this," Sam said. "But after what she
said when you left today, I reckon I should let you know so
you can decide what you want to do."

Another tree forced them to rein apart.

"Want to do about what?" Boyd asked when they rejoined.

"What are we talkin' about? My sister, you lunkhead."

"I'm not sure I savvy," Boyd confessed.

Sam sighed and rubbed his chin. "This is awkward. It's none of my business, but we've been friends awhile now and, well, it'd be a shame for her to go off to Kansas City when I like havin' her around."

Boyd had been half concentrating on Harvey Dale, but he switched all his attention to Sam. "Kansas City?"

"That's where we're from. From outside it, actually. I wouldn't go back in a million years. There's nothin' there for me. Our folks are dead. We have some kin left, but we hardly know them."

"Why would Cecelia want to go?"

"She's got nowhere else. Between you and me, I think she's kind of lonely, bein' a widow and all. Then you showed an interest and that perked her up, but you've been such a lunkhead about it she's havin' second thoughts."

"That's twice you've called me that."

"If you don't want to be called it, you shouldn't be such a lunk. What does she have to do? Throw herself at you? She told me she's made it as plain as plain can be that she'd like you to court her, but all you court is our fish."

"Well, hell," Boyd said.

"So today she came in and mentioned Kansas City again and I thought I should come into town and tell you to quit straddlin' the fence. It's root hog time, if you take my drift."

"You farmers and your hogs."

"Don't change the subject," Sam said. "Once this bank robbin' business is over, you'd better put on your Sunday best and come callin' with flowers in your hand."

"Why, Sam, you romantic devil, you."

"Damn it, Boyd. I don't need a grumpy female on my hands. And if you don't come courtin', she'll fall into a sulk that might last days or even weeks."

"I can't imagine Cecelia ever sulkin'," Boyd said. "She's always struck me as havin' a pleasant disposition."

"Seems to me you have a lot to learn about females. They have two faces. One they put on when they're out and about, and the other they wear at home."

"By golly, you're a philosopher too."

"I could just hit you," Sam said. "I'm doin' you a favor and you're pokin' fun. If you'd ever been married or had sisters, you'd know I'm right. You've only seen the sweet side of her. But she can be stormy, on occasion, and that's when you have to watch out. The only thing worse than a female in a snit is comin' down with smallpox, and I can do without either."

Boyd became serious. "Set your mind at rest. I was fixin' to ask her out when Mitch showed up bellowin' about the bank."

"Good," Sam said, nodding. "Do you mind if I sort of suggest to her that I heard somewhere you are interested?"

"Somewhere?" Boyd said. "Who told you if not me? The barber?"

"It wouldn't do for her to know I talked to you," Sam said. "She'd be upset that I poked my nose in."

"She won't hear it from me," Boyd assured him.

Up the slope, Harvey Dale was wisely skirting some talus.

"To tell you the truth," Sam continued, "you'll be better for her than her first husband. He was too bossy and always wanted things done his way."

"I haven't asked her out yet and you have us married?"

"I'm just lookin' ahead," Sam said.

"I'm grateful for the advice," Boyd said. "And now that you've said your piece, you might as well turn around and head back to town. There's no need for you to go any farther."

"I'm no quitter."

Boyd hesitated. It wasn't that he minded Sam being there. But the others all had something to contribute, and Sam didn't. Sam couldn't track and wasn't much of a rider and was an even worse shot. Boyd didn't want to come right and say that, so he settled for "It's your sister I'm thinkin' of. You should let her know my intentions so she doesn't fall into one of those sulks."

Sam gazed up the mountain at their tracker. "I've come this far. I reckon I'll set it through."

Boyd shrugged and said, "Suit yourself."

When they reached the crest, Harvey Dale was waiting. The old scout had dismounted and was sweeping the country below and beyond with a spyglass.

"I didn't know you had one of those," Boyd remarked, hooking a leg over his saddle horn. "We'll rest for five minutes," he announced to the others. It wasn't much, but it was all they could spare. He'd like to be closer to their quarry before sundown.

Without taking his eye from the telescope, Dale replied, "It's from my scoutin' days. Saved my hide more times than I can count."

Deputy Mitchell had brought his horse up and now he removed his hat and mopped at his brow. "Why am I sweatin' so much? All we're doin' is ridin'."

"You're soft, Deputy," Dale said. "You're not like me or those punchers. We can ride all day and all night and still keep goin'."

Sherm and Lefty had reined to one side and were swapping words and grins. They had overheard, and Sherm said, "We thank you for the compliment, old-timer."

"Listen to you," Lefty said, and laughed.

Boyd liked the pair. They were easygoing and a lot alike except in how they looked. Sherm was the lady's man of the two, tall and broad-shouldered, with blue eyes and black hair. Lefty was shorter and thinner and had buckteeth that made his upper lip bulge.

"It weren't no compliment," Dale said, still raking the countryside with his spyglass. "It was fact. Any hombre who can't sit a horse has no business nursin' cows for a livin'."

"Ain't that the truth?" Lefty said.

Harvey Dale suddenly stiffened and took half a step. "Hold on. There they are. Eight, like we figured."

"Can you make out Cestus Calloway?" Deputy Mitchell asked.

"How would I know what Calloway looks like?" Dale replied. "I've never set eyes on the man. And what difference would it make if I could?"

"I was just askin'," Mitch said.

"Are you sure about the count?" Boyd was anxious to learn. Now and then Calloway added to his bunch, and there might have been more of them waiting outside town when the outlaws fanned the breeze.

"One, two . . . ," Dale began, then stopped and nodded. "Yep. Eight of the skunks. They're almost to Alpine Lake." He lowered his spyglass, the brass gleaming bright in the sunlight. "Could be they're goin' to water their horses and rest a spell. This is our chance to gain on them."

"Provided we don't exhaust our own animals," Boyd cautioned.

"You're the law dog," Dale said. "Do we pussyfoot or take the gamble?"

"I vote we gamble," Sherm Bonner said. "Lefty and me can't be all week at this. We have to be back to the Circle T by the day after tomorrow or the big sugar will skin us alive."

"Whatever you decide, Boyd, is fine by me," Sam Wilson said.

Boyd made a quick decision. "We ride like hell."

Nodding in agreement, Harvey Dale folded his telescope in on itself. "I reckon an hour, no more, and we'll be there."

Mitch cleared his throat to ask, "What do you think the chances are that they'll surrender without firin' a shot?"

Everyone looked at him.

"What?" Mitch said.

Dale assumed the lead. His small pinto could move like

a mountain goat over the rugged terrain, and soon he was well ahead of them. He looked back once and shook his head as if to suggest they were a sorry bunch of riders.

Any other time, Boyd would have been amused. Now he was worried. There were eight of them and eight outlaws. Even odds. But some of the outlaws were known killers and had no qualms about adding to their tally. His posse, on the other hand, was made up of amateurs, at least when it came to gunning men down. Mitch, Vogel, Parsons, and Sam had never shot a soul, so far as he knew. Sherm Bonner had shot two or three, but he didn't know about Lefty. That left Harvey Dale. Boyd had a hunch the old scout had snuffed the wicks of more than a few hostiles, if nothing else. But that didn't necessarily mean that Dale was in the same class of killer as those with Cestus Calloway.

No, Boyd told himself, he must be mighty careful not to get them massacred. People claimed that Calloway went out of his way to avoid killing anyone, but that might change if the outlaws were cornered.

It seemed they had hardly reached the bottom of the ridge when Mitch hollered, "There's the lake!"

They were near the south shore. The wind wasn't blowing and the lake's surface was so still it made Boyd think of a sheet of glass. Waterfowl were out in the middle, and an osprey winged over the eastern portion in search of fish.

Dale had stopped to wait for them and was using his spyglass again. He swept the far end and both sides, and swore.

"Don't tell me," Boyd said.

"I don't see hide nor hair of them. They must have . . ." Dale stopped and rose in his stirrups. "Hold on. I see them! No. Wait. It's just horses. Six, seven, eight of them, at the other end. They're just standin' there with their heads hangin'. They look plumb wore out."

"The outlaws had a relay waitin'," Mitch said to Boyd, "just like you reckoned."

"That's that, then," Clell Parsons said. "Our animals are tuckered out too. We can't chase after fresh ones."

"We'll collect those they left and take them back," Boyd proposed. They might as well have something to show for their effort. Disappointed, he looped around to the west shore.

Sam Wilson caught up and made a clucking sound. "Don't look so glum. You tried your best, and now you can see my sister that much sooner."

"I wanted to be the one who brought Calloway to justice," Boyd said.

"He's long gone, him and all his curly wolves," Sam said. "We won't get within twenty miles of them now."

No sooner were the words out of Sam's mouth than his horse's head exploded.

Chapter 5

Or so it seemed to Boyd.

There was a loud fleshy *thwack* simultaneous with the distant boom of a shot, and the animal's left eye and part of its forehead burst and flew every which way. The slug cored its brain and the animal pitched forward, causing Sam to yelp in surprise and clutch his saddle horn to keep from being thrown. At the last moment he tried to leap clear, but his leg became caught and the horse fell on top of it, pinning him.

All this Boyd caught out of the corner of his eye as he reined his own horse toward the trees. He used his spurs, and the chestnut, spooked by the splash of gore and the scent of blood, gave a long bound. "Hunt cover!" he hollered.

Harvey Dale and the cowboys were already turning their animals, but everyone else was slow to react. Shock had riveted them to their saddles.

Deputy Mitchell started to haul on his reins just as his horse was struck. Blood and bits of hide showered from its neck, and it whinnied stridently. Mitch used his spurs and his horse took a couple of steps, but the shower of scarlet had become a torrent and its front legs gave out. "Oh hell!" Mitch bawled. Like Sam Wilson, he attempted to push clear and he succeeded, hitting hard on his head and shoulders. His hat fell off and he lay still, apparently dazed.

Boyd almost went to get him. But no, his animal might be brought down. He reached the pines about the same moment as Dale and the cowhands and they all vaulted off and grabbed their rifles.

Vogel was almost to cover too.

Clell Parsons, though, was farther out, having trouble. His zebra dun was terrified and wouldn't respond to his spurs or the reins. "Move, consarn you! Move!" He had leaned down and raised his hand as if to swat it on the neck when without warning part of his cheek and his nose were separated from his face.

The boom of the distant shot reached them an instant later.

"Clell!" Dale shouted.

The stable owner sprawled half out of his saddle, lifeless, and the zebra dun just stood there, a perfect target for the shooter. The next slug cored its head and it sagged in its tracks.

Vogel reached the trees. Coming to a stop, he sprang down and slid his hunting rifle from the scabbard.

Mitch still wasn't moving, but Sam Wilson was cussing and pushing at his saddle, to no avail.

Bile rose in Boyd's gorge. One man dead and three horses down. His posse had become a disaster.

"Did you see that?" Lefty said. "The polecat shot Parson's face off."

"I think he was going for the horse and hit Parsons by mistake," Boyd said.

"The hell you say," Harvey Dale declared in fury. "Mistake or not, whoever it was will by God pay."

Vogel had squatted next to a small pine and was peering around it. "Where's the shooter?"

"Careful," Boyd cautioned. "Don't show too much of yourself." Whoever the shooter was, the man was good.

The blacksmith pressed the Maynard .50 caliber to his shoulder and put his eye to a scope. "This is a Davison," he said, referring to the sight. "I'll see him before he sees me."

"Unless he's using a telescopic sight too," Boyd warned.

"He has to be at that range."

"Maybe not." Boyd knew of shooters who made remarkable shots using the sights a rifle came with. "Be careful," he said again. He didn't want to lose anyone else.

"Marshal Cooper?" Sherm Bonner said, and pointed.

Deputy Mitchell was stirring. Groaning, he raised his head and looked around as if unsure of where he was.

"Mitch, stay down!" Boyd shouted. He might be wrong about the shooter killing Parsons by mistake. "Play dead."

"Play what?" Mitch said confusedly, and gave a start. "Is that Parsons lyin' there?"

"Don't move!" Boyd yelled. "The shooter might go for you."

Mitch gazed to the north, and gulped. Laying his head back down, he said, "My horse. My poor, poor horse."

Just then Vogel exclaimed, "I see him! At the far end of the lake. Just part of him is showing."

Boyd went over and sank to a knee. "Has he seen you?"

"No. He's behind a log he's using for a rest. He has a Sharps, I think. And damn, you were right. He's not using a scope. That is damn fine shooting."

"A man is dead, mister," Lefty said. "What's fine about that?"

"What is the shooter doing?" Boyd said.

"He has his head up and he's looking this way," Vogel said. "I think I can drop him."

"You think?"

"I can only see part of his head and one shoulder. He's crafty, whoever he is."

"Which one do you reckon it is?" Lefty asked. "And do you see any sign of the others?"

"I don't know, and no, I don't," Vogel said.

"It might be just the one," Boyd reasoned. "Calloway left him there to delay us while the rest make their escape."

"I have a question," Sherm Bonner said. He was hunkered by his horse with his hand on his Colt.

Boyd looked over. "Ask it."

"Where did that old scout get to?"

Startled, Boyd looked around. The puncher was right. Harvey Dale had disappeared.

Dale ran as he hadn't run in years. He ran as he had run in his younger days when he scouted for the army and went up against the likes of the Sioux and the Arapaho. Folks sometimes said he was spry for his age, and he proved it now by doing what might daunt a man half his age.

As he ran, Dale fumed. He was mad at himself. In all his years as a scout, he'd never once led a patrol into an ambush. He'd always sniffed out trouble before it struck. But not this time. He'd been overconfident and reckless, and now a good man like Clell Parsons was dead on account of it.

Dale had liked Parsons. The man let him do pretty much as he pleased so long as he kept the stable clean and the animals fed and groomed. Dale didn't earn much, but the work wasn't hard and he'd been content. Now someone else would take over the stable, and who knew how he would be?

Dale would avenge Parsons. An eye for an eye, that was what the Bible said. He'd heard a preacher say that once, and liked it a lot. Whoever shot Parsons had to pay.

Dale only hoped the killer hadn't ridden off.

His Winchester '66 in his left hand, he wound through the pines until he was near the north end of the lake and slowed so the shooter wouldn't hear him.

Dale had bought his Winchester the year it was first manufactured. Scouts were allowed to use whatever they wanted, and he'd liked the notion of having a repeater. The soldiers had to take whatever the army issued—at the time, single-shot rifles. Dale often reflected that if Custer and his troops had repeaters at the Little Bighorn, things might have turned out differently.

Called the Yellow Boy, the Winchester '66 sported a brass receiver. His had a round barrel, not the octagonal, and a saddle ring. It was the prettiest gun he'd ever set eyes on and he wouldn't part with it for anything.

Now, molding his other hand to the trigger and the hammer, Dale cat-footed toward the log where he'd seen the shooter.

It brought back memories of his Injun-fighting days. Of the time he snuck up on a Minneconjou war party that had slain several settlers and blasted three of the warriors before they knew what was happening. And the time he and a bunch of soldiers surrounded a group of Blackfeet who had scalped four trappers.

Stopping, Dale gave a toss of his head. Now wasn't the time to be recalling the good old days.

Crouching, he moved from tree to tree. He glimpsed the horses the outlaws had left behind off to his right, near the lake. As bait, he bitterly realized. And he'd fallen for their ruse.

That was what getting old did to a man, Dale reflected. He got soft and careless. He made mistakes he'd never have made in his younger days. Well, Dale vowed, never again. He'd learned his lesson.

A slight sound brought Dale to a stop. Straining his ears, he heard it again. He couldn't tell what it was, but he wasn't taking any chances. Flattening, he crawled.

Dale came to a small blue spruce. Its lowest limbs were a foot and a half off the ground, enough space for him to crawl under and peer out. A tingle of excitement ran through him, and he scarcely breathed.

Not thirty feet away lay the log. Behind it was the shooter, an older man, like Dale, holding a Sharps, as fine a buffalo gun as was ever made. Dale had used a Sharps himself before he switched to the Yellow Boy, and he fondly remembered how powerful and accurate that old rifle was.

Dale racked his brain for everything he'd heard about the outlaws. Their leader was Cestus Calloway. That much everybody knew. There was the gun hand, the Attica Kid, who always used a pistol. Mad Dog Hanks was also halfway famous, and there was another one with a cockeye. But which one was this?

A vague memory bubbled. One of the outlaws was supposed to be an old buffalo hunter. This must be him, Dale reckoned. Absently biting his lip, he concentrated, and suddenly the name came to him. The man's name was Larner. Ben Larner.

Well, Mr. Larner, Dale thought, *you're about to meet your Maker.*

Dale wedged the Yellow Boy to his shoulder. At this range he couldn't miss. Inwardly smiling, he thumbed back the hammer and tensed at the click. But Larner didn't hear it. Smothering a chuckle of elation, Dale put his cheek to the brass receiver, held his breath to steady his aim, and squeezed the trigger.

There was another click, and nothing happened.

Dale looked at his rifle, horrified by his own stupidity. When he'd jumped down from his pinto, he forgot to work the lever to feed a cartridge into the chamber. Something he never would have done in his younger days.

Dale glanced at Larner, hoping the outlaw hadn't heard the second click either.

But Larner had. The old buffalo hunter was swinging the Sharps toward him.

Scrambling back, Dale flung himself to one side as the Sharps went off. He swore the heavy slug missed his ear by a whisker. Then he was up and running, past several pines to a boulder he dived behind.

Dale broke out in a sweat. That had been close. Too

close. His mouth had gone dry; he had to try twice to swallow.

He listened for hoofbeats but didn't hear any. That puzzled him. By rights the outlaw should light a shuck. Why hadn't he?

The answer sent another ripple down Dale's backbone, but this time of apprehension. The old buffalo hunter was doing what hunters did best; Larner was stalking *him*.

A lot of men would be scared witless at the prospect, but Dale almost cackled. He hadn't had this much fun in a coon's age. Hell, in ten coons' ages. Sinking onto his belly, he snaked toward a pine with a broad trunk. Once there, he rose to his knees, removed his cavalry hat, and peeked around.

The forest was unnaturally still. The shots had silenced the birds and driven the squirrels into their nests.

Dreading the worst, Dale jacked the Yellow Boy's lever. The ratchet seemed terribly loud, but that was just his nerves. He peeked out again, and almost lost an eye when the Sharps thundered and the lead struck the trunk and sent sharp slivers flying at his face. Jerking back, Dale snatched his hat and bolted, jamming it on as he went.

Dale was counting on the fact that a Sharps was a single-shot rifle and it would take a few seconds for Larner to reload. He reached another pine and darted behind it.

To his surprise, from out of the trees came a laugh.

"Not bad, you old goat," Larner called out.

"Who are you callin' old?" Dale hollered, and realized the mistake he'd just made. He'd told Larner right where he was, which was probably what Larner wanted him to do.

"Damn me," Dale muttered, and broke into another run. Zigzagging madly, he nearly tripped over his own feet when a gully appeared almost at his toes. He had to dig in his heels to keep from falling in.

Jumping down, Dale hunkered. He removed his hat again and raised his head to see over. Not so much as a leaf moved. Extending the Yellow Boy, he waited. Larner was bound to show himself. He needed to be patient.

A minute went by. More. Dale was beginning to think he was mistaken and the outlaw had snuck off when he was jolted by a blow to the back of his head that set the world to spinning and flooded him with pain. He was aware of losing his grip on the Yellow Boy, of sliding down and coming to rest doubled over with his cheek in the dirt.

Larner had clubbed him with the Sharps and now stood with his feet planted wide and a smirk on his face. "Snuck right up on you. Any last words?"

Dale forced himself to sit up. He felt weak and queasy. Licking his lips, he said, "Go to hell."

"You first," Larner said, and pointed the Sharps.

At the blast of a shot, Dale winced. There was no pain, nothing. Bewildered, he saw Larner look down at a red spot on his own buckskin shirt.

"Hell," Larner said.

Dale twisted and beheld Marshal Boyd Cooper with his Colt at arm's length. The lawman should shoot again, but he didn't. He just stared.

With a snarl, Larner raised his Sharps.

That was when Sherm Bonner burst out of nowhere with his Colt at his hip and fanned three swift shots.

Each was like a punch that knocked Larner back a step. He dropped the Sharps and, with a look of astonishment at the turn of events, oozed into a heap.

Awash in relief, Dale slowly rose. "I'll be switched," he said, and grinned. "We've killed us an outlaw."

Chapter 6

Mad Dog Hanks paced the cave entrance for the fiftieth or sixtieth time and grumbled moodily, "Ben should have been back by now. Somethin' has happened to him."

Cestus Calloway was seated by the fire, counting the last of the money they'd stolen from the Alpine Bank and Trust Company. Without looking up, he paused in his count to say, "Ben can take care of himself. Quit frettin'."

"I'll fret if I feel like it," Mad Dog said sullenly. "Him and me are friends. It would rile me somethin' fierce if he came to harm."

Cestus sighed and went on flicking bills with his thumb and forefinger. "Maybe the posse was slow reachin' the lake. Maybe Larner's horse came up lame. All sorts of things could have delayed him."

"Bein' dead could too," Mad Dog said.

"Ben wouldn't let them get close enough to plug him," Cestus said irritably. "He's been killin' a lot longer than you or me."

Across the fire, Butch McGivern was picking at his teeth with a twig. "It is sort of peculiar, though, him takin' so long. Must be on near to midnight."

Cestus stopped counting a second time. "I doubt it's even ten yet. Anyone have a watch?" He never carried one

himself. Keeping track of time had always seemed as pointless to him as working for a pittance to make someone else
rich.

Bert Varrow, seated on a small boulder, pulled his pocket
watch from his vest and opened it. He put his ear to the
glass, smiled, then said, "You were almost right. Twenty
minutes past ten."

"There. You see?" Cestus said to Mad Dog.

"Maybe one of us should go have a look-see," Ira Toomis
suggested while taking out his plug of tobacco.

"Couldn't hurt," Cockeye said.

Cestus shook his head in mild exasperation. "I am ridin'
with a flock of biddy hens."

The shadows dancing on the cave wall acquired form
and substance as out of them came the Attica Kid, his
thumbs hooked in his gun belt. "For once I'm with the rest
of them."

"You too?" Cestus said in surprise.

With his customary catlike motion, the Kid came around
the fire and sank down. "The old man has had enough time,
twice over, to get here."

"See?" Mad Dog said to Cestus. "Even the Kid agrees
with me."

Cestus trusted the Kid's judgment the most of all of
them. The Kid was young, but he was savvy beyond his
years, especially when it came to killing and robbing. Cestus
had never met anyone so naturally gifted at being bad. "If
he does," he said to spite Mad Dog, "it's a first."

The Attica Kid chuckled.

"Look down your nose at me all you want," Mad Dog
said. "But I always do as you say, don't I? I've never once let
you down."

"Except for your gripin'," Cestus said.

"I can't help that," Mad Dog said. "I was born with a
salty disposition, as my ma used to say."

"Salty, hell," Cestus said. "You were born with a cactus up your ass."

Most of them laughed.

Mad Dog colored but had the sense not to get mad. "This ain't about me. It's about Ben Larner. He can lick a posse of townsfolk without half tryin'. So why ain't he here unless somethin' went wrong?"

"No one's luck holds forever," Bert Varrow said as he slid his watch back into his vest pocket. "Ask any gambler."

"I know that," Cestus said with more heat than he intended.

"Then why ain't we doin' somethin'?" Mad Dog demanded. "Say the word and I'll go look for him. You won't have to put up with any more of my gripin'."

"You gripe like you breathe," Cestus said. "As soon as you get back, you'd find somethin' else to gripe about."

"So can I or can't I?" Mad Dog persisted.

All eyes settled on Cestus. He resented that they were siding against him, and then realized how foolish that was. They weren't set to ride off whether he liked it or not. They had left the decision up to him. He was their leader and they'd do as he said. Which was as it should be, given that he was the one who always went on about how he'd do his best to ensure that those who rode with him never came to harm. A backtrack was called for, in more ways than one. "I was goin' to wait a little longer. Ben wouldn't push hard in the dark. But you're right, Mad Dog."

"I am?" Mad Dog sounded astounded.

"Ben should have been back by now and we should send someone to look for him, but it won't be you."

"Why not? I'm as good in the dark as anyone."

"Because you're headstrong, for one thing," Cestus said. "If something has happened, you're pigheaded enough to ride into Alpine and do somethin' that will cause trouble for the rest of us."

"I wouldn't go into town without your say-so," Mad Dog said.

"I can't take the chance. Someone else has to go. Someone with less of a temper."

"I'll go," Cockeye volunteered.

"No. You'd be recognized, what with that eye of yours. So would the Kid, thanks to the newspapers printin' his description so many times."

"Can I help it if they like to write about gun hands?" the Attica Kid said.

"That leaves me, Ira, and Butch," Varrow said. "I don't mind going. Maybe sit in on a card game or two."

"I knew you would say that," Cestus replied, "which is why it won't be you. Those fancy duds might give you away. You were seen at the bank, close up, remember?"

"So now it's me or the cowboy," Ira Toomis said.

"Used to be I was," Butch McGivern said. "Not anymore."

Cestus gnawed his lip, debating. Toomis was almost as reliable as the Attica Kid. Another born criminal, but not as quick on the shoot or as quick between the ears. "It should be somebody who will fit in."

"Are you sayin' I wouldn't?" Toomis said.

"I'm sayin' a former cowpoke would be better, what with all the punchers who come from the ranches to have a good time at the saloons."

"What do you know? It's my lucky night," McGivern said. "I'll get to have some whiskey and maybe a dove if she's willin'."

"Hold on," Cestus said as McGivern went to rise. "There are rules you must abide by."

"More rules?" McGivern said. "We've already got how many? Twenty?" He began reciting them. "There's to be no killin' when we rob unless we can't help it. There's to be no drinkin' at the hideout. We're not to squabble or fight among ourselves. We're not to take anything that don't belong to us."

"You didn't mention my favorite," the Attica Kid said.

"Which would that be?" McGivern asked.

"We're not to wipe our asses with poison oak."

Everyone enjoyed that one, even Mad Dog.

"I'd forgotten I told you that," Cestus said when the mirth subsided. "Damn, I am thorough."

It provoked more laughter.

Butch McGivern stood. "What are the new rules? It better not be I have to keep my pecker in my pants. I'd like a tumble with a female."

"Who wouldn't?" Cestus rejoined. "Now listen. If you have to go all the way into Alpine, take precautions. Change your shirt so it's not the same one you had on when we robbed the bank. Don't use the main street. Use the side streets. In the saloons, be careful who you talk to. And don't do anything to draw attention to yourself."

"That's just common sense," McGivern said. "Don't worry. I know what to do. I'll find Larner or find out what happened to him, and be back here by noon tomorrow."

"If you're not," Mad Dog said, "we'll all go ridin' into that town and bring it down around its ears."

The night was moonless, the forest pitch-black. Riding faster than a walk was out of the question.

Even so, Butch McGivern was pleased as could be. It was rare that any of them were allowed to go into town alone. Usually Calloway had them go in pairs. To be on his own with money in his poke and not have to be back until the next day—Larner or no, he aimed to have a grand time.

Grand times were also rare these days, much to McGivern's regret. Back in his days of riding herd and branding and roping, he'd lived for his days off, for when he and his pards would barrel into town and let off steam by shooting into the air and whooping and hollering and drinking until they couldn't see straight. He'd liked those wild times so much he took to sneaking off now and then to treat himself. One of those times, he got so drunk it took two days to recover enough to ride back to the ranch. The foreman promptly fired him.

McGivern hadn't minded. There were plenty of ranches looking for good men. He worked at another and then another and it was always the same. He'd take to celebrating too hard and his work would suffer and he'd be told to find work somewhere else. He acquired a reputation as being more trouble than he was worth, and eventually there wasn't a rancher in the territory who'd have anything to do with him.

He'd tried his hand at gambling, but he didn't have the knack that Bert Varrow did. He'd clerked for a day at a general store, or rather, half a day. That was all he could stand of having some tub in an apron telling him what to do. It was demeaning.

Desperate for money, McGivern jumped a man in an alley one night. The man's poke yielded twenty dollars. From mugging he graduated to robbing people and then to robbing stages. It was risky, robbing them alone, but stage-coaches yielded more money than anything except a bank, and banks were even riskier unless you had others to back your play.

One day he'd charged out of the woods to stop the Denver-to-Leadville stage, and who should come out of the woods on the other side of the road but Cestus Calloway and his gang? They had a good laugh over it that night when they were dividing their spoils, and Calloway invited McGivern to join them.

Only a jackass would have refused.

That was a year and a half ago. McGivern had no regrets other than he didn't get into a town often enough to indulge his passion for liquor and women. Now here he was, soon to enjoy both.

There was no sign of Ben Larner at Alpine Lake. There was no sign of anyone. Not even the horses they'd left.

McGivern hollered Larner's name a few times, to be sure. Receiving no answer, he rode on to Alpine.

It was pushing two a.m. when McGivern got there. That late, most towns were shut down for the night. Not Alpine. About half of her saloons stayed open twenty-four hours, mainly so crews from the mines, who got done on the middle shift at midnight, would be tempted to spend their hard-earned dollars on whiskey and women.

McGivern used side streets, as Calloway had advised. He picked a saloon that wasn't well lit out front, and tied his mount to the hitch rail. Pulling his hat brim low, he sauntered in.

Some miners were at the bar and some townsmen and other miners at tables, playing cards.

In the far corner sat a pair of cowhands with a half-empty bottle between them.

McGivern smiled. Luck was with him. He paid for a bottle of his own and carried it and a glass over to the corner. "Howdy, gents," he greeted the punchers. "Mind if I join you?"

"Not at all," said the shorter of the two. He had a slight lisp on account of his buckteeth.

"Lefty and me haven't seen you in here before," said the other one. He was as tall as McGivern, with a shock of black hair.

"Just passin' through," McGivern said. Filling his glass, he took a sip and sighed. He'd like to savor every drop, but first he had business to conduct. "I heard tell one of your banks was robbed today."

"The Alpine Bank and Trust," the once called Lefty said. "We were part of the posse that went after those who did it."

"You don't say," McGivern said, scarcely able to conceal his delight. This was luck on top of luck. "Did you catch the owl-hoots?"

"It was Cestus Calloway and his wild bunch," Lefty said.

"And no, they all got away except one. My pard here, Sherm, killed him."

"I helped," Sherm said. "The marshal put a slug into him too."

"You don't say," McGivern said again, surprised he wasn't more rattled by the news. "This outlaw have a handle?"

"The marshal says it was Ben Larner," Lefty said. "Some old buffalo hunter who went bad."

"They're sure it was him?" McGivern asked to make small talk, since he knew very well it had to be. Mad Dog would be fit to be tied, and some of the others might want to take revenge too.

"You can ask the marshal or the deputy yourself," Lefty said.

McGivern grinned and shrugged. "What do I care who it was? I'm not about to bother them."

"It won't be any bother," Sherm said, and nodded toward the batwings. "Here comes the deputy now."

Chapter 7

For Deputy Hugo Mitchell, it had been a day he'd never forget.

First there had been the bank robbery. He wouldn't have reckoned that ever happening, not in a million years. Sure, the Cloverleaf Bank and the Red Cliff Bank had been struck, but Cloverleaf and Red Cliff were smaller towns. He never imagined the outlaws would try a town as big as Alpine.

Then there was the gun battle at the lake. Mitch had never expected to ever be in a gun battle either. Sure, he was a deputy, but a lot of lawmen—in fact, most of them—went their entire lives without having to shoot anyone, or even having to draw their six-shooter. The way Mitch saw it, he was lucky he'd survived.

Then there was the dead guy.

Mitch had only ever seen one dead person, his grandmother, after she'd passed to her reward quietly in her sleep. He'd been ten or eleven at the time and his mother took him to the funeral and made him stand by the open casket and bow his head. It made his skin crawl.

The truth be known, Mitch was never all that fond of her. His grandma was a crotchety biddy who'd liked to poke him with her cane whenever he did anything she didn't like, and she didn't like a lot of things: him tracking dirt into her house, him touching things she didn't want him to touch, him eating with his mouth full. The list had been as long as his arm.

Now he'd seen a second body, only this one had been shot to ribbons. The blood had made him a bit queasy, but he didn't let that show. The others might laugh at him. It wasn't manly to be a weak sister.

Mitch felt no remorse that the man was dead and he'd been a party to the killing. Not when the son of a bitch had shot Mitch's horse. By all accounts, Ben Larner had been a vicious killer. Larner got what he deserved.

No, what Mitch felt was worry.

It had dawned on him that wearing a tin star was more dangerous than he'd appreciated. Most folks respected the law. The worst he had to deal with were drunks now and then. Genuine man-killers were few and far between, thank goodness.

But all it took was one, Mitch realized, to put holes in him as Larner had put that big hole in his horse. Or, for that matter, a violent drunk who refused to calm down.

Wearing a badge could make Mitch dead, and he didn't like that. He was rethinking his decision to be a law officer when he strolled into the Daisy Mae Saloon on his usual rounds. The owner had named it after a gal he knew back in his younger days and carried a torch for ever since.

Mitch was tired. He looked forward to the end of his shift so he could crawl into his bed over at the boarding-house and sleep for eight or nine hours. He idly nodded at the bartender, scanned the room, and was about to back out when he saw Sherm Bonner and Lefty in the corner with another cowboy.

Figuring he should say howdy, Mitch went over. The other cowpoke's back was to him and Mitch didn't pay much attention to him. When you had seen one puncher, you had pretty much seen them all.

"Boys," Mitch said by way of greeting. "You're up awful late."

"We have to be back at the ranch by tomorrow night," Sherm said. "Gettin' our last drinkin' in."

"Couldn't sleep much anyhow," Lefty remarked. "Not after today."

"That was somethin', wasn't it?" Mitch said.

"It will be all over the territory," Sherm predicted.

"Thanks to the newspapers," Lefty said.

Mitch was tempted to join them for a bit. He moved to an empty chair to the left of the other cowboy and said without looking at him, "Howdy, mister."

The other cowboy grunted.

"Did you hear what the undertaker is fixin' to do?" Mitch asked, thinking the news might amuse them.

"We have not," Lefty said.

"He told the marshal he's goin' to prop Larner up in an open casket in front of his business and charge folks two bits to look at the famous dead outlaw."

"Larner ain't all that famous," Sherm said. "It's not as if he was Jesse James or somebody."

Mitch shrugged, pulled out the chair, and sat. "He's famous enough in these parts. The undertaker figures he can make twenty dollars or better."

"Well, hell," Lefty said. "He should give half of that to Sherm, since it was Sherm who sent the no-account to hell."

"The marshal helped," Sherm said.

"So you and the law dog can split the money," Lefty proposed.

"I doubt the undertaker would go for that," Mitch said. "Once he gets his hands on a body, he figures it's his to do with as he pleases."

"If I'd known we could make money from it, I'd have propped that old buffalo hunter against a tree and charged folks the same as the undertaker," Lefty said.

"You would not," Sherm said. "You're just mad that the undertaker is makin' money and we're not."

"It's not fair," Lefty said.

"The marshal said it was all right by him so long as it's done orderly," Mitch remarked. "He doesn't want the street blocked by crowds."

"Larner won't draw no crowd," Sherm said.

"All he'll draw is flies," Lefty joked.

Both cowboys chuckled.

It had occurred to Mitch that the other cowboy wasn't saying much and he turned to him and said, "What do you think, mister? Who should get the money? The undertaker or Sherm here?"

"I heard where they do that over to Kansas," the cowboy said. "Put bodies out for folks to see."

The cowboy was looking down at the table, and Mitch couldn't see much of his face because of the man's hat brim. But a feeling came over him that he'd seen the puncher somewhere before. "Do I know you?"

"Never met you before, Deputy, that I know of," the cowboy said.

"What's your name?"

The cowboy seemed to hesitate. "Hayes."

"You have the same name as the president?" Mitch said. "Are you any relation?"

"None that I know of," the cowpoke said.

"Nobody famous ever had my name," Mitch said.

"Me either," Lefty said. "And they ain't likely to."

"What's your last name, if you don't mind my askin'?" Mitch said.

Lefty glanced at Sherm.

"Go ahead and tell him," Sherm said, grinning.

"It's Barnhelm," Lefty said.

"Barnhelm? I don't believe I've ever heard that before," Mitch remarked. Which wasn't unusual. There were a lot of names he'd never heard of until he heard them.

"It's German," Lefty said. "I hardly ever use it, and you'd better not tell anybody."

"You don't like your name?"

"Do you like yours?" Lefty rejoined.

"I never thought about it much," Mitch said. "What good does it do? We're stuck with what our folks name us."

"That's not true," Sherm said. "People change their names all the time. Outlaws in particular."

"I like bein' called Lefty, but I'm not about to go around tellin' everybody I'm Lefty Barnhelm."

"I don't see why not," Mitch said. "Look at Mr. Hayes here. He doesn't mind bein' named after a president."

"Who would?" Lefty said.

"A name is a name," Sherm said.

Mitch turned to the other puncher. There was something about the cowboy's square jaw that pricked at his brain. It was about the squarest jaw he'd ever seen. Sort of like an anvil. "What's your first name, Mr. Hayes?"

"You sure are nosy," Hayes said.

"I don't mean nothin," Mitch said. "It's just that I still think I know you from somewhere."

"It's Farley," Hayes said. "Farley Hayes."

"Farley Hayes?" Mitch repeated, and had to admit, "No. I've never met anyone with that handle."

"Told you," Hayes said. He raised his glass and took a quick gulp of whiskey and set the glass down again.

Mitch caught a glimpse of his face, and for some reason, alarm spiked through him. But he couldn't for the life of him figure out why. He wondered if maybe he'd seen the man's face on a wanted poster but couldn't recollect one that matched. "What ranch do you work at?"

"I don't," Hayes said. "I'm driftin'."

"Ridin' the grub line?" Lefty said. "I've had to do that a time or two my own self. Never do like bein' out of work."

"Me either," Sherm said. "Makes me feel lazy."

"I don't mind lazy," Mitch said. "The days where I don't have much to do are the days I like best."

"Not me," Lefty said. "I have to keep busy. Sittin' around twiddlin' my thumbs drives me loco."

"How about you, Mr. Hayes?" Mitch said.

"How about me what?"

"Do you like keepin' busy or bein' lazy?"

"I like to mind my own business."

"Here, now," Mitch said. "You have no call to get mad. All I did was ask your name."

"And where I work," Hayes said. "And whether I like bein' lazy or not."

"Seems to me you're a mite prickly," Mitch said. He noticed that Sherm was looking at Hayes as if he too was puzzled by how Hayes was acting. "You should have another drink and relax."

Hayes did, another quick swallow that didn't please him much because he scowled as he lowered the glass.

Mitch had another glimpse of the cowpoke's face, and this time it triggered a rush of memory: of him coming down Main Street that morning, and of two men at the hitch rail in front of the Alpine Bank and Trust Company. One of those men had been Ben Larner. The other one had stepped in front of Mitch and smiled and said that there was someone in the bank who wanted to see him. Mitch had gone on in. He hadn't thought to question who the man was or how he knew someone in the bank wanted to talk to him.

And now it all came back.

The man who had stopped him had been dressed like a cowboy. The other thing Mitch remembered was that the man had a square jaw. A jaw like an anvil. Exactly like this puncher's jaw.

Mitch's mouth suddenly went dry. The cowboy who called himself Hayes wasn't a cowboy at all; he was one of the outlaws. Mitch tried to remember the man's name. Marshal Cooper had told him when Mitch related his encounter. It was Mc-something or other. Suddenly it came to him. McGivern. Butch McGivern.

Mitch hadn't ever heard of McGivern killing anyone, but an outlaw was an outlaw. McGivern would likely shoot rather than be taken to jail. And here they were, practically brushing elbows.

"Somethin' wrong, Deputy?" Lefty asked. "You look sickly."

"No," Mitch said quickly, his voice hoarse. Coughing to clear his throat, he said, "It's been a long day, is all. What with the robbery and chasin' those outlaws." He deliberately avoided looking at McGivern.

"I wonder how Cestus Calloway will take losin' one of his gang," Lefty said. "It's never happened before."

"They're outlaws," Sherm said. "They don't expect to die in their sleep."

"I reckon so," Lefty said. "They get what they have comin' to them for all the robbin' and killin' they do."

Mitch glanced at McGivern and wondered how he was taking this kind of talk. McGivern had bowed his head, so he couldn't tell.

"Larner sure got what he had comin'," Sherm said. "Him shootin' poor Parsons like he done."

Taking a grip on himself, Mitch realized he must do something. Any moment, McGivern might get up and walk out. As casually as he could, he placed his right hand on his hip above his holster. He was no quick-draw artist. His best bet was to unlimber his revolver unnoticed and train it on McGivern before the outlaw caught on.

As if the badman had read his mind, McGivern declared, "I reckon I'll be goin', gents. It's awful late and I need some shut-eye." He drained his glass and clutched his bottle.

Mitch took a gamble. Suddenly pushing his chair back and heaving to his feet, he drew his six-shooter and pointed it at McGivern. "You're not goin' anywhere, mister," he exclaimed more shrilly than he intended.

What happened next happened so fast that it was over before Mitch could collect his wits.

McGivern threw the bottle at him and sprang back, McGivern's chair crashing to the floor as he clawed for his revolver. McGivern was quick, but Sherm was quicker. Even as McGivern drew, Sherm was up and cleared leather and fanned his Colt twice. The booms were loud in the confines of the saloon. Both slugs caught McGivern dead center in the chest and smashed him back, causing him to trip over the chair and fall.

Mitch took a step to one side to have a clear shot, but another shot wasn't needed.

The outlaw's square jaw jutted at the ceiling, and his eyes were already glazing.

"What the hell?" Lefty said. "What was that about?"

"He was one of the outlaws," Mitch said, enlightening him. He swallowed to wet his throat. "I'm obliged for the help, Mr. Bonner." To be sure, he stepped to the body and nudged it with his toe.

"This makes the second gent I've shot since I got up yesterday mornin'," Sherm said, coming around the table. "This has been some day."

"You can say that again," Mitch said.

Chapter 8

Marshal Boyd Cooper and his deputy had become the talk of the town, if not the whole state, and Boyd didn't like it one bit. TWO OUTLAWS SLAIN! the *True Fissure*'s headline screamed the day after Butch McGivern was shot at the Daisy Mae, followed by ALPINE LAWMEN STRIKE BLOWS FOR LAW AND ORDER. The account went on to relate how Boyd had a hand in shooting Ben Larner, and how Deputy Mitchell had recognized Butch McGivern in the saloon, and how that led to McGivern being shot.

That Sherm Bonner had done the actually shooting didn't seem to matter much to the town newspaper. Bonner was mentioned, but he didn't get near the attention he should, in Boyd's opinion. Probably because Sherm and Lefty had returned to the Circle T and been sent out on the range, and the newspapermen couldn't find them to get the particulars.

Boyd had a suspicion that was deliberate on Bonner's part. The cowboy didn't want the publicity, and Boyd didn't blame him. Acquiring a reputation as a man-killer was an invite to trouble.

Boyd was being treated as if he were the best lawman who ever toted tin, and that bothered him. He was good at his job, but people were heaping praise on him he didn't merit. Why, one news account compared him to the likes of the Masterson brothers and even Wild Bill Hickok, which was so preposterous he'd almost gone to the newspaper to throttle the journalist who wrote it.

As it was, Boyd had to put up with having his hand shaken by nearly everyone he encountered, or so it seemed, to say nothing of the praise heaped on him. He couldn't walk into a saloon without someone insisting he have a drink, and twice now—to his amazement—ladies had asked him to kiss their babies.

So it was that three days after Butch McGivern and Ben Larner went to their final rest on Boot Hill, Boyd decided to get away from the hullabaloo for a while. He wanted to go fishing. Nothing relaxed him like an afternoon at the pond.

He also had something else in mind.

Boyd informed Mitch and Harvey Dale that he'd be away from the office for a while. Mitch wanted to know where he was going and Boyd simply answered, "I have business to tend to. You two hold down the fort."

"You can count on me, Marshal," Hugo Mitchell said, and rubbed his badge with his sleeve.

It bothered Boyd that Mitch was eating up the newspaper stories and the adoration that had resulted with a king-sized spoon. He feared it had gone to the young man's head, and Boyd intended to have a talk with him when he got around to it.

Now, astride his chestnut and wearing his best shirt, Boyd rode out of Alpine on the road that led to the Wilson Farm. He had decided to take Sam's advice to heart.

The sun was at its zenith, the sky a clear blue. A robin warbled and sparrows chirped. It was as pretty a day as there could be, perfect for what Boyd had in mind.

He shouldn't be nervous. Not a man his age, with his experience. But he was. This was a huge step. If things worked out, it would forever change his life. Which was all right by him.

Boyd was tired of being alone. He wouldn't mind a companion. Someone to come home to. Someone to share his bed with. Someone to listen to his complaints and have a sympathetic ear.

Someone, say, like Cecelia Wilson.

Boyd had thought of her a lot the past several days. Of her frank manner and her warm smile and especially about how fine a figure of a woman she was, even at her age. They were both in their fifties, which some would say was over the hill. Not by his reckoning, though. He preferred to think of him and her as seasoned and mature.

And dang, Cecelia sure did look fine in a dress.

The farmhouse was the same as it had always been, yet somehow it looked different. Boyd noticed details he hadn't before: the flowers on a trellis, that the pump was freshly painted, that a new birdhouse had been hung in a tree.

Climbing down, Boyd adjusted his hat and smoothed his shirt. He stepped onto the porch and over to the screen door and went to knock, but hesitated. What if she had changed her mind about him? he reflected, and then snorted at how foolish he was being and knocked.

Shoes scraped softly, and Cecelia appeared out of the shadowed hall. Her dress was the color of the sky with a splash of yellow trim at her throat and at the ends of her sleeves. "Marshal," she said, and bestowed one of those warm smiles of hers on him.

"This isn't a formal visit," Boyd said.

"You don't say," Cecelia said.

"You can call me by my name."

"I will if you will." Cecelia pushed on the screen door and stood back so he could pass her. "Come in, please. We'll repair to the parlor."

Taking off his hat, Boyd entered. For some reason he was reminded of the first time he ever went courting, and how nervous and shy he'd been. "Is Sam to home?"

"He's out in the fields," Cecelia said. "It's just us."

Boyd grew warm all over, and gestured for her to pre-
cede him, as a gentleman should. "I'm sorry about his
horse."

"It wasn't you who shot it," Cecelia said. "It was that
awful outlaw. And he's dead now. Good riddance, I say."

"Most folks in town are right happy about the fact,"
Boyd remarked. He'd rather not talk about the killings, but
she was the one who'd brought it up.

"They should be," Cecelia said. "Lawbreakers are a
blight on any God-fearing community. I'd as soon every last
one of them was hanged."

"I had no idea you were so bloodthirsty," Boyd teased.

The parlor was comfortably furnished, with a settee and
chairs and a piano. A painting of a waterfall hung on a wall.
On another hung a large cross.

"Have a seat, why don't you?" Cecelia offered, and followed him to the settee. As she sat, she said, "It's not bloodthirsty to want justice done. The world won't be a safe place
until all those like that Larner and McGivern have been
sent to hell where they belong."

This was a side of her Boyd hadn't seen before. "I don't
rightly know if that day will ever come. And it's not them
I'm here to talk about. It's us."

Cecelia sat back, her eyes twinkling. "You don't say. It's
about time. But better late than never."

"I like you, Cecelia," Boyd began.

"I like you too."

"I've liked you for a while now but didn't have the
gumption to say so to your face."

"In case you haven't noticed," Cecelia said, "I noticed."

Boyd wondered if she was laughing at him. "It's a little
awkward for me, doing this. I mean, at our age."

"What is it you're doing exactly? Besides stalling?"

Now Boyd was certain. He amused her. "I'd like to come
courting. I'd like to take you places. And visit whenever I
wanted."

"To be clear," Cecelia said, "visit me or visit the fish in the pond?"

"Oh, Cecelia," Boyd said.

She laughed merrily. "Boyd, Boyd, Boyd. I've been waiting for this day for more than a year. You are more than welcome to come courting anytime you so desire."

"Thank you."

"I have to say, though," Cecelia said, "I'm curious as to what finally brought you out of your shell."

Boyd wasn't about to get Sam into trouble by telling her that her brother was responsible. Instead he said, "I wasn't aware I was in one."

"Oh, a lot of men have shells. Women too. People put shells around themselves for protection. We can't be hurt if we don't open up to others."

"If you say so," Boyd said. "But it's not that I think I need protectin' so much as you scare me a little."

Cecelia blinked. "I beg your pardon? *I* scare *you*? You're the one who guns down outlaws, for goodness' sake."

"Outlaws can't hold a candle to a woman when it comes to bein' fearsome," Boyd said.

"You'll have to explain."

Boyd wasn't certain he could. "A woman like you is a mystery to a man. We don't know what you think or how you feel. Add to that how beautiful you are, and you can't blame me if it took a while for me to grab the bull by the horns, so to speak."

Cecelia asked softly, "Do you really find me beautiful, Boyd? An old gal like me?"

"More beautiful than a sunrise," Boyd admitted.

"Oh my." Cecelia's cheeks flushed pink. "No one has claimed that about me in a good many years."

"Probably because that shell of yours hides your face."

Cecelia grinned. "Touché, as Mr. Laurant at the restaurant would say. But you shouldn't exaggerate. Not when it comes to my looks. With young women, yes. Flattery is a given. It's expected." She paused. "A woman my age has only to gaze in the mirror to shatter any illusions."

"A rainbow doesn't think it's beautiful either, but to the person lookin' at it, it is."

"Why, that's quite profound."

Boyd's skin became prickly under his shirt. Fidgeting, he said, "No one has ever called me that before."

"Maybe you've hid it from everyone."

"If I have, I've hid it from me too."

Laughing, Cecelia reached out and placed her hand on his knee. "This is a good start. I hope we can go on being honest and comfortable with each other."

Boyd wasn't feeling comfortable. He was feeling hot. It was childish, but he couldn't help himself. To cover his embarrassment he said, "I don't suppose I could trouble you for a glass of water?"

"Why, certainly." Cecelia rose and bustled out.

Bubbling with excitement, Boyd stood and crossed to a front window. He felt twenty years old again. He envisioned her and him going on long rides together, or going into town to eat and shop, or taking strolls in the pasture, and almost laughed at how ridiculous he was being. He might have gone on fantasizing, but a rider went past out on the road and he caught sight of an older man in a well-worn black coat and a weathered hat.

The man stared at the farmhouse as he went by. It seemed strange, that stare.

Boyd couldn't rightly say why. The man's face wasn't familiar and Boyd was about to go down the hall and out onto the front porch to watch the man ride off when Cecelia reappeared with a glass of water in each hand.

"One for you and one for me."

Boyd reclaimed his seat on the settee. "I'm obliged."

"I don't mind fetching for a man so long as it's not always me who does the fetching," Cecelia said.

"Anything else I should know?" Boyd asked, half-jokingly.

"I don't like a whiner. I don't like a complainer. I don't like a man who doesn't wash regular or doesn't take care of his teeth. I don't like a man who goes around in shabby clothes. Not that you do any of that. At least, you haven't yet, but a woman never really knows."

"Good Lord," Boyd said.

"Don't sound so shocked. You must have standards of your own."

"Only one that I can think of."

"Name it, and if it's not something that goes against my grain, I'll do my best to accommodate you."

"I like my gal to be girly."

"Girly?" Cecelia said, and chortled.

"Hear me out," Boyd said. "Some ladies are as bossy as men, always sayin' how things will be. They carp all the time, about every little thing that bothers them. Or they put on airs, as if they're a queen and their man is a commoner."

"That's not me," Cecelia said.

"I hope not. I'd be powerful disappointed. Out at the pond you've always shown a lot of common sense and it would sorrow me to think that was an act and you're one of those females who likes to trick a man into sayin' I do."

"Why, Boyd Cooper, I had no idea you're such a man of the world." Cecelia paused. "Or that marriage is on your mind."

"What?" Boyd said, startled, and realized what he'd said about "I do." "Gettin' hitched is as far from my mind as bein' Wild Bill Hickok."

"You have to enlighten me with that last part."

Boyd told her about the newspapers, and all the fuss, ending with "I'll be glad when this blows over. I'm not a gun hand and never will be. I tote a badge and have to shoot my revolver now and then, but I don't carve notches on it, like some do."

"Is it true the Attica Kid does? Sam told me he heard that somewhere."

"I never met the man. I couldn't say."

"Do you know what Cestus Calloway is like?"

"A lot of folks like him. They say he's right friendly, as owl-hoots go."

"I hope so," Cecelia said.

"What does it matter?"

"For me, not a lick," Cecelia said. "But I should think it would matter to you."

"How so?" Boyd asked, hoping he didn't sound stupid for not knowing.

"Two of his friends are dead on account of your posse and your deputy and you," Cecelia said. "Some men would take that as a personal affront and want an eye for an eye. Let's hope Cestus Calloway isn't one of them."

"Amen to that," Boyd said.

Chapter 9

Ira Toomis arrived at the cave shortly after daybreak. He'd ridden all night to get there and was tired and sore. Only Cockeye was up, standing guard, and all he did was grunt when Toomis rode up and dismounted.

Going to the fire, which had almost died out, Toomis added enough wood to get the flames crackling, and warmed coffee leftover from the night before. As soon as it was hot enough, he filled his cup and drank it black with no sugar. He needed the jolt. As he hunkered, the warm cup between his fingers, he wondered how the others would take the news.

Toomis knew what he would do, but he wasn't in charge. By common consent Cestus was their leader, and that was fine by him. He'd freely admit that Calloway was smarter than he was, and he liked riding with a man who outthought everybody. That was rare in outlaw circles.

Toomis had been living on the shady side of the law for so long that the way of life was as ingrained in him as breathing. He'd stolen a lot of things as a boy, and growing into manhood hadn't changed anything. He'd only stolen more.

Stealing was in his blood, he reckoned. His pa had worked the Mississippi riverboats as a pickpocket, and his grandpa had been a footpad.

Neither ever got caught, and Toomis hoped to do the same.
He saved every cent he stole, which was why his poke
was bigger than the rest. He'd never told anyone, but he was
saving for the time when he was too old to steal anymore.
He'd take his savings and find a nice, quiet town somewhere
and spend his waning days in a rocking chair enjoying the
fruits of his stolen spoils.

Since he joined up with Cestus Calloway, he'd added
more to his poke than he ever did by his lonesome, which
was another reason why he'd like for things to continue as
they were for a good long while. He was worried they
wouldn't. Not with the news he brought. But he had to tell
them. They'd find out anyway, eventually.

Mad Dog Hanks was the first to rouse. Sitting up, he ruf-
fled his unruly hair, jammed his hat on, and saw Toomis.
"You're back."

"Seems so," Toomis said.

"Don't start on me," Mad Dog grumbled.

Toomis had never met anyone with such a sour disposition. Mad Dog was exactly like his namesake, always foam-
ing at the mouth and ready to bite. It was almost comical.
"Did you sleep well?"

"What the hell do you care?" Mad Dog cast off his blanket and stood. Coming over, he squatted and filled his own
cup. "What did you find out?"

"I'll tell everyone at once."

"Why can't you tell me now?"

"Everyone together," Toomis said. He wouldn't risk Mad
Dog riding off to town in a fury. In addition to being a great
grumbler, Mad Dog was bloodthirsty as could be.

"Keep your secret, then," Mad Dog said resentfully.

Cockeye joined them to pour coffee for himself. He
grunted at Mad Dog and Mad Dog grunted back.

"Cestus was sayin' last night we might hit the Silverton
Bank once Larner and McGivern get back," Mad Dog remarked.

This was news to Loomis. Good news. The Silverton Bank was a rich one. The town also had a marshal and several deputies. The job would need a lot of planning to do the job right.

That was another thing Loomis liked about Calloway. The man was a wizard at planning how to get in and get the money and get out again with their hides intact.

Speak of the Devil. Just then Cestus rolled onto his back, opened his eyes, and saw them. "Mornin', boys."

"Mornin'," Loomis said.

Cockeye grunted.

"Loomis here won't tell me what he found out," Mad Dog complained.

"He likes to put on airs."

"I was waitin' for everbody to get up," Loomis said.

"In that case," Cestus said, and raised his voice. "Kid! Bert! Rise and shine! Ira is back and we should hear what he has to say." Standing, he stretched and came over to the fire.

Bert Varrow was slow to come out from under his blankets, but not the Attica Kid. The Kid always sprang up like a cat, fully dressed with his pistol on his hip. The Kid moved like a cat too as he came to the fire.

Loomis waited for Bert to join them. When all eyes were on him and he couldn't put it off any longer, he took a breath and declared, "Both Larner and McGivern are dead."

"Both?" Cestus said.

Loomis nodded. "Larner was killed at the lake by the marshal and a cowpoke called Sherm Bonner. A part-time deputy named Dale was involved, but it was the other two who put the lead into Larner." He took a quick swallow. "McGivern was killed in a saloon. The other deputy, the green one, was there, but it was Sherm Bonner who shot McGivern."

"Bonner again," Mad Dog growled.

"Both of them," Cestus said sadly. "I didn't expect this. I figured McGivern was sleepin' off a drunk and that was why he hadn't made it back yet."

"I liked him," Cockeye said.

"We'll have to find men to replace them," Cestus said. "Any of you have anyone you'd recommend?"

"Hold on," Mad Dog said. "That's it? They're dead and we forget them? To hell with that."

"What would you suggest?" Cestus asked.

"What the hell else?" Mad Dog retorted. "They were good men. We rode with them a long time. We owe it to them to kill the bastards who killed them."

"We kill a marshal," Bert Varrow said, "we'll have every tin star in the state out to do us in."

"They have to catch us first," Mad Dog said.

"I'd rather we didn't," Cestus said. "Bert is right about killin' a law dog. It's not good for business."

"Business?" Mad Dog growled. "We rob folks. We're not no general store. Our business is stealin'. And killin' those who get in our way."

"We haven't had to kill anyone since we joined up with Cestus," Toomis remarked.

"You make that sound like a good thing," Mad Dog said. "Sometimes killin' has to be done whether we like it or not. We're a bunch of outlaws, not a bunch of blamed monks."

The Attica Kid surprised them by saying, "Mad Dog is right."

"Again?" Mad Dog said.

"Not you too, Kid?" Cestus said.

The Kid nodded. "We're outlaws, sure. And we take pride in what we do. In doin' it better than anyone else. And in stickin' together through thick and thin. Or am I wrong?"

"You're not," Bert Varrow said. "Go on."

"Two of our own have been bucked out in gore," the Kid continued. "We let that pass and go on as if nothin' has happened, and folks will think we're paper-backed. That as outlaws, we're worthless."

"You're exaggeratain'," Cestus said.

"Am I?" the Attica Kid said. "You know as well as me that fear is the best thing we have goin' for us when we rob a bank or a stage. The fear we put in those we're robbin'. The fear that we'll gun them or knife them if they don't turn over their money or their valuables. Or am I wrong?" he asked once more.

"You're right as rain," Mad Dog said.

"If no one is afraid of us, we become a laughin'stock," the Kid said. "We show up at a bank, they're more likely to resist. We rob a stage, the passengers are more likely to fight back." He shook his head. "I, for one, do not intend to become a laughin'stock."

Everyone looked at Cestus.

"I savvy all that," Cestus said. "I truly do. But revenge can be a costly proposition. We might lose more of us. Do you want that?"

"We owe it to Larner and McGivern to do in those who did them in," Mad Dog said. "That cowpoke and the marshal and his deputy, all three."

"I strongly advise against it," Cestus said.

Bert Varrow cleared his throat. "I'm sorry, Cestus, but I side with the Kid and Mad Dog on this. I was a gambler before I took to bein' an outlaw, and they both have somethin' in common. We live by our reputations. An outlaw no one is afraid of isn't much of an outlaw."

"That's just it," Cestus said. "I've worked hard to do the opposite. To have folks like us. That's why I always give money away as we ride out of a town. I don't want folks scared of us. I don't want them to want us dead. It's important that they don't put a lot of pressure on the law to corral us and have us hanged."

"That's worked until now," the Attica Kid said. "And if it had been only Larner they'd shot, I might go along with you. But Larner *and* McGivern? Two of us, and we do nothin'? I'd be ashamed to ride with an outfit so worthless."

"Same here," Mad Dog said. "I say we find that cowboy and then we jump the marshal and his sidekick and show everyone in the territory that we're the real article."

To Loomis it was obvious which way the wind was blowing. "For what it's worth, I side with Cestus. But if the rest of you are hell-bent on spillin' blood, I'll go along if Cestus does."

"Hell," Cestus said.

"We haven't ever bucked you in anything," Mad Dog said. "You owe us this."

"You don't know what you're askin'," Cestus said. "It could ruin everything. And I like how things are."

"So do I," the Attica Kid said. "But which do you put more stock in? The robbin' or your pride?"

"I've taken pride in not takin' life."

"So now you take pride in takin' it," the Kid returned. "Either that or we're washed up as an outfit."

Cestus stared at each of them, a silent question in his eyes. Finally he scowled and said. "It would have to be done right. With a lot of plannin'. The same as when we hit a bank or a stage."

"That goes without sayin'," the Attica Kid said.

"We need to find out all we can about the punchers and the tin stars," Cestus said. "Their habits and whatnot."

"I figured it might come to this," Loomis said, "so I nosed around at a few saloons. Talked to a bartender and some others. I learned that Sherm Bonner rides for the Circle T." He looked over at the Attica Kid. "It might interest you to know that this Bonner has a reputation as a gun hand."

"Does he, now?" the Attica Kid said.

"Bonner has a pard called Lefty. I don't know anything about him except he's not much with a six-shooter. It's Sherm Bonner who's the quick-draw artist. A fanner, they say."

"Better and better," the Attica Kid said.

"What are you thinkin'?" Cestus asked. "You and him, straight up?"

"Why not?"

"It's smarter to shook him in the back and be done with it," Cestus said. "Or better yet, pick him off with a rifle from a distance so that pistol of his doesn't do him any good."

"I'm no back-shooter," the Kid said.

"Your damn pride again," Cestus said, but not angrily.

"I don't have much else except this," the Attica Kid said, and patted his ivory-handled Lightning. "Without both I'm nothin'."

"The Circle T is a big spread," Cestus said, "with a lot of salty cowpokes who ride for the brand."

"So I take him when they're not around," the Kid said.

"Him and his pard visit Alpine a lot," Loomis informed them. "It's his favorite waterin' hole."

"There you go," the Attica Kid said.

Loomis had more to impart. "That deputy, Hugo Mitchell, you already ran into at the bank. He's as useless as teats on a bull. He can't shoot and he's not too bright. Killin' him would be as easy as killin' a puppy."

"I'm thinkin' we should let him be," Cestus said. "Doin' him in would be pointless."

"The marshal won't be pointless," Bert Varrow said.

"Marshal Cooper has killed his man," Loomis said. "Down to Kansas, it was. He's one of those sticklers for the law, but he treats folks decent and most everyone likes him."

"Good for him," Mad Dog said sarcastically.

"He's not quick on the shoot, but he might die hard if we go at him from the front," Loomis said. "He does have a habit, though, we can use against him."

"Oh?" Cestus said.

"He's friends with some farmer. I followed him to the farm. From what I can gather, he goes out there a lot. It'd be easy to catch him on the road or at the farm and do it with no one else around."

"Well, there you go," the Attica Kid said. "You've given us both of them on a platter."

Loomis appreciated the compliment. "Thanks, Kid."

Once again all eyes were fixed on Cestus Calloway.

"You have the final say," Bert Varrow said. "You know how we feel, but I'll abide by your decision."

"Do we or don't we?" Mad Dog demanded.

Cestus Calloway sighed. Standing, he gazed about the cave and then down at his wild bunch and announced, "We do."

Chapter 10

Deputy Hugo Mitchell was considerably surprised when someone tried to kill him.

Mitch was making his usual late-night rounds. He always started at the east end of Main Street and worked his way west, checking the doors of closed businesses, poking his head into saloons, and whatnot. Most of the time it bored him. Crime was rare in Alpine, or had been until recently.

On this particular night, Mitch had just made sure that the front door to a general store was locked. He gave the door a good shake to make it rattle, then moved on.

It was only eleven or so and all the saloons were still open. Except for an occasional burst of laughter, and piano music, you'd hardly know it. That was Marshal Cooper's doing. Boyd didn't like rowdy establishments, and had made it plain to each and every saloon owner that so long as they kept things peaceful, he had no objection to how long they served their liquor.

Mitch had to hand it to him. Boyd had done a good job of maintaining a quiet, orderly town. Until the Calloway Gang came along anyway.

Something would have to be done about them, Mitch reckoned. The bank robbery aside, it had been as brazen as anything for Butch McGivern to show up the way he did.

Even more so for him to sit at the same table as Sherm
Bonner and Lefty. The marshal was of the opinion that it
wasn't by accident, that McGivern might have come into
town for the express purpose of doing Sherm Bonner in for
Sherm's part in killing that old buffalo hunter.

Mitch figured Boyd must be right. Boyd usually was.
And if so, then it might be, as Boyd pointed out, that the
outlaws had embarked on a vendetta; they were out for revenge for Larner and now McGivern.

Lordy, Mitch hoped not. He hadn't shot anybody, but the
outlaws might figure he had it coming because he was a
deputy and had ridden with the posse; plus, he'd been in the
very saloon where McGivern was slain.

Mitch wouldn't fool himself. He was no Sherm Bonner.
When it came to unlimbering his six-shooter, he was molasses. As for shooting, he could hit the broad side of a barn if
the barn wasn't more than twenty feet away.

Up ahead, a batwing creaked and a man came out with
his arm over a dove's shoulders. They turned the other way
and went off whispering and snuggling.

Mitch envied him. He was too shy to dally with a dove.
Shy, and not a little afraid. Women had always scared him,
in part because they were so different, and in part because
he could never figure out what went through their heads.

He came to a pitch-black alley and glanced down it. He
was still thinking about how strange women were, so he was
slow to react at the sound of a metallic click. It sounded like
a gun hammer being cocked, but who would be cocking a
revolver in an alley in the middle of town so late at night?
Then he remembered the marshal's suspicion about Mc-
Givern and how the outlaws might seek revenge. He stiffened in sudden alarm as the dark flared with the flash of a
gunshot.

Pain seared Mitch's side. Clutching himself, he fell
against the wall and clumsily fumbled for his revolver. He
heard another click and dropped to his knees a heartbeat

before a second shot boomed. The lead blistered the air above his head. By then he had his six-shooter out. He fired at where the flash had been, but his hand was shaking so badly, he'd be lucky to have hit the assassin. Boots pounded, and he thought he glimpsed someone running out the far end of the alley. He fired again to discourage them from returning.

Shouts erupted up and down Main Street. People spilled from the saloons and yelled back and forth, wanting to know who was shooting, and why.

Mitch struggled to stand. His left hand, where it was pressed to his ribs, was wet with what could only be blood. Feeling light-headed, he staggered into the street and managed to take half a dozen faltering steps before he collapsed onto his side.

Another yell brought help on the run.

His teeth gritted against the pain, Mitch was aware of faces over him, and caught snatches of talk.

"Why, it's Deputy Mitchell!"

". . . been shot!"

". . . fetch the doc!"

"Fetch the marshal too."

A strong hand was slid behind Mitch's back and he was helped to sit up. He recognized the man holding him, the bartender from the Daisy Mae. "Floyd?"

"Stay still. The sawbones and Coop will be here soon."

"Someone shot me," Mitch gasped.

"Did you see who?" Floyd asked.

"Too dark," Mitch said weakly. He closed his eyes and would have drifted off, but Floyd shook him.

"Don't pass out. Stay with us until the doc gets here."

"I don't feel good," Mitch said.

"People usually don't when they're shot," Floyd replied. He was carefully prying at Mitch's shirt. "You might be in luck. Looks as if it only nicked you."

"I don't feel nicked," Mitch said. "I feel worse."

"Stay with us."

Mitch swallowed, and tried. There had to be twenty to thirty people around him by now, all gawking for a look-see. He wanted to tell them to go away and leave him be, but he couldn't find the energy. His ears were working fine, though, and he heard the next comment.

"You know who did this, don't you?"

"The nerve of those owl-hoots," someone else said. "Shootin' somebody as harmless as him."

Mitch objected to being called harmless, but he was too weak to argue about it. All he wanted was to sleep, but each time he closed his eyes for more than a few seconds, the bartender shook him.

Mitch's head was spinning and everything was a blur when a commotion ensued. Someone gripped his wrist and fingers were pressed to a vein to feel his pulse. "Doc?"

"It's me, yes."

A hand loosened Mitch's shirt. "Should you do that out here in the street?" he asked, worried more about being undressed in front of the women present than about the severity of his wound.

"Hush, Deputy. Leave this to me."

Mitch relaxed a little. The town physician was Tom Willowby, fresh out of medical school and as sharp as a razor. Willowby had impressed everybody by saving the life of a miner caught in a cave-in and nearly crushed. Everyone thought the miner was a goner, but Willowby performed over six hours of surgery that saved the miner's life and let him walk again. "Someone shot me."

"He keeps sayin' that," Floyd said.

"The deputy is in shock," Doc Willowby said. "We must get him to my office. If you and several others will be kind enough to carry him, I believe I can have him back on his feet in no time. The wound appears to be minor."

"That's what I told him," Floyd replied.

"He was lucky," Doc Willowby said.

"I don't know what's lucky about bein' shot," Mitch disagreed. "It hurts like the dickens and I've lost a lot of blood."

"Not as much as you might think," Willowby said. "Now let's get to it, men. Each of you take an arm and a leg."

Mitch's stomach tried to crawl out his gullet as he was jostled and lifted. Everything around him went dark and he had to struggle to say, "Doc? Is it all right if I pass out? That darn Floyd wouldn't let me."

"Be my guest," Willowby replied. "It can't do any harm."

"Thank God," Mitch said, and sank into nothingness.

Marshal Boyd Cooper had a lot on his mind.

The morning after the attempt on Deputy Mitchell's life, Boyd was at his desk, deep in thought, when the office door opened and in came Harvey Dale.

"Mornin'," the former scout said. "I just heard about the boy."

Time and again, both Boyd and Hugo had asked Dale not to call Hugo that. A twenty-year-old wasn't a "boy." This time Boyd let it go, and responded, "The doc says he's recovering nicely, to use the doc's own words. It took eleven stitches and Hugo will be hurting for a couple of weeks, but after that he'll be good as new."

Dale claimed a chair by the desk. "Provided those buzzards let him be, you mean."

"We don't know it was them," Boyd said.

"Who else? You're the one who warned everyone they'd be out for our hides. And you were right."

"What are you doin' here, Harve?" Boyd asked. He preferred to be alone at the moment.

"With Mitch laid up, I figured you'd want me to work more hours," Dale said. "Plus, we need to stick together now that we're bein' hunted."

"I wouldn't say that," Boyd said.

"What else would you call it when someone is out to plant you?"

"That was just a guess on my part. Sherm Bonner told me that McGivern didn't seem to know who they were when he sat down with Sherm and Lefty."

"What happened to Mitch proves it was a good guess," Dale said, "which brings me to somethin' else we need to talk about."

"I'm listenin'."

"General Custer used to say that the best tactic in a war was to ride to the sound of the guns. . . ."

Boyd held up a hand to stop him. "Custer is dead. He and his command were wiped out at the Little Bighorn."

"You reckon I don't know that? I scouted for him for a while on the Plains, and the man impressed the hell out of me."

"All right," Boyd said, "but how does ridin' to the guns help us here?"

"Custer didn't wait for an enemy to come to him. He went to the enemy. We should do the same thing."

"How, exactly, since we have no idea where the outlaws hole up?"

"We will if you'll let me go out after them. Instead of them huntin' us, we'll hunt them."

"Go after Cestus Calloway and his pack of lawbreakers by your lonesome?"

"I'm not aimin' to tangle with them, only to find them," Harvey Dale said. "Once I do, I'll fan the breeze back here and you can rustle up a posse and we'll put an end to their shenanigans."

"It's too dangerous."

"More so than huntin' the Sioux? Hell, Cestus Calloway doesn't worry me any. The one hunter and tracker they had, old Ben Larner, is dead. The rest are no-account."

"I wouldn't say that about the Attica Kid."

"So he's quick with a pistol. What else can he do?"

"Don't forget Mad Dog Hanks and Cockeye. They've each killed more than a few between them."

"They don't worry me any either," Dale said. "I'd have to get close for them or the Kid to drop me, and with my spyglass I don't need to."

"I don't know," Boyd said. Secretly he liked the idea, but the old scout would be taking a terrible risk. "Let me ponder on it some."

"Don't take too long," Dale advised. "If they are out to get us, they'll try again real soon. And next time it could be you or me they come after." Rising, he leaned on the desk. "Now, how about that extra work. Do you want my help or not?"

Boyd did have a use for him. "Can you hold down the fort for me while I pay someone a visit?"

"Take as long as you want. I'll keep a close watch on things."

Boyd wasn't expecting trouble that early in the day. He could make it out to the Wilson Farm and back again without anyone the wiser. "I shouldn't be more than an hour or two," he said as he stood. In his eagerness he was half out the door when he realized Dale was talking to him. "What was that?"

"Tell her howdy for me," Dale said, chuckling.

"Who?"

"Marshal, most everybody in town knows you're sweet on Sam's sister. You've been spendin' a lot of time at their farm and it ain't to milk their cows."

"Damn gossips," Boyd said. "Who did you hear it from?"

"Sam himself. I was at the saloon and he stopped in and mentioned how happy he was that you and his sis are makin' cow eyes at each other."

"Cow eyes, my ass."

"What are you mad about? His sis is a right fine lady. You ask me, you're gettin' the better of the deal."

"I didn't ask," Boyd said, "and I'll thank you to keep your opinions of her to yourself." He left before his anger got the better of him. He'd wanted to keep his relationship with Cecelia a secret in case it didn't work out. One never knew about those things.

The street was busy at that hour of the day. A buckboard clattered by as Boyd stepped around the hitch rail and forked leather. Smiling and nodding at people he knew, he headed south on Second Street and was soon beyond the town limits. Fields and forest spread before him, with stark peaks in the distance.

Boyd was so annoyed at Sam that he didn't think to look over his shoulder until he'd gone pretty near a quarter of a mile. When he did, he received a shock.

He was being followed.

Chapter 11

Boyd wanted to kick himself for not noticing sooner. He told himself that it might be someone bound for a mine or an outlying ranch, or perhaps going up into the mountains to hunt. But it made him suspicious, the way the rider hung back, pacing him.

To test his hunch, Boyd slowed. The rider slowed too. Boyd brought his chestnut to a fast walk. The rider did the same.

There could be no doubt about it. He *was* being followed.

Boyd never imagined the outlaws would be so brazen. First they'd tried to kill Sherm Bonner and Mitch, and now they were out to do him in.

It must be because of Larner, Boyd reasoned. He'd never heard of outlaws on a vendetta before, but that was what it must be. He and some of his posse had been marked for death.

Well, the outlaws wouldn't find it easy, he vowed.

Yonder was a bend in the road. Boyd tapped his spurs and trotted around it. Once he was out of sight of his shadow, he slowed and veered into the woods. Drawing his six-shooter, he waited. He would accost the rider and demand to know who he was and why he was there.

Tense seconds crawled into minutes.

The rider didn't appear.

Puzzled, Boyd broke cover and went back around the bend. The road was empty. "What the blazes?" he blurted. Had the rider suspected what he was up to, and left the road for the forest?

Jamming his revolver into his holster, Boyd continued on. He didn't like playing cat and mouse when he was the mouse. Then again, there could be a perfectly logical explanation. He just couldn't think of it.

The Wilson farmhouse came into sight, and Boyd smiled. Cecelia would help take his mind off his troubles. He liked being in her company so much it spooked him sometimes. He'd never felt so at ease with a woman.

He liked so much about her. Her calm nature. How her eyes sparkled when she laughed. How she did her hair. How she carried herself. Living with a woman like her would make every day special.

Living with? Boyd thought, and chuckled. He was getting ahead of himself. They were courting, nothing more. Maybe something would come of it and maybe not.

Boyd shifted in his saddle and scanned the road before he went to the door to knock. There was still no sign of the other rider.

Boyd smiled as the door opened, then said, "Oh. It's you."

"Sorry to disappoint you," Sam Wilson said, and laughed. Stepping aside, he motioned. "Come on in. She's in the parlor, sewing."

Removing his hat, Boyd entered.

"How is Mitch doin'?"

"The doc says he can come back to work in a few days."

"Good," Sam said. "If you need any help until then, you have only to let me know."

"I thank you," Boyd replied. "Harve is helpin' me hold down the fort, but I'll keep it in mind."

Cecelia smiled on seeing him, and came off the settee

with such grace, and looking so beautiful it brought a lump to Boyd's throat. She hugged him, and he grew warm inside. "Are you all right?"

Boyd had to cough to say, "Never better."

Sam excused himself and went to the kitchen.

"Have a seat, if you would," Cecelia said, returning to the settee. "This is an unexpected treat. You don't usually pay me a visit so early in the day."

"It's this outlaw business," Boyd confessed as he roosted. "I just wanted to get away for a while."

"And I am your excuse?" Cecelia teased.

"You're a lot more than that."

"I hope so," Cecelia said. "After the other night on the porch."

Boyd coughed a second time. He was comfortable around her except when it came to *that*. Or, rather, talking about it. "You have awful sweet lips."

"Why, Boyd Cooper, my blushes," Cecelia said, and laughed.

Boyd was sure he was blushing himself. To get her off that track, he mentioned how Deputy Mitchell was improving, and that Harvey Dale wanted to track the outlaws to their lair.

"Do you think he can?" Cecelia asked.

"If anyone, could, it's Harve," Boyd said. "He's the best at readin' sign I've ever come across."

"Then perhaps you should let him. It would be wonderful to rid the territory of those evil men, don't you think?"

Boyd couldn't agree more, and said so.

"I only ask that when it comes to confronting them, you be careful. I've grown quite fond of you, Boyd Cooper, and it would distress me greatly if something were to happen to you."

"I am bein' careful," Boyd assured her, and he went on to tell how he thought he'd been followed, and his ruse to catch the man at it.

Cecelia's brow puckered. "You say this rider disappeared?"

Boyd nodded. "He probably guessed what I was up to and went into the trees. Searchin' for him would have been pointless. I'm not the tracker Dale is."

"So you came on here?"

"Where else?" Boyd said, and grinned.

"You don't see it, do you?"

"See what?" Boyd said.

"If he was still following you, you led him right to our farm."

"The outlaws aren't after Sam or you." Boyd sought to put any unease she felt at rest. "They're after me." But even as he said it, he felt an unease of his own. He remembered that other time he thought he'd been followed. Nothing ever came of it, but that it had happened again was worrisome.

"I suppose you're right," Cecelia said. "They would be foolish to harm a woman. It would cause a public outrage. But I worry about Sam. He was with you that day Larner was shot."

"You think they're after the entire posse?" Boyd considered that, and shook his head. "They haven't tried to kill Vogel or Harvey Dale."

"So far," Cecelia said. "We should warn my brother, though, just in case I'm right."

"Of course," Boyd said. A sudden fear crawled into his chest and took root. He'd not only unwittingly led the outlaws to Sam, but led them to her. Granted, she had a point that no one in their right mind would hurt a female, but at least one of the outlaws—Mad Dog Hanks—was reputed to be as crazy as they came, and vicious besides.

"Are you sure you're not feeling poorly? You became pale there for a moment."

"I'm fine," Boyd lied. Inwardly he was in turmoil. He'd been appallingly, unforgivingly, careless.

"Don't fret too much over it," Cecelia said. "Everything will likely be fine."

Boyd hoped to God she was right.

*   *   *

The Circle T wasn't one of the largest ranches in Colorado, but it was one of the most mountainous. Four valleys and a section of prairie that opened into them provided most of the graze.

Efram Tilman was the owner. A former Texan, he'd ranched for years until he developed a lung condition and was told by his sawbones that a higher altitude would help relieve some of the pain and discomfort. He had a cousin in Colorado and went there to test the doctor's advice. Not only did his lungs improve, but he fell in love with the Rockies. It helped that his wife fell in love with them too, and it wasn't long before they had a new ranch up and running.

Efram was fussy about those he hired to ride for his brand. Punchers just learning their trade had to learn it somewhere else. He preferred seasoned men, those who could cut and rope and brand and do all the other chores cowboys had to do, and do them well. He paid above-average wages, and believed in getting top work for top dollar.

His dealings with Comanches and rustlers in Texas had taught Efram that all things being equal, a puncher who was good with a gun was twice his worth as a puncher who'd never fired a shot except to kill a snake. Some ranchers wouldn't hire anyone with a reputation as a shooter, but not Efram. He preferred them. Not that good shooters were all that numerous. Most cowpokes had neither the inclination nor the need to become uncommonly proficient with a firearm.

Sherm Bonner was one of the exceptions. Efram had heard of Bonner down in Texas, where Bonner had worked a ranch in the Staked Plains country and been involved in a couple of shooting affrays of note. The first involved three rustlers. Bonner and some other cowpokes came on the brand blotters as they were using a running iron, and the rustlers went for their guns. Sherm Bonner shot all three dead before any of the other punchers could touch their hardware. Later, he was involved in a fracas in a saloon with a pair of border ruffians. The ruffians picked on the wrong man and ended up in early graves.

Bonner was known as a gun fanner. Some shootists had contempt for those who fanned, claiming that in a fight a fanner had no chance against a man who was deliberate and aimed. But Efram had seen with his own eyes how ungodly quick Sherm Bonner was. Bonner could put three slugs into a target the size of an apple in the time it took Efram to blink. It convinced him that a gun fanner who knew his business was as deadly as anyone.

Sherm never went anywhere without his pard, Lefty, so when Bonner showed up at the Circle T looking for work, Efram had to hire them both. Not that he minded. Lefty was a top cowhand. Efram never did find out why the pair left Texas for Colorado, although from a few remarks Lefty dropped, the rancher came to the conclusion it had something to do with Sherm and a rancher's daughter and forbidden love.

It was on a sunny summer's morn that a rider showed up at the Circle T looking for work. Efram and his wife were taking their ease in the parlor, and at the knock on their door, they went together to see who it was. Efram took a dislike to the man at first sight. An older fellow, wearing a coat much too heavy for hot weather, doffed his hat to Efram's missus and asked if they had any odd jobs he might do for a meal and a cup of coffee. Efram would have told him no, but Efram's wife, always the tender heart, told the man he could pull weeds in her garden and that there was some wood that needed chopping for the kitchen stove.

Efram kept an eye on the man out the kitchen window. There was something about the stranger, a seedy quality, that raised the hackles on the back of Efram's neck. He noticed how the man kept looking all around as he worked as if he was taking stock of where things were and how the ranch hands went about their business. It bothered Efram. He sensed the man was up to no good, but he let his wife feed him and watched as the fellow rode off.

That evening, in the cookhouse, Efram told his hands about the man and asked that they keep their eyes skinned for any sign of him.

"If he's a rustler, he'll regret blottin' any of your brands, Mr. Tilman, when we get hold of him," a puncher assured him, and others nodded in agreement.

Another cowpoke set down his fork and said, "Why, that must be the gent I ran into on my way in today."

"You did?" Efram said.

"I asked him what he was doin' on your spread and he told me he'd just chopped wood for your missus and was headin' for the high country."

"Good," Efram said. "We're well shed of him."

"Only that wasn't all," the cowpoke said. "He asked me if I knew a hand by the name of Sherm Bonner."

"He never asked me that," Efram said.

The cowpoke scratched his chin. "He said as how he'd heard that Sherm had shot some outlaws and he would like to set his eyes on someone who was halfway famous. His very words, Mr. Tilman."

"Hmm," Efram said. "What did you tell him?"

"That I didn't rightly know where Sherm was. I thought he might be up in the High Valley, as we call it, and he wouldn't be back for days."

"What did the fellow say to that?"

"He shrugged and said he was obliged and rode off," the cowpoke said. "I didn't think much of it and came on in."

"I don't like it," Efram said. "I don't know why I don't like it, but I don't." He pointed at the cowpoke. "I want you to ride up to the High Valley in the mornin' and tell Sherm. It could be nothin', but he deserves to know."

"Could it have been one of them outlaws?" another puncher asked.

"Do you reckon they're out to do to Sherm like they tried to do to that deputy?" a different man brought up.

"Could be," Efram said, "which is why I want him warned."

"They try to gun Sherm Bonner," a burly hand said, "they'll learn right quick that they picked on the wrong hombre."

At that, a lot of the cowboys laughed.

Efram didn't find it as humorous. Even the quickest of shooters could be back-shot. "Forget waitin' until mornin'. Davis, as soon as you're done eatin', I want you in the saddle."

"Yes, sir, boss," Davis said. "You're worried the outlaws might try somethin', I take it?"

"We shouldn't put anything past them," Efram said.

Chapter 12

To Mad Dog Hanks, all the skulking about was a waste of time. Were it up to him, he'd walk up to Marshal Cooper or that cowboy, jerk his pistol, and shoot him in the face. That was how to do things. Not all the skulking about that Cestus Calloway had them doing.

Calloway was too cautious, by half.

No one had ever accused Mad Dog of being cautious. Ever since he could remember, way back as far as when he was a boy of five or six, he'd done as he pleased, when he pleased, and the rest of the world be damned.

Mad Dog didn't think of it in exactly those words back then. He just liked doing what he liked to do. What boy didn't? It just so happened that some of the things he liked to do got him in hot water with his folks and others.

For instance, early on Mad Dog grew to hate chickens. Nearly every farm had a coop so a family had a steady supply of eggs. It was one of his chores to go out to the coop each morning and collect the eggs laid the night before. But the coop always smelled of chicken droppings, and he'd get feathers on his clothes and sometimes up his nose, and the droppings on his shoes. To make matters worse, some of the chickens resented having their eggs taken, and would peck him or squawk and flap their wings and generally give him a hard time. It didn't help that he wasn't all that fond of eggs.

One morning a chicken acted up and pecked him on the cheek as he bent to retrieve her eggs, and Mad Dog snapped. He grabbed her by the neck and slowly wrung it, laughing with delight as the hen thrashed and squawked. Sheer pleasure shot through him when she finally went limp.

He'd liked it so much he took to strangling more. He was clever about it and wouldn't do it more than once or twice a month, and he always took the body out in the fields and tossed it so his pa and ma wouldn't find out what he'd done.

They did, though. One day his pa heard a chicken squawking for dear life and caught Mad Dog in the act.

It was the woodshed for Mad Dog. His pa took a switch to his backside and warned him that he must never kill another hen or he'd get another switching. His pa explained that eggs were a large part of the family diet, that they were used in cooking and baking, and they couldn't afford to go without them.

Then there was the hog affair. It was Mad Dog's job to feed them their slop, and he hated it. Hogs had no manners. He'd no sooner approach their pen with the bucket than they'd be at the trough oinking and slobbering. When he tried to pour, they'd get in the way, pushing and shoving each other so that it was next to impossible to fill the trough without getting half the slop on them. His pa kept telling him he must be more careful.

One day Mad Dog was feeding them, and hating it, when a hog bit at the slop oozing from the bucket and bit his hand. Hogs hardly ever bit people. It was an accident, but it made Mad Dog see red. Without thinking he grabbed a pitchfork, vaulted into the pen, and commenced to stab the offending hog again and again and again. The hog squealed in terror and tried to run, but the pen wasn't that big and Mad Dog got him in a corner and finished him off.

Just as his pa arrived.

It was the woodshed again for Mad Dog, and now he hated hogs as much as he hated chickens.

That was the thing about his childhood. Mad Dog had hated most everything about it. He hated milking cows and hated shoveling manure and hated all the chores he had to do, and he especially hated chickens and hogs.

So it was probably only natural that one day Mad Dog had decided enough was enough. Ironically the family dog was to blame. His mother had an Irish setter that she was fond of, and that didn't like Mad Dog. Probably because he'd pull on its tail when his ma wasn't looking, or upend a water bucket over its head for the fun of it.

The dog took to nipping at Mad Dog whenever he came near. Mad Dog didn't mind so much until one time the family was on the front porch after supper, relaxing, and his ma asked him for a hug. She did that now and then. She was an affectionate woman and Mad Dog didn't hug her enough to suit her, so she'd come right out and ask for one. He went to hug her, and the dog, which was lying between them, jumped up and bit him.

It hurt worse than anything. Mad Dog saw red again. He usually wore a hunting knife on his hip, and he'd yanked it from its sheath, grabbed the dog by the throat, and proceeded to bury his blade, not once but more than a dozen times, stabbing in a fury. When someone grabbed at his arm to try to stop him, without thinking he stabbed them too.

A scream brought Mad Dog out of himself. The red haze faded, and there, at his feet, lay his mother. Before he could say anything, a hand fell on his shoulder and he was spun around. He saw his pa cock a fist to hit him, and in pure reflex, he buried the knife in his father's chest.

That was the start of his outlaw days.

He'd killed his own folks.

Mad Dog fled, and the next he knew, the newspapers were writing about him. Only instead of calling him Harold Hanks, which was his name, they called him Mad Dog

Hanks. He didn't know if it was on account of the Irish setter or because he'd gone plumb mad and killed his parents.
Not that it mattered. The name stuck, and to this day he was
called Mad Dog.

Truth was, he sort of liked it. It made folks wary of him.
They were scared to be around him, scared of what he
might do.

For about ten years he'd drifted, robbin' and killin' as the
whim moved him. Then one day he ran into Ira Toomis.
He'd met Toomis before, and they got along well enough. It
seemed Toomis had taken up with an outlaw by the name
of Cestus Calloway, and Calloway was always looking for
good men. Was Mad Dog interested?

Mad Dog spent an entire night thinking about it. He'd
always been a loner. To become part of a gang was a big
step. He couldn't just do as he pleased. He'd have to take
orders from Calloway and try to get along with the others
in the gang. He didn't like that part, but he decided to give
it a try.

Now here Mad Dog was, skulking around, spying on the
marshal to learn all he could so Cestus could plan out how
and when to put windows in the lawman's skull.

Mad Dog saw it as a lot of bother when all they had to
do was ride up to the marshal's office one night, march on
in with their pistols and rifles cocked, and blow the lawman
to hell. He'd mentioned as much to Cestus, and Cestus said
that wouldn't do, that the killing had to be done just right,
whatever that meant.

Calloway had sent Toomis to nose around the Circle T
and find out what he could about Sherm Bonner while Mad
Dog was supposed to keep a watch on the marshal and
learn his habits and whatnot so Calloway could decide
when and where to strike.

It was a stupid way to go about it, in Mad Dog's opinion.
But it wasn't worth arguing about. Not when the Attica Kid
would side with Cestus, as he always did.

Mad Dog knew the Kid didn't like him. Why, he had no idea. But ever since they'd met, the Kid was cold toward him. True, the Attica Kid was cold toward everyone except Cestus. But Mad Dog sensed there was more to it. He suspected the Kid was looking for an excuse to gun him.

They'd never had cross words. Never even argued. Mad Dog was careful not to do anything that antagonized the Kid, and the Kid never did anything to antagonize him.

It wasn't that Mad Dog was afraid of him. Mad Dog had never been afraid of anyone. No, he treated the Attica Kid the same way he'd treat a coiled rattlesnake. You never provoked a rattler unless you were certain you wouldn't be bit.

If Mad Dog ever decided the Kid was actually out to get him, it would prove to be the Kid's undoing. The Kid liked a stand-up fight. He wasn't a back-shooter. He always gave the other guy a chance. Not Mad Dog. When he killed someone, he did it any way he could. Gun, knife, a rock to the head, he didn't care so long as it got the job done. As for giving them a chance—that was plumb ridiculous. Killing was killing. You didn't sugarcoat it with a right way and a wrong way. You got it done any way you could.

Mad Dog would use that to his advantage if the Kid ever showed signs of being on the peck. He'd play on the Kid's misguided sense of honor and turn the tables. It shouldn't be hard. He'd sneak up behind the Kid sometime and let him have it with both barrels from a shotgun.

If there was one thing Mad Dog was good at, it was being sneaky.

He was being sneaky now as he approached the farm the marshal had gone to. He stuck to the woods that bordered the road so he wouldn't be seen.

Mad Dog recollected Toomis saying that he'd followed the law dog here. That it was the Wilson place, and Sam Wilson had been one of those who rode with the posse.

Mad Dog would like to hunt up this Wilson and splatter his brains or slit his throat. But all he was supposed to do was follow the lawman around and note where he went and what he did. A lot of useless bother to go to, but that was what Cestus wanted him to do, so he'd do it.

The farmhouse made Mad Dog think of the farm where he grew up, and of that blood-drenched day when he killed his folks and the Irish setter. He missed his parents now and then. He sure didn't miss the damn dog.

Drawing rein under a pine, Mad Dog saw a man in overalls come out the back of the house and go over to the barn. Sam Wilson, he reckoned. But where was Marshal Cooper?

Curious, Mad Dog dismounted and tied the reins. He wasn't supposed to go too close. Cestus had made that plain. But Cestus wasn't there and Mad Dog would do as he pleased.

He was about to break from cover and make for the side of the house when he caught movement at a window. He couldn't see in from where he was, but that was easily solved. Gripping a low limb, he swung himself up and climbed.

He only had to clamber about ten feet up and he was high enough to see inside the house.

The window was to a parlor. The lawman was seated on a settee, talking to a woman with gray hair.

"Ain't this interestin'?" Mad Dog said out loud.

The woman got up and came to the window and gazed out. For a few moments he thought she had seen him, but no. She looked up at the sky and off toward the barn and then returned to the settee.

Wilson's wife? Mad Dog wondered. No, that couldn't be. He seemed to recollect that Wilson wasn't married. A sister, then? Probably. The lawman must have come to visit her, not the brother. And if that was the case, then Cooper must be courting her.

"Why, you devil, you," Mad Dog said, and grinned at his little joke.

This was good. This was something they could use when the time came.

Chuckling, Mad Dog descended. He dropped lightly from the lowest branch, climbed back on his horse, and reined around. He'd seen enough. The marshal would likely be there awhile, and Mad Dog wasn't sticking around.

He headed back to Alpine. He should ride straight through town, or better yet, go around, but he was thirsty and reckoned a quick drink wouldn't hurt. Not if he kept his head down and didn't draw attention.

It had been so long since Mad Dog had a drink that his mouth watered. He wasn't hooked on the stuff, like some, but he did like a swallow or three now and again.

Mad Dog didn't think he was taking much of a chance riding into Alpine in the middle of the day. A lot of people were out and about. The streets were busy with riders and wagons and plenty of folks on foot. He'd just be one of many. He wasn't like Cockeye, whose off eye always gave him away.

Pulling his collar higher and his hat lower, Mad Dog followed the dirt road to a side street that in turn brought him to Main. A few townsfolk gave him casual glances, but that was all.

Mad Dog passed a butcher's and came to a hitch rail in front of a saloon. The Dusty Trail, it was called. A stupid name for a saloon, but the barkeep was friendly enough and filled Mad Dog's glass to the brim.

"How about if I join you, mister, and we drink to your health?" the man proposed.

"Fine by me," Mad Dog said, "so long as you're payin' for your own drink."

The bartender laughed. "I'm not a mooch, friend." He placed another glass on the bar and proceeded to pour.

Mad Dog was aware that someone had come up on his right and was standing close to him, but he didn't look to see who it was. Raising his glass, he sipped and smiled contentedly. "It's been a while."

"I admire a man who likes his liquor," the bartender

said. Glancing at the newcomer, he asked, "What will it be, Deputy Dale?"

Mad Dog's gut balled into a knot.

"Nothin', Keller," the deputy said. "I'm workin' at the moment. I came in to talk to this gent."

So much for not being noticed, Mad Dog thought. Still holding his glass, he half turned. The deputy wore a buckskin shirt and an old cavalry hat and was twice as old as he was. "You want to talk to me?"

"Saw you ride in," Dale said. He was holding a double-barreled scattergun close to his leg.

"No law against that," Mad Dog said.

"True," the old deputy said. "But there *is* a law against robbin' banks and shootin' folks. Which is why I grabbed this howitzer and came right over. You're under arrest, Mad Dog Hanks."

"You have me mistook for someone else," Mad Dog bluffed.

"No. And I'll tell you why. I was with the posse, Hanks. It was me who tracked all of you. I also got a good look at the whole bunch through my spyglass. Ever used one? It lets you see a gent up close from far away. I saw you as clear as could be, as if you were right next to me. Hell, you're even wearin' the same clothes you wore when you robbed the bank. So I'll thank you to set down that drink and unbuckle your gun belt."

"Will you, now?" Mad Dog said, and threw the whiskey into Deputy Dale's face.

Chapter 13

Harvey Dale couldn't believe his eyes when he saw Mad Dog Hanks ride down Main Street and stop at a saloon.

Dale happened to be at the window in the marshal's office. He didn't mind watching over things while the marshal was away, but sitting at the desk with nothing to do bored him, so he'd gotten up to stretch and gaze out the window at the passersby.

Dale was sure it was Mad Dog. He'd seen them all through his telescope, and remembered every little detail. Cestus Calloway was a handsome cuss with curly hair. Bert Varrow dressed like a dandy. The Attica Kid wore black from hat to boots. And Mad Dog looked just like what you would imagine someone with that name would look like. Always scowling at the world, the stamp of violence on his features. Truth was, Hanks was as ugly as sin.

To see him come riding down Main Street surprised Dale greatly. The man was uncommonly bold or reckless or both.

Dale had been about to rush out when it occurred to him that he might need more than his pistol. Stepping to the gun rack, he took down a scattergun, opened the drawer in the desk that contained boxes of shells, and loaded both barrels with buckshot. He stuck extra shells in his pocket and hurried down Main Street to the Dusty Trail.

Pausing at the batwings, Dale surveyed the room. It could be that Mad Dog wasn't alone. Other outlaws might be there. But no, Mad Dog was at the bar talking to the bartender. No one else was with him.

Pushing on through, Dale went over. He held the scatter-gun against his leg so it wouldn't be obvious should Mad Dog glance his way. The outlaw was only interested in his drink, though.

When the bartender greeted him, Dale announced that he was there to arrest Hanks. He expected Mad Dog to go for his revolver, and he was watching the killer's gun hand. That proved to be a mistake. He should have watched both hands. He caught the movement when Mad Dog's other hand flicked—and caught the glass of whiskey full in the face. Blinking to clear his eyes, Dale backpedaled while leveling the scattergun. He cocked it, thinking he was a goner, that Mad Dog would shoot him before he could get off a shot, and heard curses and a scuffle.

Suddenly his vision cleared.

Mad Dog had indeed drawn his six-shooter, but the bartender, Keller, had lunged and grabbed Mad Dog's wrist in both hands and shoved Mad Dog's arm at the ceiling. Mad Dog was struggling fiercely to break loose, and the barkeep was hanging on for dear life.

Dale couldn't shoot with the barman that close. The buckshot would blow both men to hell. He sprang to help, ramming the scattergun's stock at Mad Dog's head. But Mad Dog ducked and swung his other fist. Dale blocked the blow, pivoted, and slammed the stock against Mad Dog's ribs. It seemed to have no effect.

Customers were shouting and chairs were scraping the floor. Someone hollered that they should fetch the marshal.

Reversing his grip and holding the scattergun by the barrels, Dale swung it like a club. He brought it down on Mad Dog's gun arm, and Mad Dog howled in pain but didn't let go of his revolver.

"Do it again!" Keller bawled.

Dale did.

The revolver fell to the bar, and Mad Dog Hanks went berserk. Roaring like a riled bear, he smashed his fist into Keller's face, knocking the barman against the shelves. Bottles wobbled and a few toppled and shattered on the floor.

Dale found himself fighting for his life. Mad Dog's hands were clamped around his throat and the outlaw's feral face was inches from his.

"Kill you!" the outlaw raged. "Kill you! Kill you!"

Breath that reeked filled Dale's nose. He tried to club Mad Dog away but only clipped him on the shoulder. Mad Dog retaliated by hooking a foot behind Dale's leg and tripping him. Locked together, they crashed down, and the outlaw's fingers gouged deeper into Dale's throat.

The scattergun went skittering.

Dale was being throttled. His breath had been choked off, and his lungs were in dire need of air. Bucking, Dale sought to throw Mad Dog off, but the man was heavier than he looked, and tenaciously clung on. Dale tried to knee him in the groin. Dale dug a thumb into Mad Dog's eye. Dale punched. But Mad Dog's fingers continued to tighten like a vise.

Then Dale glimpsed Keller, over Mad Dog's shoulder. The bartender was clambering over the bar, a full whiskey bottle in one hand. Keller straightened, raised the bottle high, and brought it crashing down on the back of Mad Dog Hanks's skull.

The bottle broke into fragments, the whiskey splashed, and Mad Dog sagged. He wasn't out cold, but he was stunned. His fingers loosened.

Dale seized the moment and tore Hanks's hands from his neck. He punched Mad Dog on the jaw, once, twice, three times, and Mad Dog slumped but shook his head to try to clear it.

Quickly Dale pushed out from under him and rose.

"Here! Use this!" Keller yelled. He had scooped up the scattergun and shoved it at Dale.

Grabbing hold, Dale looked down. Mad Dog was struggling to stand. It would be easy to blow his head off. Instead Dale said, "Try to kill me, will you?" and clubbed him. Mad Dog didn't go down. Dale clubbed him again, with all his strength. He thought he'd split the outlaw's head open, but all Hanks did was groan and slump to the floor, finally unconscious.

"Damn, he's tough," Keller gasped.

Dale's neck was a welter of pain. He sucked air into his lungs, conscious of others coming over.

"That there is one mean son of a bitch," Keller said, nodding at Hanks.

"We got him, though," Dale said. It hurt his throat to talk.

"You ain't got him yet, Deputy," someone said. "What if he comes around before you get him behind bars?"

That was the last thing Dale wanted. "I need you men to help me carry him to the jail."

"Who is he anyhow?" someone asked.

"Why, that's Mad Dog Hanks," Keller answered. "Don't you know anything?"

"I know I wouldn't want him mad at me," the same man said. "Did you see him fight? He's like an animal."

"Why do you think they call him Mad Dog?" Keller said.

"I heard it's because he likes to kill dogs. Now, who does that, I ask you? Cats I can understand. I never have liked cats. But dogs?"

"Let's get to carryin'," Dale commanded, "or we'll have to subdue him again."

"What's this 'we,' Deputy," yet another townsman said. "If Hanks wakes up, I'm runnin' like hell."

Under Dale's direction, they carried the outlaw across the street and into the jail without incident. Only when Dale heard the cell door clang did he breathe easier. Others had followed them, and a crowd was forming at the window. Dale thanked those who had helped, pumped Keller's hand, and promised to buy him a bottle for saving his life; then he shooed everyone out. He told the gawkers to scat too, and they reluctantly did.

Now, seated at the marshal's desk, Dale stared at the crumpled figure on the bunk and marveled at what he'd done. "I caught Mad Dog Hanks alive," he said to the air, and grinned.

Once word got out, he'd be half famous.

Marshal Boyd Cooper rode back to Alpine with a troubled soul. He was concerned for Sam Wilson, and Cecelia. The outlaws knew where they lived, and there was no telling what that wild bunch would do.

He was so worried that he rode into town without noticing much around him until a hand touched his boot and someone said, "Where have you been, Marshal? You missed all the excitement."

Drawing rein, Boyd looked up to find that a number of people had stopped to stare and others were coming toward him. "What's that?" he said.

The man beside the chestnut was a miner. Grubby with dirt, he grinned and said, "They say the fight was somethin'. I wished I'd seen it."

"Fight?" Boyd said in confusion.

A woman in a bonnet nodded. "Your deputy has him over to the jail. I looked in and saw him. Goodness, he's a sight. I daresay it would scare small children just to look at him."

"Look at who?"

"Why, that terrible outlaw, Mad Dog Hanks."

"Hanks is in our jail?" Boyd exclaimed in amazement.

"None other," the miner said. "Too bad you weren't around. I bet you'd have shot him like you did those six men I hear you shot over to Kansas. Or was it Oklahoma?"

"Excuse me," Boyd said to be polite, and gigged the chestnut. He trotted to his office and was out of the saddle before anyone else could accost him. Bursting inside, he stared in astonishment at the figure in a cell. "I'll be damned."

Harvey Dale had his boots propped on the desk and was grinning like the cat that ate the canary. "Got a present for you, Coop."

"So I've heard." Boyd went to the bars and peered in. "It's him, by heaven. Mad Dog himself."

Dale came over, a strut to his walk. "I should get a raise. Or hire me full-time. I can use the money."

"Tell me everything."

Boyd listened with rapt attention. "You were lucky," he said when the old scout finished his recital.

"Was I ever!" Dale agreed. "Keller saved my hash."

"Have you checked to see if any of the others are in town?"

"No," Dale said. "I haven't. I didn't want to leave him alone. But he was the only one I saw ride in."

"Better safe than sorry," Boyd said. "We'd better have a look around."

"Whatever you say."

Locking the office door behind them, Boyd took one side of the street and had Dale take the other. They went from one end of Main Street to the other, going into every saloon, every business.

"I reckon it was just him," Harvey Dale said when they rejoined in front of the jail. "No one I asked has seen hide nor hair of the rest."

"Same here," Boyd said, in relief. He'd become a laughingstock if folks learned that the outlaws were coming and going as they pleased. Inserting his key, he twisted it and went in.

"Well, look who is back on his feet," Dale said.

Mad Dog Hanks was gripping the bars, his eyes pools of hate. "You miserable sons of bitches."

"Now, now," Dale said. "You're still breathin', so don't be callin' us names. I could have shot you but didn't."

"Your mistake, you old buzzard," Mad Dog growled. "You're dead, is what you are."

Boyd stepped to the cell but stopped well out of reach. "You're goin' to be our guest for a spell. We have to send for the circuit judge. Witnesses have to be contacted, and there will be a trial. You might get prison for life, or more likely you'll be hanged."

"The rope hasn't been made that will stretch my neck," Mad Dog boasted.

"Listen to you," Dale said, and laughed.

"Where are your friends?" Boyd asked.

"Go to hell," Mad Dog said.

"Cooperate, and I'll ask the judge to give you prison instead of hemp," Boyd offered. It wasn't much, but it was the most he could do, and he'd dearly like to put an end to the Calloway Gang.

"Go to hell and take this old bastard with you."

"I'll say this for you, Hanks," Dale said. "Your disposition fits your name. You're a two-legged cur if ever there was one."

"When I get out of here, I'll skin you alive."

"Spare me your bluster," Dale said. "Your days of killin' folks are over. You might want to make your peace with your Maker."

"My days are over when I'm dead and not before. And don't give me that religion bunk. I don't believe in that."

"Explains a lot, right there," Dale said.

"Harve," Boyd interjected, "I want you to make another patrol. Let everybody see that we're on top of things."

"Sure," Dale said. Smirking at Mad Dog, he walked to the door. "Be seein' you," he said cheerfully, and gave a little wave.

"I can't wait to kill him," the outlaw snarled as the door closed.

Boyd was interested in something else. "Was it you who followed me to the Wilson place today?"

"It was," Mad Dog admitted.

"Why?"

"I was out for some fresh air."

Boyd started to move closer but caught himself. "They have nothin' to do with any of this. You should leave Sam Wilson be."

Mad Dog smiled. "Oh, it's him you're worried about, is it? Not that gal I saw you with in the parlor?"

Boyd swore he could feel the blood draining from his face. "What about her?"

"Like that gal, do you? I'd be worried as hell if I were you," Mad Dog said. "Two of us are dead and we don't take kindly to that."

"What does Calloway have in mind?"

"It's not just him," Mad Dog said. "It's all of us. We aim to show the whole territory what happens when they stand up to us."

"Show them how?" Boyd persisted.

"By goin' on a killin' spree," Mad Dog said, and grinned.

Chapter 14

Ira Toomis was returning from the Circle T, where he had gone to nose around and find out what he could about Sherm Bonner, and came on a freighter repairing a busted wheel at the side of the road about a mile outside Alpine. Toomis would have ridden past without stopping except that the freighter called out to him.

"Hey there, mister. Any chance I can buy your rope?"

Toomis reined over and stopped. "My rope?"

The freighter had one of those ruddy faces with cheeks like apples. "I'll pay you twice whatever you paid for it. I really need one."

It was the middle of the afternoon. A buckboard was down the road a piece, coming their way, and the freighter didn't look as if he had anything Toomis would want to steal, so he decided to be civil. "What do you want it for?"

Gesturing at the back of the wagon, the freighter swore. "The load shifted when the wheel gave out and the gate broke. I can't close it and I don't want the crates sliding out when I get to those steep grades between here and Denver."

"Is that where you're headed?"

The freighter nodded. "Have a delivery that can't be put off. Which is a shame. I would have liked to spend the night in Alpine. They're fixing to have a celebration like you wouldn't believe."

"What are they celebratin'?" Toomis asked. He didn't keep track of the calendar, but so far as he knew, it wasn't a holiday.

"Guess you haven't heard about the outlaw they caught," the freighter remarked while bending over his toolbox.

Careful to keep his voice calm, Toomis said, "Which outlaw would that be?"

The freighter selected a hammer. "One of that wild bunch, the Calloway Gang. Could be you've heard of them?"

"Most have in these parts," Toomis said.

Several spare spokes were on the seat and the freighter reached up and hefted one. "They robbed the Alpine Bank and now two of them are dead and this other one is in jail."

"You haven't said who he is."

"Oh." The freighter moved to the broken wheel. He had already placed a jack under the axle, and the wheel hung aslant. "It's the one they call Mad Dog. I think his last name is Hanks."

Toomis smothered an oath. "Did you happen to hear how they got him?"

"You won't believe it," the freighter said, and laughed. "He rode right into town and into a saloon in broad daylight. Can you imagine? After he'd helped rob the bank not long ago."

"He never was much on brains," Toomis said, and caught himself. "Now that I heard anyhow."

"You ask me, any hombre who rides the owl-hoot trail is short of common sense."

"Outlaws don't always set out to be outlaws," Toomis said. "Sometimes it just happens."

The freighter shrugged. "It was still mighty dumb of Mad Dog Hanks. I hear he rode past the marshal's office on his way in. Now, I ask you. Is that dumb or is that dumb?"

"Stupid is as stupid does," Toomis replied.

The freighter chuckled. "How about that rope so I can tie the gate? How much do you want for it?"

"Tell you what," Toomis said, "you can have it for free." He hardly ever used the thing, and he was feeling generous. The freighter had unwittingly done him a favor.

"Why, that's awful kind of you."

"That's me," Toomis said, "kind through and through." He handed the rope down. "What else did you hear about that dumb outlaw? Are they fixin' to hang him any time soon?"

"They're a law-abiding town. They sent for the circuit judge. It'll probably take him a week or better to get there. I hope I'm in the neighborhood when they have the trial. Or, better yet, I'd like to be there for the hangin'."

"Maybe they'll send him to prison instead."

"Mad Dog Hanks?" The freighter shook his head. "In case you ain't heard, he's half loco. They say he put up quite a fight when they arrested him. He bit people and clawed them like he's a real dog."

"No," Toomis said.

"I swear that's what they told me at the freight office. But what can you expect from somebody who calls himself Mad Dog?"

"It takes all kinds."

"Amen to that, brother." The freighter set the rope on the ground. "Well, I'd better get back to work. I want to be on my way before dark."

"Have a safe trip," Toomis said with a grin, amused by the act he was putting on. Clucking to his mount, he rode on. He'd been thinking of stopping in Alpine for a drink himself, but not now. Cestus Calloway needed to be told about Mad Dog, and something had to be done.

Toomis didn't like Mad Dog much, but Mad Dog was one of them and they couldn't stand by and let him be strung up.

Alpine didn't know it yet, but there would be hell to pay.

*   *   *

The Attica Kid practiced his draw every day. He'd go off by himself and spend half an hour or more doing nothing but drawing and cocking the Lightning. Over and over, again and again and again, until it was as much a part of him as breathing. When he could, he'd set up targets and shoot.

There was a clearing near the cave, and he'd go there, jam sticks in the ground, step back about ten steps, and go at it.

On this particular morning, the Kid was about to commence when he heard a footfall. Whirling, he had the Lightning out and pointed in less than the blink of an eye.

"Hold on there," Cestus Calloway said, smiling as he ambled out of the trees. "It's only me." He regarded the sticks. "You practice more than anybody I ever knew."

"A man doesn't practice, he loses his edge." The Kid twirled the Lightning into his holster. "I'll be damned if I'll lose mine." To demonstrate, he turned to the sticks. "Pick one."

"The second from the left," Cestus said.

The Kid's hand flashed. He drew and shot and split the stick, then twirled the Colt back into his holster. "How was that?"

"I've met some fast gents in my time, but you beat them all," Cestus complimented him.

The Attica Kid studied him. "Is this a social call or did you just come to watch me shoot?"

"I figured it was a good time for us to talk." Cestus stared toward the cave. "Away from the others. They know better than to come near you when you're practicin'."

"So do you," the Kid said. "You must have somethin' important on your mind."

Squatting, Cestus plucked a blade of grass and stuck the stem between his teeth. "It's about this revenge business."

"I thought that was settled. We kill the law dog and his deputies and everybody else on the posse."

"I want to talk about how to go about it."

The Kid cocked his head, puzzled. "I thought that was settled. You're havin' Toomis and Mad Dog find out what we need so we can do them in without bein' caught."

"It would help if we could make the marshal look like an accident," Cestus said. "So it's less likely other tin stars will come after us."

"Have one of the others run him over with a wagon. The rest of the posse, we can do any old way."

"I wish it were that simple."

"I'll brace Sherm Bonner. He's the dangerous one. With him out of the way, the farmer and the blacksmith and the rest will be easy."

"I want to hit all of them at once. The marshal, the cow-pokes, the farmer, the blacksmith, all of them at the same time."

"Why complicate things?" the Kid said. "We kill them one at a time and don't rush it so there aren't any mistakes."

"That could take months, with them on their guard," Cestus said. "If we do it in one fell swoop, as folks like to say, it will be over faster."

"They're scattered all over the place," the Kid said. "Or are you fixin' to send out invites to a social to bring them all together?"

Cestus grinned. "Even if I thought you were serious, which you're not, they'd be suspicious. No, we let them go about their days doin' what they usually do, and hit them when they least expect."

"Do we draw straws to see who kills who?"

"That would be one way. But what if Cockeye or Bert draws the straw to kill Sherm Bonner? They wouldn't stand a prayer. You, on the other hand, would."

"I can see where this is goin'."

"We match who is bein' killed with who would be best to kill him," Cestus said. "You should do Bonner. You're the only one of us who can beat him on the draw."

"Damn right I can," the Kid said.

"And while you're at it, you might as well blow out his pard's wick. That Lefty, I think his name is."

"Consider it done."

"I'd pick Cockeye to do for the blacksmith and Toomis to take care of the farmer. Neither should be hard. They're not gun hands." Cestus scratched his chin. "That leaves the young deputy for Bert and the old one who works at the stable for Mad Dog."

"And the marshal for you."

Cestus nodded. "It's only fittin', don't you reckon? I put this gang together. The marshal organized the posse. I'm in charge of things with us, more or less, and the marshal is in charge on his end. So it's only proper I be the one who runs him down with a wagon or however I decide to do it."

"You could be wastin' your time," the Attica Kid said. "Folks might still suspect it was us."

"Suspectin' and provin' are two different things," Cestus replied. "Once the law dog and his posse are dead, we'll light a shuck for Cheyenne or maybe Salt Lake and lie low for a while."

"If that's how you want to do it," the Kid said, "it's fine by me."

"I knew I could count on you." Cestus rose and was turning when a commotion broke out not far off. Hooves pounded and voices were raised, and someone came crashing through the brush at a gallop.

The Attica Kid instinctively placed his hand on his Lightning. "Maybe the marshal has found us."

"It's Toomis," Cestus said, peering into the trees. "He's back from the Circle T."

"He acts like his britches are on fire."

Cestus grinned, then had to take a couple of steps back as Ira Toomis trotted into the clearing and hauled on his reins. His horse was lathered with sweat. "What's gotten into you?" Cestus demanded. "That animal looks like you rode it to death to get there."

"I nearly did," Toomis said. "I rode all night." He was caked with the dust of many miles.

"You missed Cockeye's coffee that much?" the Kid joked. Everyone knew that Cockeye couldn't make a decent pot of coffee if his life depended on it.

Leaning on his saddle horn, Toomis said wearily, "We have a problem."

"Not another one," Cestus said.

"It can't be worse than Larner and McGivern bein' shot," the Attica Kid remarked.

"It comes close," Toomis said.

"Quit keepin' us in suspense, damn you," Cestus said. "Out with it."

"Mad Dog is in the Alpine jail. He got himself arrested and there's talk of the gallows."

Cestus swore. "How in hell did he manage that? I told him not to draw attention to himself."

"Since when does Mad Dog ever listen?" Toomis rejoined. "As to how, they jumped him in a saloon. He rode into town in broad daylight, if you can believe it."

"With him I do," Cestus said, and sighed. "When it rains, it pours."

"Ain't that the truth?" Toomis said.

"This changes everything."

"We have to get him out, Cestus."

"I don't see why," the Kid disagreed. "He was dumb enough to be caught. Let him rot. I never have liked him. All he does is gripe."

"He's one of us," Cestus said.

"A burr is still a burr."

"If we let him rot, folks will see us as weak. As not able to take care of our own."

"Hell," the Attica Kid said.

"We can't just ride in and take him out of the jail," Toomis said. "A lot of them know what we look like."

"I know," Cestus said.

"They're bound to have someone standin' guard every minute of the day and night, and maybe extra guards besides."

"I know that too."

The Attica Kid frowned. "Then do you mind tellin' us how we'll pull Mad Dog's fat out of the fire without gettin' burned?"

"Funny you should mention that," Cestus Calloway said, and laughed a strange laugh.

Chapter 15

The next week was so peaceful there were moments when Marshal Boyd Cooper was tempted to pinch himself to see if he was awake.

So much had happened in so short a time: the bank robbery, Larner and McGivern being shot, the assassin trying to kill Deputy Mitchell, arresting Mad Dog.

That seven whole days then went by without an incident of any kind was a wonderment.

Mitch came back to work. The town council agreed to employ Harvey Dale full-time for a while, which let Boyd set a work schedule of three eight-hour shifts so someone was always at the jail watching over Mad Dog Hanks.

Boyd took advantage of the quiet to sneak off and see Cecelia Wilson several times. He was clever about it and no one caught on. Mitch and Dale had to know, of course, so they could get word to him in an emergency, but the council and the rest of Alpine's good citizens had no notion their marshal was courting.

There were some who would say it was ridiculous at his age. There were some who would smirk and make some comment about old dogs and old love. He'd tell them to go to hell.

The plain truth was, Boyd was smitten. The more he saw

of Cecelia, the more he grew to care for her. She had a beauty about her, inside and out, and a sort of dignity that he found appealing.

They'd sit in the parlor and talk and laugh, or go for strolls about the farm and talk and laugh, or stand under the stars and not talk or laugh but be closer for the lack.

It got so that Boyd thought about her every moment he was away from her. He dreamed about her when he slept. And some were naughty dreams.

Now and then his conscience would prick him over the fact that he wasn't doing much about the Calloway Gang. But there wasn't much he could do, short of organizing another posse and going out day after day to scour the countryside. He saw no point to that. The outlaws could be anywhere.

He couldn't send Dale out either, because he needed Harve to work a shift at the jail each day. He consoled himself with the idea that once the circuit judge arrived and the trial was over, he'd set out to corral the outlaws in earnest.

In the meantime, why not enjoy the peace and quiet?

The eighth day started out like the others. Boyd had the six-a.m.-until-two-p.m. shift at the jail. He'd arranged for Ethel over to the restaurant to bring breakfast for the prisoner, and she always showed up promptly at seven, bearing a tray. With his hand on his revolver, he'd order Mad Dog Hanks to stay on his bunk while the food was slid inside the cell.

Mad Dog had lived up to his name. The man complained about everything. He insulted everybody. He hated the world and everyone in it. And Lord, could he cuss! Boyd told him to watch his mouth when Ethel fed him, but Mad Dog paid him no mind and called her things that turned her ears red.

That eighth morning, Mad Dog glared at her as the food was slid in. "Look at you, bitch, in that red shawl you like to wear. It's the same color your blood would be when I slit your throat someday."

Ethel blanched and took a step back.

"Stop that, you hear?" Boyd said. "She cooks you good meals. Show some gratitude."

"I'll show her somethin'," Mad Dog said, and cupped himself.

"How despicable," Ethel said. "He keeps this up, I don't know as I can go on doing this, Marshal."

"I can pay you a bit more," Boyd offered, "for the inconvenience."

"It's not the money." Ethel sniffed. "It's this animal."

Mad Dog chuckled as she went out. "Did you hear her? That's what I am to everybody. Nothin' but an animal."

"You bring it on yourself, the way you act," Boyd said as he returned to his desk.

Coming to the bars, Mad Dog gripped them. "I like it that they think of me that way."

"What good does it do you?"

"I'm Mad Dog Hanks. The rabid cur. Folks fear me. They tell their kids scary stories about me. I give them nightmares when they hear I'm around. They bolt their doors and latch their windows."

"That's the first time I've heard you brag on yourself," Boyd mentioned. "And it's loco besides."

"To want folks to be afraid of me?"

"It serves no purpose."

"That's where you're wrong, law dog. Fear is a kind of respect. I go into a saloon and men find out who I am, they step aside. I ride down a street and folks know it's me, they scurry for cover."

"And you like that?"

"Who wouldn't?"

"Anyone with common sense. Most folks would rather be treated with real respect. Not that kind."

"Real, hell. You think the people in this town respect you all that much? They respect the badge because they've been brought up to do whatever someone wearin' a badge tells them to do. But you? The man wearin' it? They don't respect you a smidgen as much as they respect me."

"You're confusin' respect with fear."

"Same thing."

Boyd saw no point in continuing their argument and instead said, "Have you changed your mind about my offer?"

"Hell. Not that again."

"Calloway has to have a hideout somewhere, and you must know where it is."

"He might have ten hideouts for all you know."

"Then give me all ten."

"Drop dead," Mad Dog said, and turned to his tray.

Boyd was glad when his shift was over. There was only so much of Mad Dog Hanks he could take. After a while, the man's griping and foul mouth got to him, and he wanted to march into the cell and beat him with a club.

Mitch had the second shift, from two until ten. He was healing nicely and not in pain anymore. Today he smiled and announced, "The docs say my bandage can come off tomorrow."

"Good for you," Boyd said.

"Don't get too happy, boy," Mad Dog said from over at his bunk. "The next time we won't miss."

Mitch swallowed and licked his lips.

"There won't be a next time," Boyd said to Hanks. "Not for you anyhow. You'll be joinin' Larner and McGivern in hell."

"I hope they have a card game goin'," Mad Dog said. "And just remember. There's still five of us out there to finish the job."

"Don't listen to him, Mitch," Boyd said. "He's tryin' to spook you. The outlaws have lain low since we took him into custody. They won't do anything so long as we have him."

"I bet you're right," Mitch said without much conviction.

Mad Dog laughed. "If you think Cestus and the Attica Kid are afraid of you, you have another think comin'. I may not like the Kid much, but he doesn't know what fear is."

"Boasting again," Boyd said, rising so Mitch could sit down.

"You'll find out," Mad Dog said. "You and that pup of a deputy, both. Your days are numbered."

"It's all right, Marshal," Mitch said. "When you're gone, I plug my ears with cotton so I don't have to listen to him."

About to go, Boyd turned back. "You do what, now?"

Mitch opened a bottom draw and took out two clumps of cotton. "I use these. I can hardly hear him with them in."

"You shouldn't," Boyd said.

"No?"

"What if a fight breaks out at a saloon? Or there are shots fired? Or someone needs us and is hollerin' for help? How would you hear any of that?"

"Oh. But none of that happens much."

"Mitch . . ."

"All right, all right," Mitch said, but he wasn't happy. "No more cotton in my ears. I'll have to try and block him out with my brain."

"What brain?" Mad Dog said, and laughed.

"Just take it easy, Mitch. I hope you have a quiet shift." Boyd smiled to encourage him, and departed. He had errands to run. First a visit to the millinery to see if the bonnet he'd seen in the window the other day was still there. It was, and he bought it. Next he visited Mrs. Rumpole, "the flower lady," as she was called, and bought a rose. By three he was in the saddle and on his way out of town.

Boyd hummed as he rode. He was happy. Genuinely happy. He couldn't recollect the last time he could say that. Before taking up with Cecelia, the best he could say was that he'd been content.

He remembered to check behind him. No one was back there. With Mad Dog behind bars, the outlaws had stopped shadowing him.

Or had they?

A puncher from the Circle T had stopped in the other

day. Efram Tilman sent him to let Boyd know that someone had been nosing around Tilman's spread. Whoever it was had done the nosing over a week ago, though, and nothing had come of it.

All was right with the world, Boyd decided, as he drew rein at the Wilson Farm. He practically skipped to the front porch and gave a light knock. He was holding the bonnet and the rose behind his back when the door opened.

"Why, Marshal Cooper," Cecelia said with a grin. "What a delight to see you again."

"I hope so," Boyd said, and held out the bonnet and the rose.

Cecelia put a hand to her throat, and her eyes sparkled. "Oh my. For me?"

"No, for Sam," Boyd said.

Laughing, Cecelia took the bonnet and fingered it. "What brought this on? It's not my birthday and it's not Christmas."

"How about just for bein' you?"

"Oh, Boyd," Cecelia said softly. Accepting the rose, she raised it to her nose and sniffed. "A flower too. I must say, your romantic streak pleases me greatly. I'd never have suspected you could be so sweet."

"Because I go around drownin' kittens and stompin' on puppies?"

"Oh, you," Cecelia said, and laughed anew. "Come in, won't you? I'll put this rose in a vase."

Doffing his hat, Boyd made himself comfortable in the parlor. He listened to the ticktock of the grandfather clock and the chimes on the half hour.

Cecelia returned with raspberry tea, a favorite of hers.

Boyd wasn't much of a tea drinker, but for her he would put up with it. They sat and sipped and chatted, the minutes flying by so fast that it was six o'clock before he knew it, and Sam came stomping in from the fields.

"You're becomin' a regular fixture," Sam joked as he

sank into a chair by the mantel. "Why not marry her and you can stay permanent?"

"Samuel Wilson," Cecelia said.

"It's not as if he hasn't thought about it," Sam said. "Or am I wrong?"

Boyd could have throttled him. "No, you're not wrong," he admitted, and felt his face once again grow warm.

"Stop that talk this instant," Cecelia chided her brother. "We're taking things slow for now."

"At your age you might not want to."

"Sam!" Cecelia exclaimed.

"Well, it's true," Sam replied. "You're neither of you whippersnappers. You like each other's company so much, you should quit pussyfootin' around and get on with it."

"I'll thank you to keep your wedlock advice to yourself," Cecelia said archly. "We're grown adults and know what we're about."

Sam winked at Boyd. "All the more reason to cut the courtin' short. We can have the ceremony here. Invite all our friends and neighbors and do it up right with a dance after the I dos."

"I will by God hit you," Cecelia said.

"Save me, Boyd," Sam said. "Sis has a mean right."

Chuckling at their banter, Boyd stood. "I hate to say it but I have to go. I can't stay too long at one stretch. Not until this Mad Dog business is over with."

"We can hurry things there too," Sam said. "I'll get some of the men together and we'll put on hoods and have a necktie social."

"Don't even joke about vigilantes," Cecelia said. "Breaking the law to hang a lawbreaker is the rankest hypocrisy."

"Do you hear her?" Sam teased. "That's what comes from all the reading she does."

"Ignore the dunderhead," Cecelia said, and taking Boyd's hand, she led him down the hall and out onto the porch. "Thank you again for the gifts."

They kissed, and all Boyd could think of on the ride back was how soft her lips were, and how sweet she tasted. He was so caught up in Cecelia that he didn't notice two men under the overhang at the jail until he had dismounted and was tying the reins.

"Marshal," one of them said, stepping out. "You have trouble comin.'"

Chapter 16

Their clothes and boots and the dirt on their faces and hands pegged them as miners, a common sight in Alpine. As well they should be, given that three mines largely accounted for the town's existence. The three were the Britenstein, the Livingston and the Tilden. Among them they employed a couple hundred workers, the backbone of the town's economy. Usually those workers behaved on their off hours, but now and then one drank too much and became too boisterous and had to spend a night behind bars to dry out. Boyd imagined that was the case now. "What sort of trouble are we talkin' about?"

"My name is Pike," the one introduced himself. "Me and Charley here work out to the Livingston."

Charley nodded.

"We were on our way in on the work wagon when we saw somethin' peculiar," Pike went on.

"Some others saw it too," Charley interrupted. "We volunteered to be the ones to come tell you."

"What exactly did you see?" Boyd asked.

"Riders," Pike said.

"Five of 'em," Charley clarified.

Boyd remembered the comment Mad Dog made about his five pards. "Go on," he said, all interest.

"They were a ways off and we couldn't see much except they were packin' sidearms and moved quicklike," Pike said.

"Quicklike?" Boyd repeated.

"Like they were in a hurry to get across the road."

Charley once again elaborated. "They came out of the woods on the north side and went into the woods on the south side. Which struck us as strange. Why ride in the woods when you can use the road?"

"Hunters, maybe?" Boyd said.

"Didn't look to be," Pike said. "They weren't dressed like hunters. And when they heard our wagon and looked our way, they used their spurs."

Troubled, Boyd asked, "Anything else you can tell me about them?"

"Not much," Charley said. "One wore a derby, I think it was. And another was dressed all in black."

Boyd bit off an oath. Bert Varrow wore a derby, and the Attica Kid was partial to black.

"Anyhow, we reckoned you might want to know," Pike said, "what with all that's been goin' on of late."

"You did me a favor," Boyd said. "I'll look you up and treat both of you to a drink when I have some free time."

"No need, Marshal," Pike said. "We just did what we thought was right."

"We're family men," Charley said. "Got wives and kids, and we don't want any damn outlaws skulkin' about."

Boyd thanked them again and shook each of their hands. Gnawing his bottom lip, he went into the jail and stopped short when he saw Deputy Mitchell with his feet propped on the desk, sound asleep. Going over, he swatted Mitch's boots and Hugo sat up with a start.

"What? Who?"

"You couldn't pick a worse time to sleep on the job," Boyd said.

Over in the cell, Mad Dog snickered. "Some lawman he is. That boy should take off that tin star and take to clerkin'."

"Quit proddin' me, you," Mitch said.

"Go fetch Harve," Boyd instructed him.

"What for? His shift doesn't start for a couple of hours yet. He's probably asleep right now."

"Do I have to tell you twice?"

Mitch blinked, and shook his head. "Sorry. And I didn't mean to doze off. Honest. It just happened."

"You need to be more vigilant, Mitch," Boyd said. He couldn't get mad at him, not after all Mitch had been through. "Now off you go."

Mitch vacated the chair, saying over his shoulder, "I didn't use the cotton in my ears, at least." He smiled sheepishly as he hastened out.

"What a jackass," Mad Dog said.

"He's a good man."

"Boy, you mean. He's so green it's pitiful."

Boyd sat and swiveled the chair so it faced the cells. Setting his heels on the edge of the desk, he folded his arms and thoughtfully regarded his prisoner. "What are your friends up to?"

"Huh?" Mad Dog said.

"Did they get word to you?"

"How in hell could they?" Mad Dog rejoined.

Boyd scowled. Mad Dog had a point. The cell didn't have a window, and he didn't let anyone near their prisoner except for Ethel when she brought the food.

"Why these questions about Cestus and the rest?" Mad Dog asked. "You must know somethin' I don't."

"I know they were seen close to town," Boyd revealed. "But I don't know why."

"Do tell." Mad Dog grinned. "Maybe they're fixin' to bust me out."

"They're welcome to try," Boyd said, although, truth to tell, the prospect continually worried him. Under cover of night they might be able to sneak in close without being spotted and burst into the jail with their guns blazing.

"Your nerves are showin'," Mad Dog said. "I like that."

"They try anything, you're the first one I'll shoot."

"Hell," Mad Dog said. "If it's the Attica Kid who comes in through that door, you won't clear leather."

"He's as good as folks say?"

"Mister, I mean to tell you," Mad Dog said, "I never saw anybody so quick with his hands. I don't like him much and he doesn't like me, but he's the real article."

Boyd was inclined to believe him. It tallied with the saloon talk about the Attica Kid. Gun sharks were a favorite topic. Men would argue for hours over who was faster and who had more kills and what would have happened if, say, Wild Bill Hickok had tangled with, say, Cullen Baker or Wes Hardin.

"Close to town, you say?" Mad Dog said, and grinned. "That's real interestin'. Don't you find that interestin', Marshal? Or are you too busy soilin' your pants?"

"Have your fun."

"They're comin' for me. You know that, don't you?"

Boyd's answer was to stand and take a scattergun from the rack. He made sure it was loaded and set it on the desk as he reclaimed his seat.

"Got you worried, does it?" Mad Dog said, and cackled.

A quiet quarter of an hour went by. Then the door opened, and in came Mitch and Dale. The old scout looked as if he'd been roused from a deep sleep, as Mitch had predicted. Dale hadn't slicked his hair back before jamming on his cavalry hat, and it stuck out at all angles.

"Here he is," Mitch said.

"What's so all-fired important?" Dale asked. "I could have used another hour in the sack."

"We might have company," Boyd said, and jerked a thumb at the cells. "His friends."

"Oh Lordy," Mitch blurted. "I hope not."

"Don't go weak sister on us, boy," Dale said, moving past him. "What makes you think so, Coop?"

Boyd related the information the miners had imparted, ending with "I don't think it's likely, but then again, outlaws are nothin' if not unpredictable."

"Damnation." Dale removed his cavalry hat, ran a callused hand over his hair a couple of times, and jammed the hat back on. "What do you want us to do?"

Boyd knew he could count on Harvey, but he entertained doubts about Hugo. The younger man had gone pale and kept glancing at the window as if afraid the outlaws would burst in on them any moment. "You scared, Mitch?" Boyd bluntly asked.

"No, not really," Mitch said. "It's just that I've been shot once this month and I'd rather not be shot a second time." He smiled thinly.

Boyd had intended to send them out to patrol the streets while he stayed at the office, but that might not be wise, given the state Mitch was in. "Since you're still on the mend, I'll give you a choice. Stay here and watch Mad Dog or take a shotgun and prowl around town."

Dale picked up the scattergun on the desk. "You don't have to ask me which I'd like. Sittin' in that chair too long makes my backside go numb."

"I reckon," Mitch said uncertainly, "I might as well be the one who stays. The doc said I shouldn't overdo it for a while."

"Are you sure you're up to it?" Boyd had half a mind to tell Mitch to go to his room at the boardinghouse and rest.

Mitch nodded. "I'm not helpless. And it's not as if those owl-hoots are comin' to town just to do me in." He added hopefully, "If they come at all."

"What puzzles me is why they were ridin' south," Harvey Dale said. "There's nothin' down that way but ranches and farms."

Sudden fear spiked through Boyd. The Wilson Farm was south of town, and Mad Dog knew about Cecelia and him. But Mad Dog hadn't had the opportunity to share that with the other outlaws, so Cecelia, and Sam should be safe.

Dale stepped to the rack, took down the other scatter-gun, and brought it over. "Here you go. Do we stick together or split apart?"

"Split," Boyd said, breaking the scattergun open to see if it was loaded. "You take the west side. I'll take the east. Poke into every saloon. And be careful around the alleys. Remember what happened to Mitch."

"I'm not likely to forget."

"Me either," Mitch said.

Boyd rose and came around the desk. "Don't doze off again."

"Not likely," Mitch said. Slipping into the chair, he placed his hands flat on the desk, licked his lips, and said, "Well."

Boyd and Dale exchanged glances.

"You know what?" the scout said. "When I was your age I fought the Sioux a few times. They're sneaky, those devils, and I was always so nervous about them I about wet myself."

"You?" Mitch said skeptically.

"When we were on patrol, I'd imagine all sorts of things," Dale continued. "Redskins springin' out and puttin' arrows into me, or sneakin' in when we were camped and slittin' my throat."

"I'd have worried about that too," Mitch said.

"But a scared scout ain't much good to anyone," Dale said. "I knew I had to stop worryin', but I had no notion of how to go about it until another scout by the name of Cody told me a trick he used to take his mind off his worries."

"Cody, you say?" Mitch said. "Not Buffalo Bill Cody, the famous one?"

"Might have been him," Dale said. "The important thing is that his trick worked for me and should work for you."

"What is it?" Mitch asked eagerly.

"Whenever you start to fret, think about your ma."

"My ma?"

Over in the cell, Mad Dog slapped his leg and laughed.

"Pay him no mind," Dale said.

"Why my ma?" Mitch asked.

"That's what I asked Cody. And he said who's the one person in the world most everybody feels kindly about? Their mas. Thinkin' about them makes us feel good inside. Think about yours and you'll forget all about the outlaws."

"I suppose I can give it a try," Mitch said.

"There's a simpleton born every minute," Mad Dog said.

"Hush up, you," Boyd said. He made for the door, held it open for Dale, and nodded at Mitch. "All you have to do is give a holler and we'll come on the run."

"Yes, sir," Mitch said.

Boyd closed the door and he and Dale walked out into the street. Traffic was light. Most people had headed home for supper. "Did you really know Buffalo Bill Cody?"

"Never met the gent. I would like to. They say no one can spin a yarn like Buffalo Bill."

"So you were spinnin' a yarn of your own about that talk he had with you," Boyd said.

"Afraid so."

"And havin' Mitch think about his ma?"

"It was the only thing I could think of. Who knows? It might help." Dale turned, but he only took a couple of steps and stopped. "What do you make of that?"

Boyd glanced around.

Smoke rose in a thick spiral coil from the far end of Alpine. More than there would be if someone were burning trash, or had a cook fire going. A whole lot more.

"I'd best go have a look-see," Dale said. "Maybe some kids are up to no good. Remember last year? The one who used a lantern to set that outhouse on fire?"

"I'll go with you," Boyd said. The smoke had increased to alarming proportions even as they talked.

No sooner did they start off than a frantic cry was borne on the breeze.

"Help! Help! A house is on fire!"

Chapter 17

Every frontier town feared fire. Nearly every building was made of wood, and with perennially dry conditions in the summer over much of the West, towns were tinderboxes waiting for the first hiss of uncontrolled flame to ignite an inferno.

A frantic cry of "Fire!" always brought citizens out in droves to fight it. Some towns were fortunate enough to have fire brigades. Many did not.

The town council of Alpine had the presence of mind to form one made up of a dozen men, townsfolk who had no experience whatsoever fighting fires. The council also invested in a double-tank fire wagon with a steam-driven pump, drawn by a four-horse team. It was regularly taken to the river and pumped out and refilled to keep the equipment functioning properly.

So far Alpine hadn't needed to put their fire wagon to real use.

Boyd knew their luck had run out before he reached the burning house. The smoke told him that much.

Dale at his side, Boyd sprinted around a final corner and beheld the house, already three-fourths engulfed. It sat on a narrow side street at the edge of town. That worked to their advantage if they could keep the flames from spreading. But the house was one of half a dozen spaced close together.

The people who lived on the street had scrambled to fight the blaze. Buckets were being filled in a water trough and passed down a line to the first man, who threw the water on the fire. It was akin to using a thimble to put out a forest fire, and wasn't doing anything to retard the flames.

Boyd began bellowing orders: for Dale to go urge the firemen to hurry, for more people to lend a hand. He shouted for more buckets and set up another bucket line between the trough and the house, and yet a third between the house and a backyard pump.

The heat was blistering. People couldn't stand to get too close. In no time the flames were a tongue of fire, licking at the sky.

Boyd kept the buckets moving, but it was a losing proposition. He dreaded that any moment the wind might cause the fire to leap the street and ignite other homes. Not only was that a threat, but burning bits were flying through the air like thousands of fireflies, and all it would take was for one to land at just the right spot, and they'd have a second fire to deal with.

What with the crackle and roar of the conflagration, and the shouts and cries of those trying to put it out, it was no wonder Boyd didn't realize the fire wagon had arrived until it was practically on top of him. He heard the bell, glanced up, and there it was.

Harvey Dale was up on the seat with the driver. Leaping down, he shouted needlessly, "We're here!"

Alpine's volunteer firemen practiced twice a month. They had the procedure down: how to turn the steam engine over, how to unroll the hose, how to attach it to the tank. The biggest and sturdiest held the nozzle while others held on to the hose to steady it.

At a command from the fire brigade captain, a powerful stream was unleashed.

Cheers went up from many of the onlookers, but Boyd didn't join in. The water wasn't having much effect. For a harrowing couple of minutes it appeared that the fire wagon was too little, too late.

The captain had the bucket lines concentrate on the adjacent houses to keep them from going up while the hose team pressed nearer to the main blaze. Bit by bit the water began to tell. Bit by bit the flames shrank. Once the fire was reduced enough, the captain commanded the bucket lines to join in the assault. The combined attack prevailed.

Even so, it was slow going. Boyd didn't realize how slow until the last of the flames were being put out and people were applauding, and someone near him remarked that it had taken over two hours.

Boyd was exhausted. His shoulders ached from all the buckets he'd handled, and he was soaked with sweat and stank of smoke. When the brigade captain came over and thanked him for his help, he swallowed and nodded.

"We were damn lucky," the captain said.

"Were we ever!" Boyd agreed. His throat was sore and raspy, another result of the smoke.

"It was a close thing," the captain said. "We used up nearly all the water in the tanks."

Some of the firemen were carefully moving about the debris, searching for hot spots.

"What I'd like to know," the captain went on, "is how it started."

Harvey Dale was nearby, and Boyd told him to find the owner. No sooner did the old scout turn than a woman stepped forward. She had a small child in her arms and two others at her side. Tears moistened her eyes, her hair was a mess, and soot splotched her face and neck.

"That's our house," the woman said, and let out a sob. "We lost everything."

"I'm sorry, ma'am," Boyd said.

She stared aghast at the blackened ruins. "My husband is at work. He has the middle shift at the Livingston. Wait until he sees this." She coughed, and composed herself. "Where are my manners? I'm Mrs. Shaw. These are my little ones."

The captain was all business. "How did this fire start, Mrs. Shaw? Was a lamp knocked over?"

"As God is my witness, I have no idea," Mrs. Shaw said. "Except that it wasn't a lamp. We took precautions, Woodrow and me. We know how children can be, so all the lamps were up high where they couldn't reach."

"It had to be something," the captain said, almost accusingly. "Were you starting a fire in the stove and it somehow got out of hand?"

"No."

"Are you sure?"

"No, I tell you," Mrs. Shaw said angrily. "Do you think I wouldn't say if I knew how it started?"

A girl of ten or so was clinging to her dress. Looking up at her, the girl tugged and said something too softly for Boyd to hear.

"What was that, Elizabeth?" Mrs. Shaw said.

The girl tugged harder and motioned for her mother to bend down. When Mrs. Shaw did, the girl said something in her ear.

Startled, Mrs. Shaw said, "What men, Beth?"

"Men?" the captain said gruffly. "What are you talking about, child? Is this some fancy of yours?"

The girl pressed her face into her mother's dress.

"Answer me," the captain said.

Boyd looked at him and shook his head. Squatting, he lightly touched the girl's shoulder. "Beth, I'm Marshal Cooper. You can talk to me. Are you sayin' you saw who started the fire?"

Her face still pressed against her mother's dress, Beth nodded.

"Would you tell me about it?" Boyd said.

Beth didn't respond.

"If there are men going around startin' fires, we'd very much like to know," Boyd said. "You can help us."

Her left eye peeked out of a fold.

"Please," Boyd said.

Beth slowly faced him.

The captain went to speak, but Boyd gestured him to silence. Smiling, he said, "Please, Beth. You see my badge? It's my job to stop people from doin' bad things. I need to find whoever did this and make sure they don't do it to anyone else."

"Tell him, Beth," Mrs. Shaw said. "He's the law. You can always trust the law."

"I wish Pa was here," Beth said softly.

"But he's not. So do as the marshal wants," Mrs. Shaw said.

"Honestly," the captain said, sounding irritated.

"You're not helpin'," Boyd warned him.

"Tell the marshal," Mrs. Shaw said.

Beth clasped her fingers in front of her and said something that Boyd didn't catch.

"You'll have to speak up," Mrs. Shaw said. "They can't hear you when you mumble, child."

Beth coughed, then said softly, "There were five."

"Five men?" Boyd said, and a ripple of ice ran down his spine.

"Yes, sir."

"Where did you see them?"

"Out the window," Beth said. "When two of them ran up with torches."

"What's that you say?" Mrs. Shaw interrupted. "Torches?"

"Who would deliberately set a house on fire?" the captain snapped. "This is preposterous."

Boyd gently squeezed the girl's shoulder. "Talk to me, Beth. Tell me more. What were you doin' when you saw them?"

"Helping Ma get ready for supper," Beth said quietly. "She told me to get wood for the stove from the wood box."

"It's near the back window," Mrs. Shaw said.

Beth nodded. "I looked out and saw them."

"The five men?" Boyd said.

Beth nodded again. "The others were on horses, but two were running toward our house and they had torches."

The captain turned to Mrs. Shaw. "Are you and your husband at odds with anyone? Who would do such a thing to you?"

"I have no idea."

"Hush up, both of you," Boyd said curtly. "Let the girl finish." He squeezed her shoulder. "Go on, Beth. Tell me about the two men."

"They ran up to our house and threw the torches."

"Dear Lord," Mrs. Shaw exclaimed. "Why didn't you tell me?"

"It happened so fast, Ma," Beth said, and broke into tears. Pressing her face to the dress again, she sobbed uncontrollably.

Boyd glanced up in annoyance at the mother.

"Sorry," Mrs. Shaw said. "It's a shock, is all. We don't have any enemies, Woodrow and me. He's a miner. I'm a mother. We're peaceable people. Who would want to do this to us?"

"Exactly my point," the captain said. "The child is making the story up. She must have started the fire herself."

"I don't see how," Mrs. Shaw said. "There are no lamps near the wood box, and we keep our matches in a drawer that's out of her reach."

"I tell you, she must have."

"No!" Beth cried into the dress. "It wasn't me. It was those men!"

Boyd had had enough. "Not one more word out of either of you," he said to the mother and the captain. "And this time you'd damn well better listen."

"You heard the marshal," Harvey Dale said, and put his hand on his six-shooter.

"How dare you threaten me!" the fire brigade captain replied.

"I'll do more than threaten," the old scout said.

"Please," Mrs. Shaw said. "No violence."

"Then let the marshal do his job, lady," Dale said to her. "The girl can't talk with you two buttin' in all the time."

Boyd made a mental note to thank Dale later; the mother and the captain finally shut up. To the girl he said, "Beth? Would you tell me more? Did you get a good look at them out the window?"

"Some of a look," the girl said.

"What do you remember about them? Can you describe them for me?"

Taking her face from the dress, the girl wiped at her eyes and nose with a sleeve. "Sorry," she said.

"Go on," Boyd urged. "The two men."

"They ran up to the back of house. One had a round hat and dressed real nice. Like Pa would in his Sunday-go-to-meeting clothes."

"Round hat?" Boyd said. "Do you mean a bowler or a derby?"

"I don't know how to tell," Beth said. "But it was round."

"What else?" Boyd prompted.

"The other one scared me."

"What did he do? Did he see you?"

"No, but I saw him," Beth said. "He was looking up at the roof and he threw his torch." She shuddered. "I saw his face."

"What about it?"

"It scared me. It's why I didn't yell for Ma or anything. I was too scared." Beth stopped and sniffled.

Boyd wished she would come right out with the rest of it. Getting her to talk was like pulling teeth. "What about his face scared you so much?"

"Was it scarred?" Mrs. Shaw asked. "Like your uncle Dillon's from that time he got hit on the cheek with a shovel?"

The girl shook her head. "It was the man's eyes."

"What about them?" Boyd asked, knowing what she would say, and dreading it to his marrow. Not that there could be any doubt.

"They were spooky," Beth said. "One eye looked one way and the other eye looked another."

"Cockeye," Dale said. "And the other one must have been Bert Varrow. But why would they set some miner's house on fire . . ." He stopped and stared toward the middle of town, and the jail. "Oh hell."

Boyd exploded into motion, running as if a life depended on it—because it did.

Chapter 18

"What's all the ruckus about?" Mad Dog Hanks growled. "I'm tryin' to get some sleep over here."

Deputy Hugo Mitchell peered out the front window of the jail at the people hurrying past. Craning his neck, he glimpsed a column of smoke to the west. He had to squint to see it because it was directly in line with the sun. "Looks to be a fire," he replied.

"You'd better go help," Mad Dog said.

Mitch turned. "I'm not goin' anywhere. The marshal said I'm to stay put and guard you, and that's exactly what I aim to do."

"Some gents never learn."

"What's that supposed to mean?"

"You were already shot once," Mad Dog taunted, and laughed.

Mitch returned to the desk. No sooner did he sit than the door burst open and in rushed Arthur Hunnecut, the president of the Alpine Bank and Trust Company, in a state of great agitation.

"Where's Marshal Cooper?" the banker demanded.

"He went off to make his rounds with Deputy Dale," Mitch said. "Can I help you?"

"There's a fire," Hunnecut said, gesturing at the window.

"I know," Mitch said.

"Then why are you just sitting there? Go help fight it. Don't you realize it's on my side of Main Street?"

"Your side?" Mitch said in confusion.

"My bank's side, rather," Hunnecut said. "If it spreads out of control, my bank could burn to the ground."

"So could a lot of homes and other businesses," Mitch said.

"Was that supposed to be funny?"

"Land sakes, no," Mitch said. The banker's attitude flustered him. He wasn't used to dealing with important people. "I was only sayin' that your bank ain't the only place we could lose. There are others to think of."

"Now I know you're jesting. What else can possibly be as important as my bank?"

Mitch had no answer to that one.

"Do more than flap your gums," Hunnecut said. "Get out of that chair and go lend a hand."

"I can't."

"Why in hell not?" Hunnecut asked angrily.

Before Mitch could respond, loud clanging broke out in the street. "Do you hear that? It must be the fire wagon."

Wheeling, Hunnecut stuck his head out the door. "It is. Why am I wasting my time with you when I should be talking to the fire crew? They must protect my bank at all costs." With that he ran out, slamming the door behind him.

"The salt of the earth," Mad Dog said, and laughed.

"What do you know about salt?" Mitch said. "You rob and kill for a livin'."

"I know a . . . What's that word?" Mad Dog's brow puckered.

"Which?"

"I recollect now," Mad Dog said, snapping his fingers. "I know a hypocrite when I hear one, and that banker is at the top of the heap."

"He's not a very likable man," Mitch agreed. Absently

running his hand along the edge of the desk, he wondered if he was doing the right thing. Maybe the banker was right. Maybe he should go help fight the fire.

Just then the fire wagon went past, the bell clanging and the team straining. The driver flicked a whip to hurry them.

"I hope this whole town burns down," Mad Dog said.

"What a mean thing to say," Mitch said. "Think of all the women and children. Think of the old folks."

"They can all fry to a crisp, for all I care," Mad Dog said scornfully, "and you can fry with them, boy. The only person I care about is me."

"There's a shock." Mitch leaned back and propped his feet up. It eased the discomfort in his side somewhat. "Outlaws sure ain't saints."

"I don't recollect any of us ever claimin' to be," Mad Dog said. "I live my life my way. I take what I want and do what I want and no one can tell me different."

"You're ten years old. Is that it?"

"What do you know?" Mad Dog snapped. "Look at you. I bet you think you're doin' good by wearin' that tin. Bet you think you're helpin' folks and makin' the world a better place."

"I do what little I can," Mitch said defensively. Unknown to the outlaw, Mad Dog had struck a nerve. Ever since he was little, Mitch had always tried to do what was right. Part of that came from his folks, especially his ma. She had impressed on him that there were two kinds of people in the world, good people and bad people. The good ones were looked up to and respected, while the bad ones were looked down on and shunned. Even more important, the good ones went to heaven and the bad ones burned in hell.

"I reckoned as much," Mad Dog was saying. "But what has bein' good ever got you, boy? Are you rich? Do you have a big house with servants to wait on you hand and foot?"

"No, but neither do you."

Mad Dog ignored that. "You risk your life, and for what? Hardly more money than a cowpoke makes, I suspect."

"I get by."

"That's all you do," Mad Dog said. "That's all bein' good has ever done for anyone."

Mitch was growing annoyed. "Don't you ever have anything nice to say about folks?"

"Nice?" Mad Dog said, and guffawed so hard he sat on his bunk and doubled over.

Mitch decided that was enough. Opening a drawer, he took out an old copy of the *True Fissure*, the town newspaper. He'd already read it twice, but it was something to do. And he could always use the practice. He'd only gone as far as the third grade in school and had to wrestle with a lot of words. Coop told him once that if he hankered to be a marshal someday, he should get better at it.

"You're as green as grass and that's no lie," Mad Dog said.

Mitch paid him no mind.

"Why would the marshal hire somebody as dumb as you?"

Mitch pretended to be interested in an account of a town council meeting from weeks ago. Not much had happened. The minutes had been read, and the mayor proposed an ordinance to prohibit hogs and chickens from running loose in the streets. Not that it happened all that often. But then, the mayor loved to pass new ordinances.

"Don't act like I'm not here, boy," Mad Dog said. "It riles me."

"Leave me be," Mitch said. "Can't you see I'm busy?"

"You're really readin' that?"

"Of course."

"I never learned how," Mad Dog said. "My pa used to say it was a waste of time. He had better use for me in the fields."

"Your father was a farmer?"

"What of it?"

"Farmers are usually nice people."

"We're back to that again," Mad Dog said. "You're won-derin' how a farmer raised a whelp like me?"

"Now that you mention it."

"Farm work bored me, boy. There was nothing' about it I liked. Not milkin' the cows or feedin' slop to the pigs or plowin' or any of it."

"So that's your problem," Mitch said. "Life doesn't please you."

"I didn't say all life," Mad Dog replied. "I said farmin'." He stepped to the bars. "Fact is, there's a lot about life I like. Stealin' other folks' money. Spendin' a night with a whore. Killin'."

"No one likes to kill," Mitch said. "That's not natural."

Mad Dog gripped the bars. "Let me out and I'll show you how much I like it by killin' you."

"No, thanks," Mitch said. He was almost to the end of the council account, and trying to remember what *unanimous* meant.

That was when the front door opened, admitting a blast of noise from up the street.

Mitch idly looked over, expecting it to be a townsman or maybe Arthur Hunnecut again. But no. The man who filled the doorway wasn't much older than he was, and dressed all in black. Even as Mitch looked, the man's hand flicked and a Colt Lightning appeared, pointed squarely at Mitch.

"Stay right where you are, law dog."

"Kid?" Mad Dog said

Belatedly Mitch recognized the Attica Kid. He felt as if ice-cold water had been poured into his body, and froze.

The Kid moved to one side and Cestus Calloway strolled in as casually as could be. Behind him came the old outlaw, the man called Ira Toomis, with his six-shooter out.

"It was plumb easy," the Attica Kid said.

"Told you it would be," Cestus Calloway said. Smiling

grandly, he stepped to the desk, roosted on the edge, and rested his wrists on his leg. "How do you do, Deputy?"

Mitch had to try twice to say, "Mr. Calloway, sir."

"Sir, is it?" Cestus said, and chuckled.

"Where are the others?" Mad Dog asked.

"Bert and Cockeye are out back with the horses," Cestus said. "Some of the animals are skittish from the smoke and all the yellin', and we don't want them runnin' off."

Mad Dog tried to shake the bars, but they were firmly embedded. "Let me out. I hate bein' caged more than I hate just about anything."

Cestus bent toward Mitch. "Are those the keys yonder, on that peg?"

Even though Mitch knew that they were, he looked and nodded. "Yes, sir. They are."

"Ain't you polite?" Cestus said. He pointed at Ira Toomis and the grizzled outlaw crossed to the wall, slid the ring from the peg, and moved to the cell door.

"I'll have you out in two shakes of a lamb's tail, Hanks."

"About damn time," Mad Dog growled. "I was beginnin' to think you were goin' to leave me here to swing."

"We're here, ain't we?" Toomis said. Inserting the key, he twisted, and there was a click.

Mad Dog didn't wait for Toomis to open the door. He pushed, forcing Toomis to move aside or be struck. Storming out, his fists clenched, Mad Dog strode to the desk. Suddenly bending, he relieved Mitch of his revolver, stepped back, and cocked it.

"No," Cestus Calloway said.

"Why the hell not?" Mad Dog demanded.

"Because he said so," the Attica Kid said. He was still holding his Lightning, and trained it on Hanks.

"Don't you dare," Mad Dog said.

"Do as Cestus says."

"He's a tin star," Mad Dog fumed, and wheeled on Calloway. "Give me one good reason why I shouldn't?"

"I'll give you a heap of reasons," Cestus said. "You shoot him, someone will hear. Most folks are out at the fire. That's why we started it. But not everyone is, and if some hear the shot and come runnin', we might have to shoot them too."

"So?"

"So robbin' banks is one thing. Shootin' up a town is another," Cestus said. "Word will spread. Folks from Cloverleaf and Red Cliff and Alpine and others will band together to stamp us out—"

"You don't know that," Mad Dog said.

"I'm a hell of a good guesser. And that's not all. There are bound to be—"

Mad Dog wasn't listening. He barreled toward the door, muttering, "Some outfit I'm with. They kill two of us, but we can't kill any of them." He slammed the door so hard the walls shook.

"I'm sorry I let him out," Toomis said.

"He's so mad he forgot to collect his own hardware," Cestus mentioned. Sliding off the desk, he pushed his hat back. "How about you hand his things over, Deputy? Then I'll put you in that cell. We'll light a shuck and you get to go on breathin'."

"I'd like that a lot," Mitch said. He'd taken it for granted he was a goner when they walked in. To find out different made him want to whoop for joy. He opened a drawer and took out Mad Dog's gun belt and effects.

"Let's go," Cestus Calloway said.

Raising his hands to show he wouldn't resist, Mitch rose and backed toward the cell. He saw the Attica Kid twirl the Lightning into its holster, saw Ira Toomis wink at him, saw Cestus Calloway looking as pleased as could be. Then the door opened and in strode Mad Dog Hanks. Before Mitch or anyone else could guess his intentions, Mad Dog pointed the revolver he'd taken from Mitch.

"Hold on there!" Mitch blurted.

"Like hell," Mad Dog said, and shot him.

Chapter 19

Marshal Boyd Cooper was several blocks from the jail, with Harvey Dale running at his side, when a woman with two small children pointed toward it as they drew near her.

"There was a shot from down that way, Marshal," she said anxiously. "People should know better than to shoot where there are women and children out and about."

Boyd kept on running. It took effort. Fighting the fire had taken a lot out of him, and now this. He was winded and his legs were close to giving out.

Dale, despite his age, was hardly panting at all. "Are you thinkin' what I'm thinkin'?"

Boyd puffed and strained and didn't answer.

"The outlaws started that fire to draw us away from the jail so they could free Mad Dog Hanks," Dale guessed.

Boyd grunted.

"I thought so," Dale said. "Damn, I hope that boy is all right."

So did Boyd. His gut was bunched in a knot from worry. Mitch was a good deputy but inexperienced, and in law work that could get a man killed.

"Look!" Dale exclaimed. "The front door is open."

Boyd peered ahead. The scout must have good eyes. He couldn't tell if the door was or wasn't open, but he did see a small crowd forming. "No," he gasped, and dug deep inside for a reserve of stamina he didn't know he possessed. He covered the last twenty yards at a sprint, shouting, "Let me through!" to part the gawkers.

Boyd burst into the jail, and stopped cold. "No," he said again, softly, and went numb with shock. He was barely aware of Harvey Dale moving past him to the body.

Sinking to a knee, Dale put his fingers to Mitch's neck and after a bit shook his head. "There's no pulse. Not that I expected there would be."

Neither did Boyd. Mitch's eyes were wide and glazed, his face rigid with the horror he'd felt at being shot in the forehead. A lot of his hair and most of his brains were splattered on the floor.

"Poor kid," Dale said.

A constriction in Boyd's throat kept him from replying. He stared at the cell, feeling as empty as it was.

"Wonder which one shot him," Dale said.

"Does it matter?" Boyd got out.

The ferocity of his tone caused Dale to jerk his head up. "No, it surely doesn't. They have to pay for this. Every last one."

"They will," Boyd vowed. Moving around his desk, he sat. His legs were trembling. He'd liked Mitch, liked him a lot. Ernest and likable, Mitch would have made a great lawman given time to grow in the job. That potential was why Boyd had taken Mitch under his wing as another lawman once took him.

"Is there anything we can do, Marshal?" someone called out from the doorway.

Boyd had forgotten about the townsfolk. Swallowing, he said, "Fetch the undertaker. And I need some of you to go to the saloons. Ask around, find out if Sherm Bonner is in town, and bring him here. If he's not, find any Circle T hand who can take him a message."

"Glad to help," the same man said, and several of them hastened away.

"The rest of you," Boyd said, "close the door, if you please." He said that last because there were women and children present, and they shouldn't be looking at the blood and the brains.

"I'll do it," Dale said, going over.

Boyd stared at Mitch. He hadn't expected anything like this. Certainly not a jailbreak. The only other time he'd ever heard of such a thing was years ago, and it happened down to Texas.

"I'll get a blanket," Dale offered, and went into the back.

Boyd didn't care what Dale did. He was drained. Sitting back, he closed his eyes and wearily rubbed them. This was the lowest day of his career. Of his life. He would bear the burden the rest of his days.

A soft sound caused him to look up.

Harvey Dale was spreading a blanket over the body. "I can go after them and mark their trail for you and a posse. There's still some daylight left."

"Not enough," Boyd said. "The sun will be down before I can get the men and the horses together." He shook his head. "No, we'll start after them in the mornin'. With any luck, we'll have Sherm Bonner along."

"We don't need him."

"Like hell we don't. He's the only gun hand we have. We need Vogel too. Him and that rifle of his."

"I'll spread word about the posse, and have them meet here at the jail. What time do you want it to be?"

"The crack of daylight," Boyd said.

Dale nodded and went out.

Grateful to be alone, Boyd sagged in his chair. It was hard to believe that just a couple of weeks ago, all had been right with his world. Now it was in shambles, except for Cecelia. She was the one bright spot. He wished he could be with her now and take comfort from her presence.

Coughing, Boyd sat back up. "What in hell is the matter with me?" he said out loud. Pity was a poor substitute for grit. He needed to stop feeling sorry for himself. There were outlaws to go after in the morning, and revenge to take.

Yes, revenge, Boyd told himself. By rights he should arrest them and bring them back for trial. By rights he should stick to the letter of the law. But for once, he wasn't going to. To hell with the law, Boyd thought, and startled himself. He would order his posse to shoot to kill, on sight. No one would hold it against him. Not after Parsons and now Mitch.

Hanging the outlaws would take too long. Hot lead was quicker. And if there were any justice in the world, he'd be the one to personally snuff out Cestus Calloway's wick.

Yes, that would please Boyd greatly.

They rode hard through the woods south of town for a short way and then slowed to a walk. There was no sign of pursuit. Cestus hadn't reckoned there would be, not with most of the men off fighting the fire.

The sun was setting, the shadows lengthening. They came to a clearing and Cestus drew rein and wheeled his chestnut. He had held his anger in, but now he let it out. "What the hell did you think you were doin', Hanks?"

The Attica Kid came up next to Cestus and turned his animal, his hand on his Lightning.

Behind Mad Dog, Bert Varrow and Toomis and Cockeye sat their saddles and listened.

"Answer me, damn you," Cestus said.

Usually so quick to bristle, Mad Dog acted surprised. "Doin' what we agreed on. To kill everyone who was in that posse."

"We agreed to spare the deputy. He was a kitten."

"You wanted us to, but I never agreed to any such thing," Mad Dog said. "He had it comin' and I gave it to him."

"You stupid son of a bitch."

"I wouldn't make callin' me that a habit."

"Or what?" the Attica Kid said.

A crooked smirk twisted Mad Dog's lips. "No, you don't, Kid. You're not goadin' me into drawin'."

"You consarned jackass," Cestus said. "You gunned down an unarmed boy."

"Boy, hell. He was full-growed and you know it."

"Everyone will want our hides for this."

"That's another thing," Mad Dog said. "You're always so worried over what people will think. Who the hell cares? Let them hate us. It doesn't matter."

"That's where you're wrong," Cestus said. "Why do you think I went to so much trouble to curry public favor? Why did I give money away after we robbed each bank? So people would like us. So they wouldn't put pressure on the law to bring us in. Are you so stupid that you can't see that?"

"That was all well and good, and it worked for a while," Mad Dog said. "But in case you've lost count, we're not as many as we used to be. Larner and McGivern are dead, and their dyin' changed things. We can't go around bein' nice anymore. We'll be a laughingstock if we do."

"He's right, Cestus," Bert Varrow said.

"I think so too," Cockeye said.

"There. You see? I'm not the only one," Mad Dog crowed. "Shootin' that deputy will bring the marshal and some of those others into our rifle sights, and ain't that what we want?"

Cestus could have hit him. There was no reasoning with the man, none at all. He regretted ever letting Hanks ride with them; Hanks truly was a mad dog. And he wasn't the only one who took exception.

"It bothers me, Hanks, you not listenin' to Cestus," the Attica Kid said coldly. "It bothers me you make trouble for us."

"I already told you, I won't let you provoke me," Mad Dog said. "I'm not as dumb as your pard seems to think."

"You want to go on ridin' with us, you'd better start listenin'."

"Who made you boss?"

Toomis gigged his mount up next to Hanks's. "Enough of this bickerin'. We're wastin' time. We have somethin' to do and we need to get to it."

"You shouldn't butt in, Ira," the Kid said. "He's not worth it."

"I'm not doin' it for him," Toomis said. "I'm doin' it for all of us. We've timed things so the posse won't come after us until mornin', but they might not wait, and here we sit squabblin' like a bunch of biddy hens."

"He has a point," Bert said. "We should get it done."

Cockeye nodded.

Some of Cestus's anger faded, and he put the rest aside for the time being. They'd need Mad Dog later, when the shooting commenced. "Hanks, no more killin' unless I say so."

"Yes, Ma," Mad Dog said.

Disgusted, Cestus reined around. The road would be faster, but he stuck to the woods where they were less likely to be spotted. They rode in single file until the chestnut acquired a shadow.

"I've about had my fill of him," the Attica Kid said, "but he's right about one thing."

Cestus looked over but couldn't read the Kid's expression in the gloom. "You're takin' his side again?"

"We agreed the posse has to pay. You argued about the deputy, but most were for it. Now it's done, and as much as you don't like it, you need to accept things as they are."

"I thought I could count on you."

"Always," the Attica Kid said. "I wasn't provokin' Mad Dog because he killed the deputy. I did it because he was buckin' you."

"So you don't mind he shot the deputy?"

"Not a lick."

Cestus sighed. "I am the lone voice in the wilderness."

"You're what?"

"I heard that somewhere."

The Kid let half a minute go by, then said, "Mad Dog is right about you when it comes to curryin' favor with folks. Givin' all that money away. You ever hear of an outlaw doin' such a thing? I went along with it because it worked for a while, but that was then and this is now."

"I did what I thought best for all of us," Cestus said grumpily.

"We know that," the Kid said. "It's why the others have stuck with you as long as they have. But now things have changed and we have to change too or we're done for."

"I don't know if I can," Cestus admitted. "Robbin' is one thing. Killin' is another. I'm not a killer at heart, not like Hanks, and not like—" He stopped.

"Me?" the Kid said.

"We've got money squirreled away," Cestus went on. "Maybe it's time we let the others go their own way and you and me go off to Montana or anywhere that no one knows us and live straight for a change."

"And do what? Work cattle? Clerk at a store? No, thank you. I'd rather breathe dirt."

Cestus didn't press the issue, but now that the notion had taken root, he liked it. He liked it a lot. He'd never aimed to be an outlaw forever.

"What's that?" the Kid said suddenly.

The woods were thinning, the trees almost at an end. A grassy pasture spread before them, and something moved in the starlight, a blocklike shape.

"It's a cow, you infant," Cestus said, and laughed.

"For a second there I thought it was a bear."

The glow of lit windows appeared, and Cestus sobered. "That must be it," he said. Drawing rein, he waited as the others came up on either side. "There's the farmhouse. Any questions before we pay the marshal's friend and his sister a visit?"

"We've been all through what to do," Bert Varrow said.

"Two in one night," Toomis mentioned. "We'll be the talk of the territory."

"What are their names again?" Varrow asked.

"Wilson," Ira Toomis said. "Sam and Cecelia Wilson."

Chapter 20

Cecelia made beef stew for supper. Her brother was fond of soups and stews of all kinds, and had been since he was a boy. She humored his craving by making it a point to prepare some sort of soup at least once a week.

This particular evening, Sam got in from the fields late. He'd been hard at work all day preparing a new section for plowing. It involved clearing trees and removing more than a few large boulders and a lot of smaller ones that might damage the plow.

"I'm hungry enough to eat one of our cows," Sam announced as he came in the back door. He'd washed up at the pump and his face and hands were clean, if not his clothes.

Cecelia had his silverware and bowl waiting on the table, and ladled the stew. She didn't mind waiting on him when he toiled so hard each day for their mutual benefit. He handled almost all the field and barn work, and she handled the house and the vegetable garden.

"No Boyd tonight?" Sam teased.

"He was out early today but had to go back," Cecelia said. "That outlaw business."

"Mad Dog Hanks," Sam said. "The judge will do a service to the town and the territory when he sentences Hanks to hang."

"The man hasn't put been on trial yet."

"He will, and that will be the end of him. Or should be," Sam said, "if the judge doesn't go easy."

Cecelia decided not to pursue the topic. Sam was quite set in his ways when it came to the legal system. He often complained that judges mollycoddled criminals too much. "Eat your stew," she said, setting his bowl in front of him.

Sam didn't need urging. When it came to meals, he jumped in like a starved bear and ate as if it were his last meal on earth. When he was eating soup, he slurped now and then, much to her annoyance. Just now, smearing butter on a piece of bread, he licked his lips and said, "Smells delicious. You're about the best cook who ever lived, except for Ma."

Cecelia moved to the other end of the table and sat. Placing the napkin in her lap, she spread it out. "Your flattery is appreciated, kind sir."

Chuckling, Sam was about to spoon stew into his mouth, and froze. "I just had a thought."

"Oh no," Cecelia said.

"I'm serious." Sam lowered the spoon. "What happens to me if Boyd and you get hitched?"

"Pshaw. You're getting ahead of yourself," Cecelia said. "We've barely begun our courtship."

"You've been at it long enough to spend a lot of time on the porch swing at night."

"That's hardly your concern," Cecelia said archly.

"My stomach is."

About to dip her own spoon, Cecelia paused. "How's that again?"

"My stomach," Sam repeated. "Who's going to feed me if you marry Boyd Cooper and move out?"

"First off," Cecelia said, "you're old enough to feed yourself. Second thing, who says I will? Maybe Boyd wouldn't mind moving in here."

"No married man in his right mind wants to live with his

brother-in-law. He'll want a place of his own. Or your two's own, rather."

"And why wouldn't he live with both of us?" Cecelia asked.

"It's just not done," Sam said. "He'll want his own place to raise his own family."

"Sam, neither Boyd nor I are spring chickens," Cecelia reminded him. "There won't be children. There won't be a family. Just him and me."

"Say, that's right," Sam said. "You're both a little long at the tooth to have children."

"Thank you so much," Cecelia said.

"I didn't mean anything," Sam said quickly. "Finding a man at your age, that's some feat."

"You can shut up now."

"All I'm trying to say is that maybe you're right and he won't mind living here. Although we'd have to arrange things so that you two are at one side of the house and I'm at the other. I don't know how noisy you two will be."

"Oh, Samuel."

"Don't 'Oh, Samuel' me. I'm not the one who thinks she is sixteen again. But you know, sis"—Sam beamed with warmth and affection—"I couldn't be happier for you. Who knows? It could be lightning will strike twice and I'll find a woman my age willing to put up with the dirt and the smells."

"You don't stink that much except when you've been shoveling mature," Cecelia said gaily.

"I had that coming, I suppose, for pointing out your gray hairs are a factor."

"Eat your stew."

Laughing, Sam bent to his meal.

As for Cecelia, she ate slowly, thinking of Boyd and the possibilities ahead, and how she would love more than anything if her brother's prediction came true. She didn't like living single. If her previous marriage had taught her anything, it was that having someone to love increased her happiness tenfold. Always doing things together, laughing together, snuggling together, it filled a body's heart close to bursting with joy.

"What are you thinking about?" Sam asked unexpectedly.

"Nothing much. Why?"

"You looked like you were about to cry."

"No, not that. I was—" Cecelia stopped. She'd heard the front door open and now saw someone coming down the hall toward the kitchen. The lamp in the parlor wasn't lit yet and all she saw was a dark silhouette. "Who on earth is that?"

Sam twisted in his chair. "Boyd? Is that you?"

The back door opened and in came three men with drawn revolvers. They spread out as they entered. The oldest of them had a beard, another had a stray eye, while the third wore a derby and an expensive suit. "Ma'am," the third one said politely.

"Good God!" Sam blurted.

Out of the hall came three more.

Startled to her core, Cecelia recoiled in dismay. She'd recognized them from what Boyd had told her: Cestus Calloway, the Attica Kid, and Mad Dog Hanks.

"Lord help us," she gasped.

Calloway strolled to the table while the other two moved to the right and the left, respectively. Picking up a piece of corn bread, Calloway took a bite. "Yum-yum," he said. "Did you bake this yourself, Miss Wilson?"

Cecelia couldn't seem to find her voice.

"What is this?" Sam demanded. "How dare you come marching into our home? You have no business here. Get out."

"I wouldn't be bossin' folks around, if I were you," Cestus Calloway said. "Not with five six-shooters pointed in your direction."

"Let me do him and we can be on our way," Mad Dog Hanks said.

Calloway gave him a sharp glance. "Didn't you learn your lesson back in town? We talked this out and you're to behave."

"He better," the Attica Kid said.

"Oh hell," Mad Dog growled.

Cecelia had regained enough control to say, "Mr. Calloway, isn't it? What is the meaning of this? Would you please explain?"

Cestus came around the table and, to her surprise, doffed his hat. "Listen to you, ma'am. As polite as anything. You remind me of my ma, some. She was always goin' on about bein' polite."

Not sure what to make of his friendliness, Cecelia glanced at each of the others. They weren't nearly as friendly. The Attica Kid showed no emotion at all, Mad Dog Hanks was worthy of his nickname, and the bearded man and the man with the mismatched eyes seemed almost bored. The only one who did her the courtesy of smiling was the one in the derby.

Sam's own confusion was apparent. "Whatever it is you're after, take it and go. Just don't hurt her. She's never done anything to you."

"Hurt *her*?" Cestus said. "Farmer, you have it wrong. It's not her we're here for."

"No," Cecelia gasped.

"What?" Sam said.

"It wasn't your sister who rode with the posse," Cestus Calloway said. "It wasn't your sister who had a hand in Ben Larner bein' blown to hell."

"I didn't shoot that old buffalo hunter."

"You were with those as did."

Sam started to rise but froze when a revolver hammer clicked. Sinking back down, he said, "Now, see here. I only rode with the posse to have words with the marshal."

"Words about what?" Cestus asked.

"That's none of your affair."

"You might live longer if you tell me."

Mad Dog Hanks uttered a string of oaths. His jaw muscles had been twitching the whole while, and now he wagged his revolver at Sam and rasped, "What the hell difference does it make? He was part of the posse. That's all we need to know. Quit playin' nice and finish this."

"You're tryin' my patience," Cestus said. "You truly are."

"I can say the same," Mad Dog said. "Did we come here to kill him, or not? If we did, put one in his brainpan and we can go."

Cecelia tried to think of a way to use their bickering to her advantage. It was plain they didn't like each other. Plain too, given the looks they shot at Hanks, that some of the others didn't like him either. "May I interrupt?"

"You certainly may, good lady," Cestus said.

"I can't take this," Mad Dog fumed. "Are we outlaws or a sewin' circle? If the rest of you want to stay here and listen to this, fine. But count me out." Wheeling, he stomped off down the hall like a mad bull.

"So much for the nuisance," Bert Varrow said.

Cecelia was only concerned with saving her brother's life. "Sam," she said, seizing the opportunity. "You can tell them why you went to see Boyd." She had suspected the truth when Boyd brought up courting her the very next day.

"Boyd, is it?" Cestus Calloway teased her.

Cecelia was sure she blushed. "Please, Sam. It's for your own good. I don't mind them knowing."

"It's not proper," Sam said.

"Hang proper," Cecelia said, and inwardly winced at her choice of words. "If you don't tell them I will."

Sam glared at the leader of the outlaws. "I went to see the marshal about her behind her back. She was taken with him, and he wasn't doing anything about it, so I suggested he should come courting."

"And I thank you for that," Cecelia said.

Cestus Calloway laughed. "Well, now. I believe this is a case of true love, boys."

"Don't poke fun at her," Sam said.

"I wouldn't think of it."

Sam mumbled something, then said, "When I got to town, the bank had been robbed and the marshal was leavin' with a posse. The only way I could talk to him was if I rode along."

"So we didn't enter into it at all?" Cestus said.

"In what way?"

"It never dawned on you that if the posse caught up to us, lead might fly? That you could be shot helpin' your sister with her romance?"

"I didn't think that far ahead."

"I believe you," Cestus said, and laughed even louder.

The Attica Kid came closer to the table. "Don't tell me you're thinkin' what I think you're thinkin'."

"You heard him," Cestus said. "We can't shoot a man over romance."

"I don't believe this," Ira Toomis said. "First you wanted to spare that deputy and now you want to spare this farmer?"

"You missed your callin', Calloway," Cockeye said. "You're so fond of sparin' folks, you should have been a parson." That was more words than he'd uttered in months.

Whatever Cestus was about to say in response was cut off by the slamming of the front door. Boots thudded in the hall, and down it ran Mad Dog Hanks.

"Not you again," the Attica Kid said.

"You'll want to hear this," Mad Dog said. "I was out by the road and heard a rider. I looked, and caught a gleam on his shirt. It must be a badge. I suspect the marshal is comin' to court his farm gal."

Cestus jammed his hat on and drew a revolver. "Don't this beat all? What is it religious folks like to say? Ask and you will receive."

"Let's blow out the lamps and ambush him," Mad Dog said.

"And make him suspicious, the house bein' all dark?" Cestus shook his head. "We'll let him ride up and walk in as natural as you please, and then we'll blow him to hell."

"Finally you want to kill somebody," Ira Toomis said.

"When it comes to the marshal," Cestus Calloway said, "I truly do."

Chapter 21

Marshal Boyd Cooper told himself he should turn in early. He needed rest. He was to lead the posse in the morning, and he was worn out. Fighting the fire had exhausted him. Mitch's death had made a wreck of his emotions. Competing tides of fury and sorrow were ripping at him, and something else. A growing sense of worry.

According to a witness, the Calloway Gang had headed south after they murdered Deputy Mitchell. At the time, Boyd hadn't thought anything of it.

But after the undertaker had removed the body and Dale had gone to make his rounds, Boyd had a troubling thought. After they'd robbed the bank, the outlaws had gone north. Boyd had figured—and Harvey Dale agreed— that they had a hideout somewhere.

To the north, not the south.

So why, Boyd asked himself, had they gone south this time? No one had ever reported seeing them south of town before. Had they done it to throw pursuers off their scent, or was there a more sinister purpose? Because the Wilson Farm was south of town, and Sam had been with the posse that killed Ben Larner.

Boyd told himself he was fretting over nothing. That the outlaws wouldn't break Mad Dog out and then kill Mitch *and* go after Sam. They'd expect the whole countryside to be roused against them. They'd head for their hole-in-the-wall to the north and lie low.

The more Boyd thought about it, though, the worse he worried. He'd suspected that the outlaws sent McGivern to murder Sherm Bonner and Lefty, and now they'd killed Mitch. It could be they were doing the unthinkable: wiping out every member of the posse.

Finally it reached the point where Boyd couldn't stand the worrying. He had to do something about it. Saddling his horse, he took the south road out of Alpine. He would check on the Wilsons, and if all was well, stay for a short visit with Cecelia and head back to get his much-needed sleep.

Everything appeared normal. A couple of their windows were lit and the farm lay peaceful under the sparkling host of stars.

Boyd dismounted and was almost to the front porch when he stopped in his tracks, troubled. The farm was *too* quiet. Sam and Cecelia might be sitting quietly in the parlor, Sam reading and Cecelia knitting, as they liked to sometimes do after their evening meal, but a sense of unease warned Boyd that wasn't the case. He was probably being foolish, but he palmed his revolver and moved around to the side of the house.

The first window that was lit was to what Cecelia called her sitting room. It contained a lot of female knickknacks and a flute she played on occasion. She wasn't there.

The other lit window was to the kitchen.

Boyd crept forward, still feeling a bit foolish. Removing his hat, he inched an eye to a corner.

Sam and Cecelia were at the kitchen table, eating.

Exhaling in relief, Boyd was about to put his hat on and go around to the back door and knock when a shadow moved by the stove. He looked, and his blood ran cold. A man was crouched beside it where he wouldn't be seen by anyone coming down the front hall.

The man was Mad Dog Hanks.

Ducking, Boyd moved to the other side of the window and again raised his eye.

Cestus Calloway and the Attica Kid were to either side of the hall doorway, their backs to the wall, their revolvers out and cocked.

Boyd ducked down again. The whole gang must be in there. Somehow they were expecting him. He must do something, quickly, before they came out to investigate what was keeping him. Replacing his hat, he moved to the rear of the house.

No one was out back.

Careful not to let his spurs jingle, Boyd stalked to the back door and hesitated. All the outlaws must be inside. All six of them. By bursting in he'd take them by surprise and might get one or two or maybe even three, but the rest would surely fill him with lead, and where would that leave Cecelia and Sam?

Boyd was in a quandary. What else could he do? Shoot through the kitchen window? That wouldn't work any better than charging on in

Boyd needed to draw the outlaws out of the house somehow. On open ground, in the dark, he stood a better chance of holding his own. He could knock and run, but where would that leave Cecelia and her brother?

Stumped, Boyd gazed about him. Not far off a pile of chopped wood was ready for use in the stove. An ax leaned against the wall. The barn door was closed for the night, the chicken coop still.

The barn. There might be something he could use. He was about to cross over to it when he heard an oath from in the kitchen, and pressed his ear to the door.

"What the hell is keepin' him?" Mad Dog Hanks rumbled. "He should have been here by now."

"Hush, damn you. You'll give us away."

"I tell you he should be here," Mad Dog said. "Somethin' is wrong, Calloway. I can feel it."

"Could be he's right," someone else said.

"I'll go have a look-see out the front," another volunteered.

"Go ahead, Kid," Cestus Calloway said. "But don't let him catch sight of you."

"Do you think I'm as stupid as Hanks?" the Attica Kid said.

"You have your nerve," Mad Dog declared.

Boyd was unsure what to do. The Attica Kid would see his horse and warn the others. Should he retreat to the barn, or fight?

The decision was taken out of his hands.

The back door was jerked open, splashing him with light. The man known as Cockeye, about to step out, froze in surprise.

Boyd shot him.

Cecelia was beside herself with worry. She yearned to shout a warning to Boyd, but she might be shot. Or, worse, Sam might. Her brother was fidgeting in his chair and glowering at the outlaws. She recognized the signs. Sam was contemplating something. That worried her even more. He'd be filled with lead before he took two steps.

Cecelia tried to catch Sam's eye, but he wouldn't look her way. She tapped her bowl with her spoon, thinking that might draw his attention, but he was looking over at Mad Dog Hanks, the nearest of the outlaws, crouched beside the stove.

Dear God, no, Cecelia thought. Jumping Hanks was the last thing Sam should do. But they had to do *something*. If not, Boyd would walk in and be cut down with no chance to defend himself.

Desperate, Cecelia glanced about. Her gaze was drawn to the sugar bowl and her matching repoussé salt and pepper in the middle of the table. She'd special-ordered the shakers through a catalogue at the general store. They were sterling silver, and engraved with a floral pattern. As casually as she could, she reached for the saltshaker. No one was looking at her. She brought the shaker to her bosom and commenced to remove the top. She wanted a handful to throw into their eyes. It wasn't much, but it was the best she could think of at the moment.

Just then Mad Dog Hanks growled, "What the hell is keepin' him?"

An exchange took place. The outlaws were suspicious that Boyd was taking so long. The Attica Kid went down the front hall, and the outlaw called Cockeye moved to the back door.

Cecelia was ready. She would cause a distraction. She gripped the saltshaker and was set to dart over and dash the salt into Mad Dog's face when her brother exploded out of his chair.

"Look out!" Ira Toomis hollered.

Mad Dog was looking toward the front hall and was a shade slow to react. Before he could bring his revolver to bear, Sam slammed into him, smashing him against the stove. Mad Dog cursed, Sam grabbed both of the outlaw's wrists, and they grappled.

A revolver boomed, but it wasn't Mad Dog's. It came from behind Cecelia. She turned and saw the man known as Cockeye tottering backward from the open back door, a hand pressed to his gut. Boyd was framed in the doorway; he had shot Cockeye in the stomach. Even as she looked, Toomis spun and snapped a shot at Boyd that sent splinters flying from the jamb. Bert Varrow fired too. Boyd bounded to one side, out of sight.

Toomis and Varrow dashed toward the back door.

So did Cestus Calloway. As he came abreast of the table, Cecelia rose and threw salt from the saltshaker at his eyes. As it struck him, he instinctively turned his head away, but the harm had been done. Lurching to a halt, he cursed and swiped at his eyes with his sleeve. It had to sting like the dickens.

Cockeye had sunk to his knees with both hands splayed over a spreading scarlet stain.

Toomis and Bert Varrow had rushed out the back door.

The Attica Kid was coming back down the hall on the run.

And over at the stove, Sam and Mad Dog Hanks continued to grapple, with Mad Dog trying to point his revolver at Sam and Sam doing his utmost to prevent him.

Cecelia sprang to help her brother. There was still some salt in the saltshaker and she intended to throw it into Mad Dog's eyes. That should give Sam the advantage he needed. She was almost to the stove when Sam rammed Mad Dog's gun arm against it in an apparent attempt to make Mad Dog drop the six-shooter. Instead the gun went off.

Cecelia felt as if a fist punched her in the head. A searing pain spiked her and she stumbled, suddenly weak all over. "Sam?" she said as her vision swam and her legs gave out. She heard him shout her name, and the cuff of blows. Then she was on the floor, on her side, dizzy and nauseated and wishing very much that she could get back up.

She had been shot. It didn't seem real, somehow, yet it was. She had been shot in the head. The pain wasn't as terrible as she'd always imagined it would be, but it was enough that she closed her eyes and gritted her teeth to keep from crying out.

A revolver thundered twice from over near the hall, so swiftly the shots were as one.

Cecelia heard the thud of a body. She opened her eyes, but the room was whirling around and around. Bile rose in her gorge and she swallowed it back down and closed her eyes again against the dizziness.

"I'm obliged for the help," Mad Dog Hanks said, sounding surprised. "He was a tough bastard."

Boots drummed, and the Attica Kid asked anxiously, "Are you hit? Who shot you?"

"Salt," Cestus Calloway gasped. "She threw salt in my eyes."

"She got hers. She's down," the Kid said.

"You shot her?"

"No. Mad Dog did."

"Like hell," Hanks said. "My pistol went off when that stupid farmer jarred my arm."

"Water," Cestus Calloway said. "I need water to wash out my eyes."

"Comin' right up," the Attica Kid said.

"Mad Dog?" Cestus said.

"Right here."

"I can hardly see. Where are the rest?"

"Toomis and Varrow ran out after the law dog. Cockeye is sittin' on the floor, bleedin' like a stuck pig."

"Damn. Get him to his horse. Holler for the others. We're lightin' a shuck."

"What's your hurry?" Mad Dog asked.

"The marshal might not be alone."

"I only saw him."

"Just do it," Cestus snapped.

Cecelia might have heard more, but she blacked out. The next she knew, she experienced the sensation of moving, but that couldn't be; she was too weak to even open her eyes. She realized someone must be carrying her, and blacked out a second time.

More motion. This time Cecelia felt something under her. A horse, unless she was dreaming. She had been propped up and was slumped against someone, her back to his front. An arm was around her waist. In a panic, she groped blindly about and her hand came to rest on a saddle horn. "What . . .?" she got out.

"It's all right, ma'am," a voice said in her ear. "I have a good hold on you. You won't fall off."

Cecelia recognized Bert Varrow's voice. It must be his

horse. The outlaws must be abducting her. Or were they merely taking her somewhere to dispose of her body when her wound took its toll? She struggled weakly.

"Be still, ma'am," Varrow said. "It's hard enough ridin' at night in these woods without you actin' up."

Cecelia clutched at his arm, and her own went limp. She wanted to scream for help but couldn't. She wanted to jump off and hide, but her body wouldn't move. She had the illusion of falling into a well with no bottom, and then there was nothing, nothing at all.

Chapter 22

Marshal Boyd Cooper had no choice but to hunt cover.
Lead was striking the jamb and buzzing past his head.
Whirling, he sprinted for the barn. He hoped the outlaws
would come after him and leave the Wilsons alone.

He went a dozen feet, glanced back, and tripped. His
boot snagged in a rut or a hole and he crashed down hard.
He went to push up and keep going, but Ira Toomis and
Bert Varrow rushed outside and turned from side to side,
looking for him. They hadn't spotted him in the dark, but
they would if he stood, so he stayed put.

Voices were raised in the kitchen. There were the sounds
of a struggle. A revolver boomed, and seconds later there
were two more swift shots.

Anxious about Cecelia and Sam, Boyd came close to
charging back in. But Toomis and Varrow blocked the doorway.

Muffled talk didn't tell Boyd much. He thought he
caught the word *salt* a few times.

Mad Dog appeared. He was supporting Cockeye, who
could barely stand. "The horses, Toomis," Mad Dog barked,
"and be quick about it. Calloway thinks we might have a
posse down on our heads."

Boyd wished that were true. He could use the help. As it

was, the outlaws might spot him at any moment. Twisting, he crawled toward Cecelia's flower garden. Her rosebushes were high enough to hide him.

Toomis hurried into the night. Mad Dog and Varrow were staring after him. Cockeye's head had slumped to his chest.

Boyd reached the roses.

Mad Dog hefted Cockeye and grumbled, "Damn. You weigh more than I reckoned."

"How bad is he?" Bert Varrow wanted to know.

"You've got eyes, don't you?" Mad Dog replied.

"Quit bein' so damn contrary," Varrow said. "All I did was ask."

"He's gut-shot," Mad Dog said. "What does that tell you?"

"Hell," Varrow said.

It told Boyd that Cockeye wasn't long for this world. Stomach wounds were nearly always fatal. Sometimes the victim lingered for days in the worst agony imaginable. He supposed he should feel a shred of regret, but he didn't. It had happened too fast. He'd shot in reflex, not aiming at all.

"Hell is right," Mad Dog said. "We lose him, that makes three. This outfit is becomin' a dangerous proposition."

"Things were fine until we robbed the Alpine Bank," Bert Varrow said. "That's when it all went to hell."

"The worst might be yet to come," Mad Dog said, "with Cestus so worthless these days."

"Don't let him hear you say that."

"He doesn't scare me any," Mad Dog said. "Him nor the Kid neither."

"Anyone with any sense is afraid of the Attica Kid."

As fate would have it, the Kid picked that moment to emerge. "What was that about me?"

"Nothin'," Varrow said.

"I heard my name," the Attica Kid said.

"I was tellin' Mad Dog that most folks are scared of you

and should be. You're hell on wheels with that smoke wagon of yours."

"I can shoot too," Mad Dog said.

"Not as fast or as accurate," Bert Varrow said. "Compared to the Kid, we're a bunch of beginners."

"Lick his boots, why don't you?" Mad Dog said.

Rising onto his knees, Boyd parted a rosebush to see better and winced when a thorn pricked his hand.

A horse nickered, and Ira Toomis hurried up, three sets of reins in each hand. One of the horses was giving him trouble and resisted being pulled. "Your damn animal," he griped at Mad Dog. "It's as cantankerous as you are."

"It should be," Mad Dog said, grinning. "I trained it."

Groaning loudly, Cockeye was boosted onto his mount and clutched the saddle horn. "I hurt," he said.

"You've been shot, you simpleton," Mad Dog said.

Boyd wondered where their leader had gotten to and found out when Calloway came out of the house carrying Cecelia. She appeared to be unconscious. Boyd went to stand but caught himself. He'd be cut down before he reached her.

"What the hell are you doin' with the farm gal?" Mad Dog said.

"We're takin' her with us," Cestus replied. "Bert, you'll have the honor. Climb on your critter."

"Why me?" Yarrow said.

"Why take her at all?" Mad Dog said. "Leave her with her brother. It's fittin' they die together."

"That's just it," Cestus said. "We don't want her to."

"Here you go again," Mad Dog said.

"I can think of no surer way to have the whole countryside out for our hides than to harm a woman."

"We weren't to blame. Her brother was."

"Who'd believe that? Who'd take our word for anything?" Cestus moved to the horse Bert Varrow was mounting. "If we can we'll patch her up, sneak into town, and leave her for the sawbones. If it's hopeless, we'll bury her where no one can ever find the body."

"I savvy," Mad Dog said. "Without the body they can't prove a thing."

"Are you done arguin', then?"

"He better be," the Attica Kid said.

The hardest thing Boyd ever had to do was kneel there while the woman he cared for was hoisted up to Bert Yarrow and her leg slid over his saddle so Yarrow could hold her in front of him. Five to one, Boyd kept reminding himself. Five to one. Five to one. Cockeye didn't count. He was in no condition to shoot.

Cestus Calloway wiped a sleeve at his face. "Consarn that salt anyhow. I still can't see straight."

"Can you see good enough to ride?" the Attica Kid asked.

"We'll find out," Cestus answered. Forking leather, he did more wiping, then reined his horse to the north. "Back to the cave, boys. It has been a long day and I'm plumb tuckered out."

"At least you ain't shot," Cockeye gasped.

Spurs tapped and reins were lashed, and the outlaws trotted to the barn and on around.

Boyd was up the second they were out of sight. He flew into the kitchen, digging in his heels when he saw the form crumpled by the stove. A pair of bullet holes low in Sam's back were dribbling drops of blood.

"Sam!" Boyd cried, and dropped beside his friend. "Sam? Can you hear me?" Carefully turning him over, Boyd cradled Sam's head on his leg.

Sam groaned and his eyelids fluttered.

"Sam?" Boyd said. "Don't you die on me." He felt for a pulse. It was terribly faint, barely a tick of the vein. "Lord, no."

"Boyd?" Sam opened his eyes and gazed blankly about. "What happened? Where am I?"

"Don't you remember?" Boyd said. "One of them shot you."

Memory returned, and fear lit Sam's eyes. "Sis? Where's Cecelia?" He tried to sit up but couldn't.

"Be still," Boyd cautioned. "You're in a bad way. I'll get you to your bed and go fetch the doctor."

"Where's my sister? Why haven't you said?"

Boyd could hardly say the words. "They took her."

"Lord in heaven, no." With sudden strength, Sam gripped Boyd's wrist. "Forget about me. Go after them. Save Cecelia."

"I can't track at night."

"Save her," Sam said again. "She's more important than me. Leave me here and go."

"You're not listenin'. I can't find them in the dark. I'll have to wait until dawn, and set Harve on them."

Tears filled Sam's eyes and his grip tightened. "Damn it, Boyd. Don't make excuses. You care for her, don't you? Or have all your visits been a sham?"

"You know better."

"Then *go*."

"Maybe I will, at that," Boyd said. To town, to bring the physician and tell Dale to have the posse at the jail before the break of day. He eased Sam off his leg and rested Sam's head on the floor. "Are you comfortable? Do you want a blanket?"

"All I want is my sister, safe."

Boyd began to stand but stopped when Sam uttered a sharp cry and shuddered. "Sam?"

"I hurt, Boyd. God, I hurt."

Boyd sank back down. "How about if I dig the slugs out? I'm no doctor, but it may keep you alive until the real doc gets here."

"Too late," Sam said. Arching his back, he opened his mouth wide as if to scream, but instead he exhaled and gazed wildly at the ceiling. "Boyd? Where did you go."

"I'm right here," Boyd said.

"Did the lamp go out?"

Boyd glanced over. The wick burned as brightly as ever.

"It got dark all of a sudden. Is the back door open? Did the wind blow the lamp out?"

Boyd didn't have the heart to tell him there wasn't any wind, that the night had been perfectly still.

"I feel strange," Sam said, "like there's something inside me that's crawling up my chest. What can that be?"

The only thing Boyd could think of was blood. Sam must be bleeding inside. That was bad. That was very bad.

"Do me a favor, would you? Tell Cecelia I'm sorry I couldn't protect her. I failed her when she needed me most."

"You did no such thing. Hush and rest."

"I don't even know who shot me. I was grappling with Hanks and it felt as if I was kicked in the back, and then I was on the floor and not sure how I got there."

"You should stop talkin'."

"My sister likes you, Boyd. She likes you an awful lot. Do me another favor and ask her for her hand."

Boyd saw blood trickle from a corner of Sam's mouth.

"It would please me to know you're looking after her," Sam said. "Not that she needs to be. Cecelia can take care of herself just fine. Don't ever tell her I said this, but I'm as proud of her as a brother can be." A trickle seeped from the other corner.

"Sam, please."

"I know," Sam said. "I know."

Boyd took Sam's hand and squeezed it. "Can you feel that?"

"Feel what?"

"You've been a good friend," Boyd said, suddenly feeling congested.

"We never know, do we? When I got up this morning it was just another day. And now I—"

When he didn't go on, Boyd said, "Sam?" and bent down. There was no answer, and never would be.

Boyd folded Sam's arms across his chest, sat back, and bowed his chin. Of all the days of his life, this had been the worst. His best friend, gone. The woman he cared for, shot and taken by outlaws. His deputy, murdered. He stared at the tin star pinned to his shirt and asked out loud, "Is it worth it?"

The silence ate at him. He faintly heard the ticking of the grandfather clock in the parlor and the lowing of a cow in the pasture.

Boyd half thought he might shed a few tears, but no. The emotion building in him wasn't sadness. It was rage. A rage such as he'd never known. A rage that boiled so red-hot he struggled to contain it. Rage at the perpetrators of the misery in his life.

The outlaws.

Boyd never considered himself a violent man, but his mind raced with violent images. Of him shooting Cestus Calloway. Of him taking a club to Mad Dog Hanks. Of putting nooses over the necks of the others and laughing as they dangled and gurgled and died.

"God help me."

Rousing, Boyd stood. He had a lot to do. He must notify the undertaker. And see to it that someone came out to look after the farm until Cecelia returned, if she ever did.

Despair tore at him, and Boyd fought it off. He focused on his rage. His rage would sustain him. His rage would keep his head clear so he could do what needed doing.

He closed and bolted the back door, blew out the lamp, and wearily walked down the hall past the parlor. The sight of the settee reminded him of the last time he sat there with Cecelia. The memory fanned his rage into an inferno.

The night air was cool, but Boyd felt hot all over as he stepped onto the front porch. *"I failed her when she needed me most,"* Sam had said. Boyd had failed both of them. He should have done more. He should have protected them somehow.

Boyd vowed to make it up to them when the posse caught up to the outlaws.

This time the outlaws weren't getting away. This time Boyd was going to do what he should have done the first time.

Kill all of them dead, dead, dead.

Chapter 23

Some folks might think it was ridiculous, but Cestus Calloway tried hard to be a good outlaw. He wasn't cold-blooded.
He wasn't a natural-born killer, like the Attica Kid. Or a
vicious sidewinder who liked to hurt people, like Mad Dog
Hanks. No, his main failing in life, as most would regard it,
was that Cestus was lazy.

Not a little bit lazy either. Cestus was as lazy as hell, and
would be the first to admit it. Ever since he could recollect,
he'd hated work of any kind. Even as a boy, when his ma
and pa made him do chores, he hated it. He'd much rather
loaf the day away. Every day.

Cestus couldn't rightly remember when it first occurred
to him that there was a way of life that involved a lot of
loafing. It was called "crime." Rob somebody, or rob a stage
or a business or a bank, and he had enough money to loaf
for as long as the money lasted.

He was always polite about the robbing, always friendly.
Why be mean to folks when there was no need? Why put
fear and resentment and hate in them, and have them wish
he were dead?

Cestus had found that the robbing went easier when he
was nice. So he smiled and made small talk and generally
gave people the impression that he was the nicest gent

around. That was partly why he gave money away after a bank robbery. It wasn't just to crowd a street and slow pursuit. Cestus *liked* giving the money away.

For a couple of years now things had gone better then he'd dared hope. He'd formed a good gang and they mostly did as he wanted and didn't give him a lot of guff. There was an exception, as there was to just about everything in life, and that exception was Mad Dog Hanks.

Mad Dog was one of those people who were born with sour acid in their blood. They were never happy, even when things were going their way. Hanks was a grumbler, but usually he did as Cestus told him once he got the grumbling out of his system, so Cestus tolerated him.

Of late, though, Cestus had begun wondering if Mad Dog wasn't more of a bother than he was worth.

Cestus was thinking that now.

It was the middle of the day and they were still miles from the cave. They'd had to stop because Cockeye had fallen from his saddle. Cestus had been first to reach him, and propped him against a boulder.

"Lordy, I hurt," Cockeye had said.

Cestus had squeezed his shoulder and joked, "Don't die on us. We don't have any shovels to bury you."

That was when Mad Dog said, "Let's put him out of his misery and leave him for the buzzards."

"You could do that to a pard?" Cestus said.

"Pard, hell. Him and me ride for you, is all. I can't rightly say I'm pards with any of you."

"Is that so?"

"What's eatin' you?" Mad Dog said. "Are you mad because all your highfalutin notions have gone to hell?"

"Which notions, exactly?" Cestus asked.

"Let's start with bein' an outlaw but not actin' like one," Mad Dog said. "That's plumb silly."

"Stop insultin' him," the Attica Kid said.

Mad Dog frowned and leaned on his saddle horn. "Here

we go again. What is with you, Kid? Nobody can so much as sneeze in his direction and you get your spurs in a snit."

"Be real careful," the Kid said.

Bert Varrow cleared his throat. "If you three can quit your squabblin' for a minute, what do you want me to do about the lady here?"

Cestus stood and went over. Cecelia Wilson was still unconscious. "Help me get her down so I can take a look at how bad she is."

They laid her on her back in the grass next to Cockeye, and Cestus examined a gash in her head. It wasn't deep, but it was long, five or six inches. It started above her left eyebrow and ended above her ear. "We're lucky," he announced. "The bullet glanced off."

"Why are we lucky about that?" Mad Dog said.

"I told you before," Cestus said. "She dies, and we'll have the whole territory up in arms. Nothin' stirs folks up worse than killin' a woman."

"What do you aim to do with her?" Bert Varrow said.

"We'll take her to the cave, patch her up, and when she's fit enough, drop her off in Alpine, like I said. Folks will see that as a good gesture on our part."

"Oh hell," Mad Dog said. "You beat all, Calloway."

"Is it wise to let her see the cave?" Ira Toomis asked.

"What can it hurt?" Cestus replied. "We'll blindfold her when we take her back. She'll have no idea where it is."

"That should work," Bert said.

"Cestus?" Cockeye said. "Can I have some water?"

Cestus got his canteen, opened it, and carefully tilted it to Cockeye's lips. Cockeye swallowed a few times, and thanked him. Setting the canteen aside, Cestus pried at Cockeye's shirt so he could see the wound. Gut shots were always nasty, and this was no exception.

"That damn law dog," Cockeye said. "He took me by surprise."

"It happens," Cestus said.

"I should have shot first."

"We all make mistakes."

Cockeye did a rare thing for Cockeye. He smiled. "That's what I've always liked about you. You forgive folks."

"Does anyone hear harp music?" Mad Dog said.

"Pay him no mind," Cockeye told Cestus. "He doesn't savvy you like I do. You're all right, Calloway."

"Thank you," Cestus said. He'd never been all that close to Cockeye and it surprised him the man felt this way.

"It's why I stuck with you so long," Cockeye went on. "You're just about the nicest outlaw anybody ever saw."

Mad Dog snorted.

"If I could draw my six-shooter I'd shoot you, Hanks," Cockeye said.

"I might anyway," the Attica Kid said.

Cockeye's mouth curled in a lopsided smile. "I'm fadin', Cestus. I can feel it. I'm sorry to go out like this. Sorry for inconveniencin' you."

"It's no bother," Cestus said.

"You know somethin' else I always liked about you?"

"No."

"You're one of the few who never saw me as ugly. I could see it in your eyes that you didn't. You looked at me the same as you looked at everybody else."

"Now I've heard it all," Mad Dog said.

"Go to hell, Hanks," Cockeye said. "I know you think I'm ugly. You think it every time you look at me."

"Forget about him," Cestus said.

"Don't worry. I don't want to die thinkin' of his ugly puss," Cockeye said. He smiled, exhaled, and was no more.

Cestus squatted there another minute, wrestling with his emotions. Then, slowly standing, he turned to Mad Dog Hanks. "You couldn't let him die in peace, could you?"

"What did I do?"

"You didn't leave him any dignity."

Mad Dog appeared bewildered. "What the hell does that

even mean? I didn't treat him any different than I treated him all the rest of the time."

"You need to watch yourself," Cestus said. "You truly do."

"First the Kid and now you," Mad Dog said. "This outfit is becomin' a flock of mother hens."

"You're welcome to light a shuck anytime," Cestus said, hoping Hanks would take him up on it.

Mad Dog didn't respond.

"What about Cockeye?" Ira Toomis said. "Do we leave him for the coyotes to eat or the posse to find?"

"We do not," Cestus said. "We take him with us and bury him at the cave. We owe him that much."

"And now there are only five of us," Toomis said.

Bert Varrow helped Cestus place Cockeye belly-down over his horse and tie the body so it wouldn't slide off. Then Varrow climbed back on his own mount and Cestus hoisted Cecelia Wilson up.

Cestus rode hard, despite the wear to their horses. The last mile, they resorted to a trick they liked to use. They veered west to a long stretch of caprock and followed that to within a holler of the cave. Horses didn't leave tracks on caprock.

They were a weary bunch of outlaws when they finally drew rein. Cestus had Bert and Toomis take care of the horses and told Mad Dog to get a fire going. With the Kid's help, he carried Cecelia Wilson in and Cestus spread his own blankets and they gently set her down.

Cestus filled a pot with water from the spring and put the pot on the fire. He didn't know much about doctoring, but his ma had taught him that hot water was the best thing in the world for cleaning wounds. He needed a cloth for a bandage, so he took a small towel of his, cut it into strips, and washed them once the water was warm enough.

No one said much. They were drained. They'd suffered the loss of three of their own, and that rested heavy on their shoulders.

Once the pot was boiling, Cestus took it over to his blankets. He had to wait a bit for the water to cool enough for him to dip a cloth in. He wrung it out and pressed it to the wound, and Cecelia Wilson groaned.

Cestus made sure to clean the wound good. Infections from being shot killed more people than being shot, and he was sincere about wanting her to live. He was wiping the last of the dry blood from above her ear when he happened to look down and discovered her eyes were open and she was staring at him. "Ma'am," he said.

"Where am I? What has happened?"

"We brought you back with us so we could tend to you," Cestus said. "I'm just about to bandage you."

Cecelia stared past him at the others and then at the roof and the sunlight outside. "It's a cave."

"Right the first time," Cestus said, smiling.

"You surprise me, Mr. Calloway. You're going to a lot of bother over an old woman you could have left for dead."

"You're not that old, ma'am," Cestus said. "And leavin' folks for dead isn't somethin' I do."

"I see." Cecelia tried to sit up, and grimaced.

"You might want to lie still. A wound like this, you try to stand, you'll get woozy and maybe sick."

"I'm already woozy," Cecelia said, and stiffened. "Wait. My brother. What happened to Sam? The last I saw, he was fighting that awful Mad Dog Hanks."

Cestus debated whether to tell her. She'd likely take it hard, and she was feeling poorly enough as it was. "I don't know, ma'am," he hedged. "The last I saw, your brother was lyin' on the floor. He was still breathin', I think."

"You think?"

"We had to fan the breeze," Cestus said. "That marshal friend of yours was somewhere near, and I didn't want any more of my men shot." He paused. "He killed Cockeye."

"I'm sorry."

Cestus studied her, then said, "Damn me if I don't think you mean it."

"No one should die like that. Being shot. We should all of us die peacefully in our sleep. In an ideal world we would."

"I don't know much about ideal," Cestus said. "In the world I live in, folks are shot all the time. But I thank you for the kind thought."

"You're not what I expected, Mr. Calloway."

"I hear that a lot," Cestus said. "Now be still a bit." He gently applied the bandage and tied the knot on the opposite side of her head from the wound. "Is that too tight?" he asked when he was done.

"It feels just right. Thank you."

Cestus sat back. "Would you care for somethin' to drink or eat?"

"Water would be nice," Cecelia said. "I'm not all that hungry. My stomach is queasy still."

"I'm sorry you were shot. I never meant for you to be hurt."

"Only my brother," Cecelia said bitterly.

"That wasn't my idea," Cestus admitted. "The others wanted him to pay on account of he was with the posse that killed Larner."

"You're their leader, aren't you?"

"Yes, ma'am. But sometimes I don't so much lead as go along with what they'd like even though I don't want to."

Cecelia's eyebrows puckered. "Mr. Calloway, I don't quite know what to make of you. You're a strange sort of outlaw."

"I'm just me," Cestus said.

Chapter 24

"We keep goin' like we are," Lefty remarked, "we'll ride our animals into the ground."

"We are pushin' sort of hard," Sherm Bonner agreed.

Boyd turned to the cowboys. He'd called a halt in a clearing in the woods, but only because the pair was right; he was pushing too hard. "We'll rest for half an hour," he announced, and at least half of the ten posse members smiled or sighed in relief.

Vogel, the blacksmith, gigged his sorrel over and climbed down. Sliding his Maynard .50-caliber rifle from the scabbard, he cradled it in both of his big arms. "We need to talk, Marshal."

"We do?" Boyd said. He was tired and irritable. He hadn't gotten much sleep. Not as worried as he was about Cecelia.

Vogel gestured and moved away from the others.

Annoyed, Boyd followed. "Well, what is it?" he demanded when they were out of earshot of the rest.

"You," Vogel said.

"How so?"

"It's not what you're doing so much as how you are," the blacksmith said. "Sure, you're pushing to catch the outlaws. That's to be expected. They murdered poor Sam and they took his sister, and everyone knows you're sweet on her."

Boyd's annoyance grew. "Her and me are none of your affair."

"It is when you put my life and the lives of the rest of these men in danger," Vogel said.

"Like hell I have."

"Not being yourself can get us killed as sure as being reckless," Vogel said. "And you're not yourself."

"What the hell do you expect? Besides Sam and Cecelia, my deputy was murdered. Of course I'm not myself."

Vogel shook his head. "It goes deeper than that." He paused. "I'm a hunter, Marshal. You know that. I'm good at it. To be good, you have to notice things. Little things that others usually don't. The signs that game leave. Their tracks. Their habits. You learn a lot that way."

"So?"

"It works with people too. You learn to read them like you do game. Not so much what they do or say, but the little things. Their expressions. Their eyes. Even how they walk and sit. It tells you a lot."

"Again, so?"

"So what I see in you has me worried. You're mad, and I don't blame you for that. In your boots I'd be mad too. But there's more than that. I see hate in your eyes whenever someone mentions the outlaws. I see hate, and something else. Something I never saw in you."

"And what would that be?" Boyd said, half sarcastically.

"A hankering to kill."

Boyd didn't say anything. How could he when it was true? He refused to lie and say it wasn't.

"I'm right, aren't I?"

Boyd didn't answer.

"All right. Be that way," Vogel said. "But I'll be watching you. And if you do anything that I think puts the rest of us at risk, I won't be shy about speaking up."

"Was that a threat?"

"You know better."

Boyd closed his eyes and rubbed them. What he wouldn't give for six or eight hours of sleep. He looked at the blacksmith and nodded. "You're bein' honest, so I'll be honest with you. I've been pushed to the brink. Yes, I want those sons of bitches dead. Wouldn't you? But I give you my word I won't act recklessly and get us all killed. I still have my wits about me."

"That's good to hear," Vogel said. "And for what it's worth, I want them dead too. So when we catch up, I'll pick off as many as you want me to and swear under oath, if need be, that it had to be done even if it didn't."

Boyd realized what the man was offering to do on his behalf, and was moved. "I'm obliged."

Vogel nodded and walked off.

Wanting a few minutes to himself, Boyd moved to the edge of the clearing and sat. He couldn't stop thinking about Cecelia, couldn't stop worrying about her. The outlaws would have to be loco to harm her, but they *were* outlaws. He doubted that Mad Dog Hanks, in particular, had any qualms about murdering a woman. He could only pray the others wouldn't let it come to that.

Boots crunched and spurs jingled, and Sherm Bonner and Lefty ambled up, and Sherm nodded.

"We need to talk," Lefty said.

"Now you two too," Boyd said.

"Pardon?"

"I'm listenin'," Boyd said.

"My pard and me want to be clear on somethin'," Lefty said. "Namely what do you aim to do when we catch up to these polecats?"

"And by that," Sherm Bonner said, "we mean do you aim to arrest them or shoot them or what?"

"You wear that badge and you have to abide by the law," Lefty said, "but we want you to know we're fine with not abidin' by it."

"Is that a fact?" Boyd said. First the blacksmith, and now the cowboys.

"This is personal with us," Sherm said.

Lefty nodded. "They sent that McGivern to kill us, didn't they? So long as they were just bank robbers, we didn't much care how they met their end. But now we'd just as soon do to them as they tried to do to us."

Boyd went to speak, but Lefty raised a hand.

"I know what you're goin' to say. That it's wrong to want them dead. That we have to go by the letter of the law and take them into custody so you can take them back to town and they can be put on trial. But we'd be just as happy if it was otherwise."

Sherm nodded.

"I'm glad I'm not the only one," Boyd said, and chuckled.

"Marshal?" Lefty said.

"I have no objections to otherwise, as you put it," Boyd informed them. "In fact, between you and me, I'd prefer it."

"You do?"

"That makes things easier," Sherm Bonner said.

"Oh, I doubt they'll die easy," Boyd said.

Sherm shrugged and placed his hand on his Colt. "Easy or hard, it's all the same to me."

The sudden crackle and crash of undergrowth brought Boyd to his feet with his own hand on his six-gun. Within moments a horse and rider burst into the clearing, and the man drew sharp rein.

"It's the scout," Lefty said, stating the obvious.

Harvey Dale looked around and spotted Boyd. Alighting, he came right over.

"I have bad news."

"I don't want to hear you lost their trail."

"About half a mile ahead is a lot of caprock," Dale reported. "I looked and I looked and I rode in circles, and I couldn't find any sign."

"I told you I didn't want to hear that," Boyd said.

"I'm sorry. What else can I say? They've gotten away."

Boyd stared to the north, and scowled. "Like hell they have."

Cecelia Wilson was beside herself with worry. Not for herself. For her brother. When she'd asked Cestus Calloway about Sam, she sensed that he was hiding something. The only thing she could think of that he'd want to keep from her was that Sam was dead.

Her heart grew heavy with dread. She lay as one dead, numb in mind and body. She hardly noticed the pain from her wound, and it was considerable. She thought of Sam, of how good a brother he was, of the many pleasant times they'd had, and her eyes dampened with tears.

Turning her face away from the fire and the outlaws, Cecelia started to weep, then caught herself. No, she thought. She wouldn't be weak. She would be strong for Sam's sake. Time enough for crying later. Right now she must keep her head and find a way out of her dire predicament.

For it was dire. Cecelia had no doubt of that. Cestus Calloway was kind enough, and the dandy, Bert Varrow, treated her with cordial respect. But the others were cause for concern.

First there was the Attica Kid. He showed no kindness toward her at all. She was nothing to him. Or, to put it differently, she didn't amount to much more than the dirt under his boots. He'd shoot her as quick as look at her if it wasn't for Cestus Calloway.

Ira Toomis had hardly spoken two words to her. He wasn't cold or mean, but her woman's intuition told her Toomis regarded her as a liability they were better off without. He didn't trust her not to turn on them, and of all the outlaws, he kept the closest watch on her.

Then there was Mad Dog Hanks. Now, there was a genuinely scary man. The looks he gave her, and his comments to Calloway, left no doubt he'd just as soon kill her where she lay and be done with her.

Outside the cave, twilight had fallen. The outlaws were preparing their supper. To her surprise, Hanks did the cooking. Pork and beans, it turned out, and the aroma set her stomach to growling.

"Ma'am?"

Cecelia dabbed at her eyes and turned her head. "Yes, Mr. Varrow?" She hadn't heard him come over.

"Are you hungry? I'll bring you a plate and some coffee to wash the food down, if you're of a mind."

"That's considerate of you," Cecelia said. She wasn't all that hungry, but she needed to keep her strength up. "I'd be ever so grateful."

Varrow smiled and returned to the fire.

Cecelia wondered why the gambler was treating her as kindly as Calloway.

For that matter, she wondered about Cestus Calloway too. Calloway puzzled her. He seemed like a nice person. He acted nice, talked nice, treated her as nice as anyone ever had. Yet he was a notorious outlaw. Sometimes the world just made no sense at all.

As if he was aware she was thinking about him, the outlaw leader sauntered over and hunkered. "How are you feelin'?"

"Tolerable," Cecelia answered.

"That's better than before. I'm glad, awful glad. By mornin' you should be feelin' fit enough to ride, I hope."

"You do?"

"Yes, ma'am," Cestus said, bobbing his chin. "The sooner we get you back to Alpine, the better it will be for all of us."

"We are in agreement there," Cecelia said. Every moment she spent in their presence heightened the risk of her coming to harm. She could see that even if Calloway couldn't.

"I must say, you're takin' this with less fuss than I reckoned you would," her captor mentioned. "A lot of gals would be cryin' and screamin' at us to take them home along about now."

"I'm not prone to hysterics, Mr. Calloway," Cecelia informed him.

"I can see that, ma'am," Cestus said, and grinned. He glanced at the others and bent toward her. "Mind if we gab awhile?"

"About what?"

"Anything you'd like. I can't recollect the last time I got to be with a lady like you. It's a treat, you might say."

"You're awful peculiar," Cecelia said.

Cestus laughed. "Not that again." He grew serious and regarded her while gnawing on his bottom lip. "It's like this, ma'am. We don't ever have females here. Or with us at all. It's a rule of mine. If the men are randy, they're go find a dove in a town somewhere."

"Your love life couldn't interest me less," Cecelia said harshly.

"Sorry, ma'am. I'm not makin' love to you. I promise. If I was, I'd have brought flowers."

Despite herself, Cecelia smiled.

"It's just that female company is like apple pie. I'm powerful fond of both and I don't hardly get either these days."

"Whose fault is that?" Cecelia asked bluntly. "You chose the life you lead. No one twisted your arm to turn you into an outlaw. Or did they?"

"No, ma'am, you have me there," Cestus conceded. "I reckon we are what we make of ourselves."

Bert Varrow returned with a tin plate heaped with pork and beans, a tin cup brimming with coffee, and a wooden spoon. Without saying a word, he set them down next to Cecelia, touched his derby, and went back to the fire.

"I'm grateful for the hospitality you've extended," Cecelia remarked.

"Be sure and tell the marshal that when you see him, will

you?" Cestus requested. "I reckon he's out for our blood after Mad Dog went and shot his deputy."

"That won't be the only reason," Cecelia said as she picked up the plate and placed it in her lap.

"Oh?"

Her belly aching with hunger, and intent on her food, Cecelia said without thinking, "Have you forgotten he's been courting me? True love, I think you called it back at our farm." She dipped the spoon into the beans, raised it to her mouth, and stopped.

Cestus Calloway was staring at her in shock. "Lord in heaven. I've been as dumb as a stump."

"In what regard?"

"This courtin'? How serious is he about it?"

"As serious as anything. I wouldn't let him come calling if he wasn't," Cecelia said. "Why are you so upset? What difference does it make?"

"The difference, ma'am," Cestus Calloway said, "is that it changes everything."

Chapter 25

The posse was in a surly mood. They all knew that Harvey Dale had lost the trail, and many of them resented being forced to continue north into the wilderness with little hope of finding it again.

By nightfall, Boyd was forced to admit to himself that if he didn't change his mind and turn around, he'd likely have a mutiny on his hands. The scout and the two cowboys and Vogel hadn't complained, but the rest were giving him hard stares and talking in hushed tones among themselves.

They had three fires going.

Boyd guessed what to expect when a grocer by the name of Malcolm and several others left their fire to come to his.

"We'd like a few words with you, Marshal," Malcolm said. He was portly from an addiction to sweets, and always smelled of lilac water.

"Do you, now?" Boyd said, and took a sip of coffee.

Some of the others nodded. Malcolm took courage from that and said, "You bet we do. We've spent most of the day riding ourselves ragged, and for what? Your scout has admitted he's lost the sign. What can we hope to accomplish by pushing on?"

"We might find their trail again."

"Might," Malcolm stressed, and gestured. "These mountains go on forever. It's like looking for a needle in a haystack."

"He's right, Marshal," another man said.

"We have families," Malcolm declared. "We have livelihoods. It upsets us to be away from both for little practical purpose."

"You volunteered for this posse," Boyd said. "I didn't force you."

Malcolm nodded. "We volunteered, yes, out of a sense of civic duty. For the benefit of the town, and because a woman was taken. But it seems to us that now all we're doing is for the benefit of you only and to the detriment of us."

Containing his temper with an effort, Boyd said, "You need to be plainer."

"You have a personal stake in this that is affecting your judgment."

"Plainer still," Boyd said.

"Very well. Since you're forcing me." Malcolm paused. "Cecelia Wilson."

"Are you sayin' she doesn't matter to you?"

"Don't put words in our mouths," Malcolm said. "Of course she does. But she matters more to you, to the point where you aren't thinking clearly."

"We're wasting our time," another townsman complained.

"We want to go home to our families," said a different man.

All of them nodded.

Boyd swirled the coffee in his tin cup. He was mad enough to hit each and every one of them, but that wouldn't get him anywhere. A good lawman had to know when to be forceful and when to be diplomatic, as the politicians liked to say. "I don't blame you for bein' upset."

"You don't?" Malcolm said.

"If I had a family, I'd want to be with them too. And you're right. It's no secret, I reckon, that I'm fond of Cecelia."

"It's decent of you to admit it," Malcolm said.

Boyd saw his opening. "How decent would it be to abandon her? Or any woman, for that matter? What if it wasn't someone I cared for? What if it was a woman you cared for? Or a woman none of us knew? Would that change things?"

"I don't see—" Malcolm began.

"It could just as well be any woman from Alpine. Would we be right in abandonin' her because we don't know her?"

"It's not abandoning that's the issue," another man said.

"It sure as hell is," Boyd said. "You want to give up. You want to leave a woman taken against her will to God knows what fate. Who she is doesn't matter. She's alone, helpless, in the hands of a pack of curly wolves. And you want to turn your backs on her?"

"You're twisting our words against us," Malcolm said.

Boyd didn't relent. "I'm tellin' you the truth. But if you want to turn back, if you can find it in your hearts to let an innocent woman be murdered, or worse, I'll bow to your will and we'll head back at daybreak." Inwardly he held his breath at the gamble he just took.

"When you put it that way," a man said.

"But we can't go on forever," Malcolm said uncertainly.

"I'm not askin' you to," Boyd said, and smothered a smile that he had won. "I'm willin' to compromise. Give me half a day. Until noon tomorrow. We'll keep lookin', and if we don't come across any sign of them, I give you my word we'll head back to Alpine. Is that fair?"

"I suppose," Malcolm said.

"More than fair," another man admitted begrudgingly.

"Thank you," Boyd said. "Let the others know, would you? And you better turn in early. We're all pretty beat."

They returned to their own fire, only to be replaced by a figure in a buckskin shirt who made no more noise than a Sioux or Blackfoot warrior would.

"You handled that real well," Harvey Dale said as he took a seat.

Boyd grunted.

"What happens if noon rolls around and we haven't come across the owl-hoots' trail?"

"I'll cross that bridge when I get to it," Boyd said. "But I'm countin' on you not to let that happen."

"I appreciate the confidence," Dale said. "I truly do. But I can't work miracles. And I've plumb lost them. They could have gone in any direction."

"South?" Boyd said.

Dale snorted. "Hardly. That would take them back to town."

"Southwest? Southeast?"

"Why would they go south at all when they headed north before and now this time after takin' Miss Wilson?"

"That narrows it down, don't you reckon?"

"Not nowhere near enough. We're still lookin' at hundreds of square miles of some of the most rugged country on God's green earth."

"Think, then," Boyd said. "If you were them, which way would you go? To the northeast?"

Dale considered a few moments, and shook his head. "No. You'd run out of mountains too soon. And there are a lot of valleys with people, ranches, and homesteads and the like. Wherever they hide, it's probably somewhere no one hardly ever goes."

"So that leaves north or northwest."

"I see what you're doin'," Dale said. "And if you're askin' me to pick, I'd say northwest. Only a few ore hounds have ever been out that far, to the best of my recollection."

"Northwest it is, then, at first light," Boyd said. And with any luck at all, they'd strike the trail again. They had to.

For Cecelia's sake.

By midnight the fire in the cave had burned so low so that the faces of the five men ringing it were partly in shadow.

"What's so damn important that we all had to stay up for this palaver?" Mad Dog Hanks griped.

"I wanted her to be asleep," Cestus said, "so she doesn't hear."

"Ain't you considerate?" Mad Dog said.

"Don't start on him," the Attica Kid warned. "I've had my fill of you and your carpin'."

Bert Varrow asked. "What's this all about anyhow?"

"Her," Cestus said, with a nod at the sleeping woman. "I learned somethin' that changes things." He had been mulling it over ever since, and come to a decision he hoped the rest would go along with. "But before I get to that, there's somethin' else on my mind."

"This ain't goin' to take all night, is it?" Ira Toomis asked, and yawned. "I'm old and I need my sleep."

"Hear me out," Cestus said. "We've robbed the Alpine Bank. We've robbed the Cloverleaf Bank. We've robbed the bank in Red Cliff. We've robbed all the stages at one time or another, and that mine payroll besides."

"We've robbed just about everybody," Toomis said, and chuckled.

"Not quite, but enough that everyone in these parts knows who we are. And they're always on the lookout for us. That makes it harder for us to pull a job without bein' caught."

"We've done all right," Bert Varrow said.

"Until now," Cestus said. "Until we lost Larner and Mc-Givern and Cockeye. I wouldn't call that all right. I'd call that an omen."

"An omen how?" the Attica Kid said.

"An omen in that maybe our luck here has run out. An omen in that maybe we should think about movin' to greener pastures." Cestus held up a hand when Toomis went to speak. "I'm not done, Ira. We've robbed almost all the banks for fifty miles around. What are we goin' to do? Rob them again? The stages have shotgun messengers ridin' along now. And every time we go into a town for supplies, we have to be mighty careful not to be recognized."

"That's true," Bert Varrow said. "Things have gotten a lot harder."

"Why not change that?" Cestus said. "Go somewhere we're not known. Where the banks and the stages will be easy again."

"You bring up a good point," Toomis said.

"Always thinkin' ahead," the Attica Kid said. "That's our Cestus."

"Yours, maybe," Mad Dog said. "What does any of that have to do with the Wilson woman?"

Cestus sat back. He had a trump card to play in his effort to persuade them, and now was the time to play it. "What's the one thing that makes a man madder than anything else?"

"Bein' kicked in the crotch," Ira Toomis said.

"Bein' spit on," Mad Dog said.

"No, you lunkheads. The one thing is havin' a man's filly messed with. Say the wrong thing, act the wrong way, and a man in love will get mad quicker than you can blink."

"What is this?" Mad Dog said. "A lesson in love?"

"How soon they forget," Cestus said, and shook his head. "The marshal is smitten with her, remember?"

"Good for him," Mad Dog said. "She's too old for my taste."

Ira Toomis got it first. "Oh hell."

"That's right," Cestus said. "The marshal and her have been courtin'. And it's gotten serious." He paused. "In other words, for those of you with rocks between your ears, Marshal Cooper is in love with her."

"Good for him," Mad Dog said.

"You dang idiot," Toomis said.

A look of great concern had come over Bert Varrow. "We took the woman the marshal is in love with?"

"Afraid so," Cestus said.

"All we have is bad luck anymore," Varrow said. "This cinches it. Ask any gambler and he'll tell you that when the cards turn cold, there's nothin' for it but to quit the game and try your luck at another. Cestus is right. We should find somewhere else to do our robbin'."

Toomis stared at their captive. "We have to be shed of her first. That law dog won't give up this side of the grave unless we do."

"I agree," Bert Varrow said.

"I do and I don't," Cestus said, and pressed on. "I agree that Marshal Cooper would follow us clear to Canada to save the gal he's sweet on. Most any man would. By the same token, he's not likely to jump us so long as we have her and risk her takin' a stray slug."

"What are you proposin'?" Toomis asked.

"That we head for greener pastures and take her along," Cestus said, and again held up a hand so they wouldn't interrupt. "Only part of the way. As insurance, you might say, to keep the posse at bay until we're clear of these parts."

"We're not goin' to get clear with the posse doggin' our steps because of her," Ira Toomis said.

"They won't be," Cestus said. "We use her to bargain with. Strike a deal with the marshal. In return for him and the posse turnin' around and lettin' us go, we'll let her go the first town we come to."

"He'll never go for a thing like that," Toomis said.

"It can't hurt to try," Cestus said. "It depends on how much he cares for her on whether it will work or not. If he's in love with her, he'll back off."

"How do we get word to him?" Bert Varrow asked. "Do we leave a message in a stick for them to find?"

"Do you have any paper to write on?" Cestus said. "Or anything to write with? I sure don't. The surest way is for one of us to ride up to them and give them our terms."

"And be shot out of the saddle before we get close," Toomis said.

"I don't know as I'd take the chance," Bert Varrow said.

"I'm not askin' any of you to," Cestus said. "I'll do it myself."

"No," the Attica Kid said.

"It has to be me. Cooper leads the posse and I lead you. It should be the two leaders, man to man."

"What's to keep him from clappin' leg irons on you and demandin' we turn his woman over to them or he blows your brains out?" the Attica Kid said.

"You."

"Me?"

"Will you or will you not shoot her if I ask you to?"

"Say it right now and I'll show you," the Kid said.

Cestus smiled. "The marshal knows your reputation. I'll tell him that if he lays a finger on me, you've promised to splatter her brains. That should keep me safe so him and me can parley."

"You hope," Ira Toomis said.

Chapter 26

More than half the morning had gone by and Boyd was debating whether he'd insist they push on if Harvey Dale didn't strike sign by noon, when the old scout came galloping back as if a horde of hostiles were after his hide. Hollering for the posse to halt, Boyd placed his hand on his six-shooter.

Vogel was riding beside him, and slid the Maynard rifle out. "Must be trouble ahead."

Sherm Bonner and Lefty gigged their mounts up on the other side of the blacksmith and Lefty said, "Look at that old buzzard, ridin' like a bat out of hell. He's liable to break his fool neck if his horse takes a spill."

Harvey Dale brought his zebra dun to a sliding stop and didn't bother greeting them. "There's a hill yonder," he announced excitedly, "and someone is waitin' for us on top of it, holdin' a white flag."

"A what?" Lefty said.

"You heard me," Dale replied. "A piece of white towel or somethin'. A flag of truce. He's sittin' there as calm as you please, and when I yelled up to ask what he was up to, he said he wanted to talk to the marshal."

"Who is it?" Sherm Bonner asked the pertinent question.

Dale hadn't taken his eyes off Boyd. "Cestus Calloway."

"No foolin'?" Lefty said.

"Well, I'll be," Vogel said in amazement. "He's got his nerve."

"What do you think of it, Marshal?" Sherm Bonner asked.

Boyd didn't know what to think. It was the last thing he'd expected. The outlaws had made good their escape. Why would Calloway show himself, and under a flag of truce, no less? "Maybe it's a trick," he speculated. "Maybe the rest are lyin' in wait to ambush us when we ride up."

"I did a quick sniff around before I lit a shuck back here," Dale said. "I didn't see hide nor hair of any of the others."

"Well, this is peculiar," Vogel said.

"Let's go find out what he wants," Boyd said. "Lead the way, Harve."

A trot bought them to a flat stretch of mostly grass, and there, in the middle, rose a low hill. Silhouetted against the sky, his white flag waving in the breeze, was none other than Cestus Calloway, leaning on his saddle horn and smiling. He raised his other hand and gave a little wave.

"Don't that beat all?" Lefty said in admiration.

"The gent has grit," Sherm Bonner said. "We have to give him that."

Malcolm and some of the other townsmen were bewildered by the turn of events, and not a little afraid. They'd shucked their rifles or drawn their revolvers and were glancing anxiously about in fear of imminent attack.

"What's going on?" one of them kept saying.

"I don't like it," another exclaimed.

"Calm down, all of you," Boyd commanded. "Keep your eyes peeled. Harve and me will ride up there and see what Calloway wants."

"Take Sherm instead of the scout," Lefty said. "He's quicker on the shoot."

"I want your pard here with the rest of you in case it is a trick and the outlaws attack," Boyd said. Bonner was the only gun shark among them, and the one most apt to hold his own should lead begin to fly.

Boyd nodded at Dale and they started toward the hill, but their animals had only taken a couple of steps when Cestus Calloway cupped a hand to his mouth and hollered down, "Just you, law dog. No one else."

Boyd and Dale drew rein.

"What's he up to?" Dale wondered. "Why only you?"

"I don't rightly know," Boyd said, "but for now we'll play along. He has Miss Wilson, remember?"

"I'm not likely to forget," Dale said.

Boyd clucked to his horse and kept his hand on his six-shooter. It wasn't until he was almost to the top that he saw that Cestus Calloway wasn't wearing a gun belt and the out-law's saddle scabbard was empty. "Forget your hardware?" he asked as he drew rein.

"Needed you to know I'm harmless," Cestus answered, "so you'd hear me out."

Boyd scanned the other side of the hill and the forest about fifty yards away. "Where's the rest of your bunch?"

"Nowhere near here."

Struggling to keep his voice even, Boyd said, "What about Miss Cecelia Wilson? Is she still breathin'?"

"She was right fine when last I saw her," Cestus said. "Whether she stays that way depends on you."

"You'd kill an innocent woman?" Boyd said in undis-guised disgust.

"Not me," Cestus said, putting a hand to his chest. "I was the one who brought her from the farmhouse in order to save her when she was accidentally shot."

"You expect me to believe that? How do I know she's even still alive?"

Cestus grinned. "I reckoned you'd bring that up. So I let her know I was comin' to talk to you about freein' her. I told her I needed somethin' to prove she's still breathin', somethin' only she and you would know. And she gave me a question to ask you."

Boyd held his breath without being conscious of doing so.

"Your sweetheart acted embarrassed about it, but she said I should ask you what took you so long to ask her out."

Boyd gave a start. No one except Cecelia and Sam knew about that, and Sam was dead.

"Took a while to get up the nerve, did you?" Cestus Calloway said, and grinned.

"Go to hell," Boyd said. He'd be damned if he'd let the outlaw talk about his personal life.

"Fair enough," Cestus said, his grin widening. "But you'll agree I couldn't have known that on my own? I had to get it from her, which means she's still alive and will stay alive so long as you do as I want."

"You bastard," Boyd said.

"Save the name-callin'," Cestus said. "I already told you I wouldn't harm a hair on her head. But there's someone who rides with me who would."

"Mad Dog Hanks."

Cestus, oddly enough, acted surprised. Then he laughed and said, "Why, yes, sure, why not him? I tend to forget he has his uses."

"How's that again?"

"All that keeps Mad Dog from killin' her is me," Cestus said. "Somethin' to keep in mind if you start gettin' ideas."

Boyd's temper was fraying. He thought of Mitch and Sam, and it was all he could do not to jerk his pistol and put a slug in Calloway's chest. "Is this why you were waitin' for us? To rub my nose in what Mad Dog might do?"

"Not exactly, no," Cestus said. "It was to give you some good news and some not so good news."

"Do I get to pick which I hear first?"

"The good news is that this neck of the country has become too hot for my boys and me," Cestus informed him.

"We have a hankerin' to find safer pastures, so we're packin' our war bags and leavin'."

"And Cecelia? Turn her over to us first, and I give you my word I'll give you half-a-day head start before we come after you."

"You're awful generous," Cestus said drily, "only I have a better idea. You don't follow us at all, and I'll set your gal free at the first settlement or town we come to."

"No," Boyd said.

"I wasn't offerin' you a choice."

"It's still no."

"You're forgettin' Mad Dog Hanks."

Boyd couldn't believe the outlaw's nerve. To sit there and threaten the woman he cared for. It was insult piled on injury. "Let me make myself clear. There's no way in hell I'll trust you not to harm her. You'll keep her alive only as long as it suits you. Once you've gotten clean away, you'll do her in and bury her body where it'll never be found."

Cestus Calloway frowned. "You have an awful low opinion of me."

"You're a damn outlaw, for God's sake," Boyd snapped. "What do you expect?"

"Have you ever heard tell of me shootin' anyone?" Cestus asked. "Man or woman?"

"No."

"Have you ever even heard of me hurtin' anybody at all?"

"Not that I can recollect," Boyd was forced to admit. "Folks say you're the friendliest cuss who ever rode the owl-hoot trail."

"There you go," Cestus said. "I'm givin' you my word that I won't let Mad Dog or anyone else do anything to your lady. All I want in return is for you to take your posse back to Alpine and wait for her to get word to you that she's all right."

"She'd never forgive me if I run out on her."

"She will once I explain," Cestus argued. "She knows I came to see you, but I didn't tell her why."

"You ask too much."

"Would you rather that Mad Dog got his hands on her? You had him in your jail. You know how he is. Is there any man alive you'd trust less with her than him? I sure as hell wouldn't."

"Yet he rides with you."

"I can't be that choosy about who does. Outlaws ain't the cream of the crop, if you take my meanin'."

Boyd was set to argue until doomsday that he'd never, ever leave Cecelia in their clutches. It went against everything he believed, against how much he cared for her, against the badge pinned to his shirt. Then a brainstorm sprang full-blown into his head, an idea that could turn the tables and save her at the same time.

Calloway must have sensed something because he said, "What?"

"I'm wonderin' if I've been hasty," Boyd said. "If maybe it wouldn't be best to go along with what you want."

"Now you're talkin' sense," Cestus said. "It shouldn't be more than a week to ten days and we'll drop her off somewhere and the two of you will be reunited."

Boyd believed Calloway was sincere. That it wasn't a ruse to shake the posse off, which the outlaws had already done and didn't know it. It had occurred to him that he could use that against them with a ruse of his own. "You harm her, I'll see to it that you're the guest of honor at a hemp social."

"How many times do I have to say she won't be?" Cestus thrust out a hand. "Let's shake on it and I'll be on my way."

Boyd would just as soon shoot him, but he shook. "I'll be waitin' to hear word of her."

"You're doin' the smart thing," Cestus assured him. Casting the stick and the white flag to the ground, he reined his mount around and shifted in the saddle. "Listen. I know you'll worry. I would too, in your boots. But I don't ever hurt women or kids. It goes against my grain."

"So you keep sayin'."

"I have a ma and a younger sister, just like ordinary folks. And I don't do to others what I wouldn't want done to me."

"You rob banks and stages."

"Banks and stages ain't people. We can do anything to them."

Boyd didn't bother to point out that the money most banks had on hand was placed there by their depositors, so that when Cestus and his fellow outlaws relieved a bank of its assets, they were relieving the people who had put the funds on deposit. As for stagecoaches, their strongboxes usually contained money being transported for one company or another, payrolls for workers. But the outlaws didn't stop there. They relieved the passengers of their money too.

Cestus Calloway touched his hat brim. "We'll be out of your territory by sundown tomorrow, and you can rest easy."

"Not until Cecelia Wilson is safe."

Calloway was trotting off and might not have heard. He looked back when he reached the forest, and waved.

The moment the outlaw was out of sight, Boyd wheeled the chestnut and galloped to the waiting posse. They were bound to badger him with questions, but he nipped that in the bud by drawing rein and saying, "Dale! Swing around that hill and into the woods to the west and then circle to the north and pick up Calloway's trail. This time try not to lose it. He'll lead you right to their hideout. And blaze the trail so we can follow."

Harvey nodded and was off like a shot.

"What's goin' on, Marshal?" Lefty asked. "What was all that jawin' about?"

"Tell you later," Boyd said. "Right now check your guns, revolvers and rifles both. I expect to be at the outlaws' hideout before this day is done. A lot of blood will be spilled, and I don't want any of it to be ours."

"We don't have to spill any if we take them alive," Malcolm the grocer said.

A couple of others nodded.

"I better spell it out for you," Boyd said. "There's only so much a law-abidin' community should have to put up with. We've had our citizens killed, our town set on fire, a woman kidnapped. Enough is enough. We can't let those outlaws get away to do to others like they've done to us. When we find them, we end this, permanent."

"How permanent?" the grocer said.

"We're goin' to kill every one of those sons of bitches."

Chapter 27

Cecelia Wilson had a new worry. The outlaws were up to something and she had no idea what. They had saddled their horses and tied their bedrolls on, and now they were packing things and strapping the packs on packhorses. All this after Cestus Calloway mysteriously rode off.

Calloway had startled her when he came over and asked out of the blue for something he could tell Boyd Cooper that only she would know. She'd asked why, and Calloway said he was going to have a talk with the marshal. When she wanted to know if Calloway was arranging to set her free, the outlaw had smiled and said he'd tell her all about it when he returned.

What was Calloway up to? Cecelia wondered. Why were the rest preparing to depart? She thought she might find out by asking the only other outlaw who had been friendly to her, and when Bert Varrow walked past, she cleared her throat and said, "Might I have a word with you, Mr. Varrow?"

"Of course, ma'am," Varrow replied, doffing his derby. "What can I do for you?"

"I'd very much like to know what all the commotion is about, and where Mr. Calloway got to."

"I'm afraid I can't say."

"You've always been so considerate," Cecelia said sweetly. "Why change now?"

"I do as Cestus wants, and he wants to talk to you himself once he gets back." Varrow paused. "If he gets back."

"Why wouldn't he?"

"He went to talk with the marshal by his lonesome, and wouldn't let any of us go along to cover him."

"You expect trouble?"

Varrow shrugged. "Beggin' your pardon, ma'am, but when a woman is involved, men can be hard to predict. Your friend with the tin star might not take kindly to what Cestus is goin' to propose. Could be the marshal will resort to his six-shooter."

"My word," Cecelia said in alarm. "Is that why Mr. Calloway took that little white flag?"

Varrow nodded.

"I'm terribly worried. Can't you at least give me a hint as to what it's all about?"

"It's about you, ma'am." Varrow gave her another smile and walked off.

Cecelia sat back. She had been hoping that maybe, just maybe, Calloway was arranging to turn her over to Boyd. But if so, there'd be no need for six-shooters. Boyd would be happy to have her back. The only reason she could think of that he might become angry enough to pull his pistol was that the outlaws didn't intend to release her, but had something else in mind.

Cecelia started to scratch at her bandage but caught herself. Her wound was bothering her. It itched something terrible. At least she had recovered much of her strength and was no longer dizzy.

Calloway had mentioned she'd likely have a scar. She wished they had a mirror, but evidently outlaws didn't care how they looked.

Her thoughts drifted to Sam and she grew glum with sorrow. She had loved her brother dearly. As brothers went, he was a treasure. He'd always treated her with respect and consideration. Her whole life, Sam had always been there for her if she needed him, and now he was gone. Murdered by the men around her. From what she'd overheard, she knew who was to blame, and she watched him now, wishing she had a gun.

The Attica Kid had his mount ready to go and was at the cave entrance, pacing. Waiting for Calloway, she imagined. He must be worried too, all the back-and forth he was doing. Which surprised her. He rarely showed emotion. Whenever she looked into his eyes, it was like looking at twin frozen ponds. Deep down where most people had feelings, the Attica Kid had next to none.

She understood why folks said he was a natural-born killer. She'd heard the term before, of course, but never met anyone who fit the description until she met the Kid. He wasn't normal. Either he had been born the way he was or something had happened in his past to make him less than human. Or perhaps, she speculated, he liked to kill, and made himself as he was on purpose.

Her head swam a little, and Cecelia closed her eyes. She hoped she was thinking clearly. She knew that people who suffered head wounds sometimes got concussions and their thinking was jumbled for a while. She didn't think her thinking was, but she couldn't be sure.

From outside came the clatter of hooves, and Cestus Calloway drew rein. The others quickly converged on him. Calloway glanced in her direction, then spoke to his men in low tones. Toomis and Varrow appeared quite pleased.

Cecelia unconsciously fluffed her hair as Cestus came toward her, a habit of hers when she was nervous. "Well?" she said before he reached her. "What did Marshal Cooper have to say?"

"We had us a nice talk, ma'am," the outlaw leader informed her, and sank down cross-legged. "Now you and me need to have one."

"I was hoping you would explain what this is all about."

"It's about greener pastures for my men and me, and how to get to them without bein' dogged by the posse every step of the way."

"I don't quite follow you," Cecelia said.

"It hit me last night how fond the marshal is of you. Not a little bit but a lot. It gave me an idea how my men and me can get out of this country in one piece. I've already lost three and I don't aim to lose any more."

"I still don't follow. How does the courting help you?"

"Why, that's simple, ma'am. The marshal cares for you. He cares enough that he won't do anything that might see you harmed."

An awful sinking feeling formed in the pit of Cecelia's stomach. She didn't like the sound of that. "What are you saying?"

"That I'm usin' you as a hostage, ma'am," Calloway revealed. "So long as we hold on to you, the marshal will do whatever we want. I offered him terms, and he's agreed."

Cecelia's mouth had gone dry. She had to swallow to ask, "What kind of terms?"

"That he turns his posse around and goes back to Alpine."

"Boyd would never agree to such a thing."

"Didn't you hear me? He already has."

Cecelia was shocked beyond measure. She couldn't conceive of Boyd abandoning her. Had she misjudged him that badly?

"I gave him my word you wouldn't come to harm if he agreed," Cestus continued. "I could tell it didn't sit well with him, but he's not about to let anything happen to his filly."

"So that's it," Cecelia said bitterly. "You threatened to hurt me if Boyd didn't give up the hunt."

"Not in so many words," Cestus said. "Although Mad Dog Hanks did come up a few times." He chuckled.

Cecelia wasn't the least bit amused. Mad Dog had been

giving her dirty looks all morning. It was apparent he'd love to be rid of her, and equally apparent how he'd go about it. "You're despicable, Mr. Calloway."

"Now, now," Cestus said. "I'm only doin' what I have to. You fell into our hands, so I'm makin' use of it."

"If I refuse to go along?"

"Do you really need to ask? You're comin' with us whether you want to or not, and you'll behave or I'll give you to Mad Dog and have him look after you. I doubt you want that."

"My original remark stands. You're really not as nice as you pretend to be. When it comes right down to it, you're not much different than Hanks or any of these others."

"I'm an outlaw, ma'am, not a saint."

"Don't patronize me. And what are your intentions? How long do you plan to keep me your prisoner?"

"Only until we're clear of these parts. The first town we come to, we'll set you free and you can get word to the marshal and have him fetch you."

"I look forward to that."

"I'd imagine you do." Calloway stood and stepped back. "Now if you'll excuse me, I have some last-minute things to attend to." He touched his hat brim and strolled off.

Cecelia struggled to stay calm and clearheaded. This was disastrous. Every moment spent in their company increased the chances of something terrible happening. Mad Dog Hanks was a keg of black powder that could explode at any time. Then there was the Attica Kid and that other fellow who didn't like her, Ira Toomis.

The outlaws squatted around the fire and spoke quietly. So she wouldn't overhear, she figured.

Cecelia rested her elbows on her legs and her chin in her hands. Overcome by sorrow, she stared out the cave at the forest. When something moved she didn't pay much attention. She took it to be a bird or a squirrel. Then it moved again and she focused on the spot and felt a jolt of surprise.

It was a hand.

Waving at her.

Harvey Dale was embarrassed. He'd seldom lost a trail his entire career as a scout. To lose the outlaws ate at him. He fretted he was growing too old and losing his former skills.

So when the marshal told him to follow Cestus Calloway, Dale took to the task like a hound dog to the scent of a raccoon. He had something to prove, to himself as well as to the others.

As it turned out, following Calloway wasn't much of a challenge. The outlaw only looked back a few times. Calloway appeared confident no one would come after him.

That puzzled Dale. But he wasn't one to look a gift horse in the mouth. He hung well back and now and then marked a tree with his knife. It was as easy as anything.

Calloway came to a part of the mountains Dale had never been to. Beautiful but rugged scenery, the kind that always stirred him. The kind he'd loved to explore in his younger days.

Dale hated growing old. He hated that his body couldn't do all the things it used to. Hated that sometimes his joints ached and his muscles were sore for days on end. He hated too that he rarely felt the urge to go off into the wilds anymore.

He almost envied acquaintances from his early days who'd met their end by arrow or bullet. They'd gone out young, in the prime of life, before time reduced them to pale shades of their former selves.

Dale yearned for his youth and his vigor. He remembered someone telling him once that if a person had his health, he had all that was worth having. That always struck him as silly. Then his own health started to go, to be eaten away in crumbs and pieces by the relentless maw of time, and he realized they were right.

When Calloway came to a cave, Dale forgot about everything except the job at hand. He'd found their hidey-hole. Drawing rein, he debated what to do. Should he fly back to the posse and bring them on, quick? Or should he keep watch until the posse showed up?

Faint voices reached him, one of them female, and Dale made up his mind. Dismounting, he tied his horse, shucked his rifle, and cat-footed toward the cave mouth. He could still move silently when he needed to, and the wind favored him in that it was blowing his scent away from the cave, and the outlaws' horses.

Crouched over, Dale came to a waist-high boulder and leaned against it. He cautiously peered around and saw the outlaws huddled together, talking. He also spied Cecelia Wilson, seated on some blankets. She looked sad as could be, and was staring gloomily in his direction.

Dale took a risk. It would cheer her to know help was on the way. He moved his hand where she would see it. At first she didn't notice. Then she sat up, and he quickly ducked back before she gave him away.

Now all he could do was wait. He figured it would take the posse the better part of an hour to get there, and he might as well make himself comfortable. Settling back, he placed his rifle across his legs.

This reminded him of the time he'd tracked a Sioux war party and had to wait for the cavalry to catch up. He'd blazed some trees, just as he had for Coop, but the fool captain lost the sign. Eventually the warriors rode on, and he'd had to backtrack to find what was keeping the troopers. They never did catch those Indians.

Dale prayed Coop didn't lose the sign now. That poor gal needed rescuing. He would do it himself, only there were five outlaws and two of them were notorious killers.

Not that Dale was afraid of them. He'd never been scared of the Sioux or the Blackfeet or any other hostiles. A colonel once joked that he must not have any common sense, but Dale saw fear as useless. What did it gain a man to fret over taking an arrow when it might never happen? It seemed to him that people worried too much about things over which they had no control.

Dale was thinking that when he was jarred to his marrow by something hard pressed to the side of his neck. At the same instant a gun hammer clicked.

"Got you, you old goat," the Attica Kid said.

Chapter 28

Marshal Boyd Cooper was close to his breaking point. It was bad enough his deputy and one of his best friends had been killed. It tore at his innards that the woman he cared for was in the clutches of the same killers. And now, on the verge of catching the outlaws before they could spirit her away, half of his posse was ready to quit on him.

It started when Boyd called a halt. They'd been pushing hard for two hours and their animals needed to rest. A short rest, he announced, and climbed down. He was too wrought up to sit, too agitated to stand still, so he roved about the clearing.

When Malcolm the grocer and four others approached, Boyd demanded curtly, "What do you want?" He'd rather be left alone.

"We need to talk, Marshal," the grocer said.

The others nodded in agreement.

"Not again!" Boyd was tired of their quibbling.

"We've discussed the situation among ourselves," Malcolm said, to more nods, "and we think you're going about this all wrong."

"I'm what, now?"

Malcolm thrust out his chin. "Hear us out. That's all we ask. Then we can decide how to proceed."

"I've already decided," Boyd said.

"That's the problem. We don't agree with your decision. You're putting Cecelia Wilson at great risk. We understand you have a personal stake, but you should have consulted us before you sent Dale to follow Calloway and made us ride ourselves near to death."

Even more nods.

Boyd folded his arms and reminded himself they were a grocer and clerks and whatnot.

Over by the horses, the blacksmith and the cowboys and a couple of others listened intently.

"Now, don't get mad," Malcolm said. "But you have to admit that the course of action you've chosen will place Miss Wilson in dire peril. Cestus Calloway won't like that you've broken your word, and there's no predicting what Mad Dog and the others might do."

"No one will lay a finger on her if we hit them hard and fast," Boyd said. "It will be over before they can."

"That's terribly optimistic of you," Malcolm said. "Now, I'm no fighter —"

"You're sure as hell not," Boyd couldn't stop himself from saying.

"Please, Marshal. Insults ill become you." Malcolm frowned. "As I was saying, I'm no fighter. I'm not a gun hand. I'm not an idiot either, and I know that in shooting affrays, things don't always go as we like them to. If lead starts to fly, there's no guarantee Cecelia Wilson won't take a bullet. Do you really want that?"

"The longer she's with them, the more risk she's in. We have to get her away from them as quickly as we can."

"Only that's not all you've set out to do," Malcolm argued. "Need I quote you?" And he did. " 'We're going to kill every one of those sons of bitches.' "

"It seems to us," another townsman said, "that you're more interested in wiping the outlaws out than in saving Miss Wilson."

"Don't you dare," Boyd bristled. "Not one of you here likes that lady as much as me."

"Prove it," Malcolm said. "Call this off before the unthinkable occurs. Let the outlaws leave. There's every reason to believe that Cestus Calloway will be true to his word and release her at the first opportunity."

Boyd almost grabbed him by the shirt and shook him. "Name one of these reasons of yours."

"Eh?"

"Why take Calloway's side over mine?"

"Because you're not thinking straight. You're so filled with fury and hate, all you want is the outlaws dead. Saving Miss Wilson is secondary."

"We want to turn back, Marshal," another man said.

"You're doing wrong and we don't want any part of it," declared yet another. "We won't have that woman's blood on our hands."

"No, sir, we sure won't," said someone else.

Boyd was fit to explode. "If the five of you go back, that leaves me with just five men, plus Harvey Dale."

"We're sorry," Malcolm said, "but our minds are made up."

"Damn you," Boyd said. "Damn all of you."

"Now, see here," Malcolm said indignantly. "You have no call to address us like that."

It was then that Sherm Bonner came over, his thumb hooked in his gun belt. "If'n they want to go, Marshal, it's best we let them. They won't be of much use in a fracas anyhow."

Lefty had tagged along, and nodded. "My pard is right. Not if their hearts ain't in it, they won't."

Vogel and the rest also drifted over, the blacksmith contributing his two bits. Patting his Maynard, he said, "I can drop half the outlaws before they know what hit them. We don't need these weak sisters. I say cut them loose."

"I resent your insult, sir," Malcolm said.

"Just tuck tail and go," Vogel said to him. He towered over them, and had more muscle than all of them combined. "I'm ashamed to be in your company."

"You misjudge us," the grocer said. Wheeling on a boot-heel, he sniffed and said, "Come along, those who are with me. Our words of caution have fallen on deaf ears."

"You're makin' a mistake," Lefty said.

Malcolm looked back. "No, *you* are. I only pray it doesn't get poor Cecelia Wilson killed."

Harvey Dale was seething mad. Not at the outlaws. Not at the Attica Kid for sneaking up on him. He was mad at himself for being caught. In his younger days no one could have done what the Kid did. It was added proof that he wasn't the man he used to be.

Now, standing with his arms in the air, he was careful not to twitch as the Kid relieved him of his six-shooter and his knife, then stepped back. His rifle lay on the ground at his feet.

"Cat got your tongue, old-timer?"

"That was slick of you," Dale complimented him.

Other outlaws were hurrying out of the cave: Cestus Calloway, Mad Dog Hanks, and Ira Toomis.

Dale racked his brain for a way out of the fix he was in, but for the life of him he couldn't think of one.

"What have we here?" Cestus Calloway demanded, his six-shooter out. "Why didn't you tell me what you were up to, Kid?"

"I had to do it quick," the Attica Kid replied without taking his Lightning off Dale. "I saw him wave to the old lady and snuck out without her or him noticin'."

"Slick," Ira Toomis said, and chuckled. "Real slick."

Cestus Calloway walked up to Dale and poked him in the chest with the muzzle of his revolver. "What are you doin' here? I had the marshal's promise that the posse wouldn't come after us."

Dale knew that he if admitted the truth, the outlaws would be furious. He kept quiet.

"I asked you a question." Cestus looked around. "Where are the others? Or did the law dog only send you?"

"Me," Dale said, and an idea blossomed. "Just me." His lie should buy the posse time if he could convince them to believe it. "The marshal was worried you wouldn't keep your word. Or that one of these others wouldn't. So he sent me to keep an eye on Miss Wilson."

"Let me gun him," Mad Dog said, raising his six-shooter. "It will teach the rest to leave us be."

"No," Calloway said.

"Why in hell not?"

Calloway poked Dale. "He came to watch over the woman, not to arrest us or do us harm. Isn't that so, Deputy?"

"It's so," Dale said, confirming his lie.

Cestus grinned at his men. "Then I say we let him watch over her. In fact, he can come join us and stay with us until we're ready to be shed of her."

Both Harvey and Mad Dog said, "What?" at the same time.

"Think, Hanks. Think," Cestus said. "Two hostages are better than one. We'll tie him and take him with us. The posse won't dare start somethin' if the two of them might be hurt."

"We already have the woman," Mad Dog said. "We don't need the scout."

"Are you leadin' this outfit or am I?" Cestus motioned at the Attica Kid, and the Kid moved around behind Dale. "After you," Cestus said, motioning at the cave.

His skin prickling as he walked past Hanks, Dale tried to act unconcerned. He mustn't let them suspect that the rest of the posse wasn't far behind.

Bert Varrow was standing guard over Cecelia, and said, "Where in creation did he come from?"

"The moon," Cestus said, and laughed. Nudging Dale, he

said, "Have a seat next to our other guest. Don't get too comfortable, though. We're headin' out soon."

Dale had no sooner sunk to the ground than Toomis seized him by the arms and bound his wrists behind his back. The rope was so tight it bit into his flesh and cut off the circulation.

"Let's finish up," Cestus Calloway said to the outlaws. "I want to fan the breeze inside the hour."

Cecelia had been staring quizzically at Dale. The moment they were alone, she said quietly, "I'm sorry you were caught, Deputy. I hate to see you suffer on my account."

Bending toward her, Dale whispered, "The marshal and the posse are on their way. They should be here before these varmints head out. Be ready to hunt cover when the shootin' starts."

Cecelia brightened. "I knew Boyd wouldn't desert me. In my heart I just knew it."

"Shhh," Dale whispered. "Try not to give it away. You look so happy they'll be suspicious."

"Oh." Cecelia bowed her head and stopped smiling. "I'm sorry twice over. This captive business has me rattled."

Dale looked over his shoulder at the rope around his wrists. "I'm new at it too." He scoured their vicinity for a sharp rock or something else he could use to cut himself free.

"How will Boyd go about it?" Cecelia asked. "It's not as if he can ride up and demand they surrender. They'll put guns to our heads and make him back off."

"He'll think of somethin'," Dale said. "He's crafty, that man of yours."

"Oh, Mr. Dale," Cecelia said. "Despite what you might have heard, he's not mine yet. Our romance has only just begun."

"What you just said, ma'am."

"I beg your pardon?"

"Romance."

"You're turning red. Haven't you ever had a romance of you own?"

"Let's talk about somethin' else." Dale was loath to admit that he'd had a wife, once upon a time. She died of consumption at the age of thirty. Later he'd lived with a gal who was part Cheyenne. One day he'd come home from a monthlong scout to find her gone. No note, no letter, nothing, to explain why. He'd pined for her for a good long while.

"You must have talked to Boyd. How is he holding up?"

Dale was thinking of the Cheyenne gal and answered without thinking, "Not very well."

"How do you mean?"

Figuring he should be honest with her, Dale said, "He's mad all the time. I never saw him act this way before. Not even after Mitch was shot."

"Is it because of me?"

"I don't know. It came over him after the attack on your farmhouse." Dale scowled. "I was told your brother died in his arms. Maybe that has somethin' to do with it."

"Goodness," Cecelia said. She could only imagine how horrible that must have been. Sam and Boyd had gotten along splendidly. They genuinely enjoyed each other's company.

"Mad as he is, the marshal won't let it get in his way," Dale assured her. "He'll corral these sidewinders quicker than you can blink."

"I pray you're right."

Dale saw Mad Dog Hanks glare at them and cautioned her with "But you never know. Somethin' might go wrong. When the posse gets here, be ready to drop on the ground so you don't take a slug. And stay there until we say it's safe to get up."

"I would hate for more blood to be spilled," Cecelia said. "Hasn't enough been shed already?"

"I doubt Mad Dog Hanks thinks so. Spillin' blood is what

he likes to do best. And the Attica Kid ain't likely to give up without firin' a shot neither. He has enough sand for men twice his age."

"More blood, then," Cecelia said sadly.

Dale nodded. "More blood, and a lot of it."

Chapter 29

Marshal Boyd Cooper led what was left of his posse through a high pass and descended to an imposing series of sheer cliffs. Drawing rein, he glanced over his shoulder at the remnant: Vogel, the blacksmith, Sherm Bonner and Lefty, and a pair of townsmen, Divett and Titus. Everyone else had gone back to Alpine.

A tree with a carved arrow drew Boyd on. They hadn't lost Harvey Dale's sign, thank God. The crude arrow pointed into the forest. In a short while Boyd came on another that pointed due north. He rode parallel to the cliffs until a dark maw appeared.

It could only be one thing. A cave.

Raising an arm to halt the others, Boyd put a finger to his lips to caution them to silence. He dismounted, slid his rifle from the boot, waited for the others to gather around him, and pointed at the cave. "That must be it," he whispered.

"At last," Vogel said.

"Spread out and don't shoot until I do," Boyd instructed them. "Pick a target, like we talked about, and whatever you do, don't hit Miss Wilson. Keep your eyes skinned for Harvey too. He should be around here somewhere."

Cautiously advancing, Boyd glided from cover to cover.

He smelled smoke, which told him the outlaws had a fire going.

To his left, Vogel, who hunted regularly, made little noise. The cowboys weren't quite as quiet about it, and the pair of townsmen were downright clumsy.

But that was all right, Boyd told himself. He finally had the outlaws where he wanted them. He could avenge Mitch and Sam, and put an end to the Calloway Gang once and for all.

Boyd didn't hear voices or see movement. He reckoned the outlaws were deeper in the cave. Their horses too, probably, kept close so Calloway and his pards could make a quick escape if they had to. He'd nip that in the bud by having his men circle the cave mouth. The outlaws would face a ring of rifles and be cut down as they emerged.

A tiny voice in Boyd's head warned that Malcolm the grocer had been right and he was taking a terrible chance with Cecelia's life. He smothered it in annoyance. He was doing what he had to. It was as simple as that.

The last dozen yards, Boyd flattened and crawled. He came to a wide pine, one of the last before the cliffs, and crouched. From his new vantage he could see into the cave.

Tendrils of smoke curled from a campfire that had gone out.

Rising so he could see better, Boyd swore.

The cave was empty.

His arms and legs pumping, Boyd charged in. The others took their cue from him and did likewise. Their surprise mirrored his.

"What in hell?" Lefty exclaimed.

Boyd went to the fire. The embers were still warm. The outlaws hadn't been gone long. He roamed about. There were plenty of tracks, but he wasn't Harvey Dale. He couldn't read them like the old scout. The best he could tell was that the outlaws had used the cave as their sanctuary for a long time, and that the horses had been kept along the right-hand cave wall.

Divett and Titus were looking around in confusion. "What do we do, Marshal?" the former asked. "Where did they get to?"

"I sure didn't expect this," Sherm Bonner remarked.

"They must have lit out as soon as Calloway got back," Lefty speculated. "They're long gone by now."

Vogel had squatted at the entrance and was examining some tracks. "No, not that long. I can track elk and deer, and these tracks tell me they didn't leave more than half an hour ago."

"Speakin' of the old scout," Lefty said, "where is he?"

Boyd was wondering the same thing. There had been no sign of Dale's horse either. It led him to conclude, "He must have gone off after them and is blazing the trail for us to follow."

"He should have kept them penned in here," Lefty said.

"Just him alone against the whole bunch?" Sherm Bonner said.

"I reckon not, then," Lefty said.

Boyd stared to the north. The outlaws were heading for the far end of the cliffs. "If we hurry we might catch up before dark."

"Our horses are tuckered out," Lefty said. "We push too hard and they'll be useless."

"Would you rather the outlaws got away?"

"They won't with Dale markin' trees for us," Sherm said. "We can take our time and not lose them."

Boyd knew the cowboy was right, but taking his time was the last thing on his mind. He wanted it over with, once and for all. He wanted Cecelia safe, and the outlaws maggot food.

He did what was best, though, and led them at a quick walk. Always on the lookout for arrows on trees, he went a quarter of a mile without coming across a single blaze. That puzzled him.

His puzzlement grew to worry when they'd gone another quarter of a mile and they still didn't find any of Dale's sign.

Vogel brought his mount up, the Maynard cradled in his big arm. "We should have found some marks by now."

"I know," Boyd said.

"What could have happened that Dale isn't leaving any?"

"That I don't know."

"This isn't good."

The understatement of the century, Boyd reckoned. None of them, not even the blacksmith, were anywhere near as skillful at tracking. Left on their own, they were bound to lose their quarry.

And Cecelia.

Over the course of his many years, Harvey Dale had had good days and bad days, just like everyone else. But few were as bad as this one.

At the moment he was belly-down over his horse, which was being led by Ira Toomis. His gut hurt and he'd lost his hat. He'd asked Toomis to stop and pick it up, but the outlaw ignored him.

The cliffs were behind them and they were wending through heavy forest toward the northeast.

"At least let me sit up," Dale said. "I can ride with my hands tied."

"One more word out of you and I'll shut you up the hard way," Toomis threatened.

Dale resigned himself to enduring more discomfort. He supposed he should be grateful he was still alive. He saw Cecelia Wilson look back at him. She was riding double with Bert Varrow. When she smiled he returned the favor, but his heart wasn't in it. There wasn't much to be encouraged about.

His biggest concern was how long the outlaws would keep him alive. They didn't need him when they had Cecelia. And if they found out the posse was still after them, they might take it out on him.

Dale turned his mind to getting away. He'd been working at the rope around his wrists. It was so tight he'd chafed his skin raw, and he was bleeding. But that was good. The blood made the rope slick enough that he might be able to work his hands free. All he needed was time.

Cestus Calloway called a halt on a flat-topped ridge that afforded a sweeping vista of the county behind them. He sat studying their back trail awhile, and then gigged his horse over to Dale's.

"I have a question."

Dale lay still and hoped Calloway didn't notice the blood under his sleeves. "Oh?"

"You wouldn't have lied to me, would you?"

"My ma raised me to be like George Washington," Dale said. "She used to say that if a person can't speak the truth, he shouldn't say anything at all."

Cestus cocked his head. "Would you like your teeth kicked in?"

"Not particularly, no."

"Then spare me your silly stories." Cestus placed both hands on his saddle horn. "You see, when I sent Ira there to find your horse, he found it, and somethin' else." Cestus bent and his face hardened. "Can you guess what it was?"

Dale didn't answer.

"He found a tree marked with an arrow."

"Injuns leave signs all the time," Dale said.

"This was new," Cestus said, "and there hasn't been a Ute in these parts in a coon's age."

"Beats me who made it," Dale said.

"You're a pitiful liar." Straightening, Cestus turned in the saddle. "Mad Dog?"

"I'm right here," Hanks said.

"Would you oblige me? Climb down and pull this old buzzard off his horse and stomp on him some, but don't kill him."

"Happy to," Mad Dog said.

Dale braced himself, but it did little good. Rough hands fell on his back and he was wrenched off his horse and thrown to the ground so hard it jarred him to his bones. A boot caught him in the side and the pain caused him to cry out. He heard Cecelia yell his name. More blows landed, feet and fists both, and through a haze he saw Mad Dog Hanks sneering at him. He tasted blood in his mouth and was on the verge of passing out when the assault stopped. He was aware of having his shoulder gripped, and of being rolled over.

Cestus Calloway was crouched over him, smiling. "Had enough?"

"More than," Dale got out.

"Good. Answer me true or I'll have Mad Dog stomp on you some more. Are you ready?"

Dale swallowed blood and nodded.

"It was you who carved that arrow in the tree."

"It was."

"For the posse."

"For them."

"So you weren't sent just to watch over Miss Wilson. You were to blaze sign for the marshal and lead the posse to us."

"Why else?"

Cestus Calloway sighed. "I am plumb disappointed. Marshal Cooper gave me his word, and I believed him. I promised him I wouldn't let his gal come to harm and he promised me that he'd take the posse back to town. He's broken his word. A man should never do that."

"Coop is doin' what he thinks best," Dale said. Truth to tell, though, he agreed with Calloway. A man never *should* break his word.

"This changes things," Cestus said, and straightened. "All of you hear? Folks like to say there's no honor among thieves. There's no honor among tin stars either."

"Honor is for jackasses," Mad Dog Hanks said. "I get by without any."

"What do we do?" Bert Varrow asked. "They can't be that far behind. How many are there anyhow?"

"Dale?" Cestus said.

"Eleven countin' me."

"That's a lot of guns," Varrow said.

"Not if they can't shoot worth a damn," the Attica Kid said.

"They don't have to be marksmen when they can fill the air with lead," Varrow said.

"That don't scare me any," Mad Dog boasted.

"Hold on, boys," Cestus said. "I'm tryin' to think." He gnawed on his lip and stared down the mountain. "Ira, did you get a good look at that mark you found in the tree?"

"Good enough to tell it was an arrow," Toomis said. "Why?'

"Could you carve one just like it?"

"I reckon I could, yes."

Calloway faced his men. "I'm through bein' nice. The marshal played me for a fool and I aim to give him a dose of his own medicine."

"About damn time," Mad Dog said.

"What do you have in mind?" Bert Varrow said.

"You ever heard that what's good for the goose is good for the gander?"

"Sure."

"We're goin' to use their own trick against them. Ira, I want you to ride back a ways. Say, about half a mile or so. Carve an arrow in a tree just like the one you saw, pointin' this way. Carve another about halfway between there and here. We'll be waitin' for you."

Harvey Dale stifled a groan. Not because of the pain he was in, but because the posse was in for it.

"I savvy," Toomis said. "We're goin' to lead them right to us and blow them out of their saddles."

"We are," Cestus said. "But this ain't the place for that. There's too many trees for them to hide behind. No, we'll lead them on until we find the perfect spot for an ambush and can pick them off like ducks on a pond."

"You wouldn't," Cecelia Wilson exclaimed.

"My dear woman," Cestus said, "your tin star has done the worst thing he could. I plan to wipe him and those others out like the redskins wiped out Custer. To the very last man."

Chapter 30

So far Boyd and the posse were lucky. They hadn't lost the trail. The tracks were fresh enough that Vogel stuck to them without much difficulty, although twice, on rocky ground, they drew rein and waited while the blacksmith climbed down and searched on foot.

They were climbing toward a distant ridge when Titus, a stocky young man of twenty or so who worked as a butcher's apprentice, hollered and pointed at a pine tree.

"Marshal! Look there! Isn't that one of the scout's?"

Boyd had ridden past the tree and not even noticed an arrow cut into the bark. He ran a finger along it, and smiled. "Good eyes."

"Then Dale is still on their trail," Vogel said.

"Maybe he left others and we missed them," Lefty guessed.

"We won't lose the outlaws now," Sherm Bonner declared.

Boyd let himself relax a little. They could take their time now, to spare their horses.

Divett, who worked as an accountant out of a small office over a barbershop, and who wore a suit and bowler, said, "I guess this means we won't be turning back any time soon?"

"You're welcome to if you want," Boyd said. The pencil pusher would be next to worthless in a fight anyway.

"By myself?" Divett said. He looked hopefully at young Titus. "How about it? If I go back will you go with me?"

"And leave that lady in the clutches of those outlaws?" Titus shook his head. "What do you take me for?"

"I was only suggesting," Divett said.

Boyd assumed the lead. A glance at the sun, which was sinking to the west, left no doubt they wouldn't overtake the outlaws before nightfall. He stayed on the lookout for a site to camp in, and just as twilight fell, as they were passing through thick timber, a wide clearing opened before them. There was no water, but they had enough in their canteens to see them through the night.

Boyd called a halt. The horses were stripped and picketed, a cook fire was kindled, and coffee was put on to brew. For supper they had beans and jerky. Everyone was so hungry they ate with relish. The exception was the accountant, who picked at his beans and wouldn't touch the jerky.

"You should eat to keep your strength up, Mr. Divett," Titus said to him.

"I'm not that hungry," Divett said. "I miss my wife's cooking. I could be home right now, having roast beef and mashed potatoes, or a thick steak with all the trimmings. Instead we have fare fit for a field worker."

"A what?" Titus said.

Boyd was irritated by the accountant's attitude. "Why did you come along if you don't want to be here?"

Divett shrugged. "It seemed like the right thing to do. To help rescue Miss Wilson, I mean."

They were high up on the mountain, and the wind out of the northwest chilled them unless they sat close to the fire or draped a blanket over their shoulders.

Boyd had finished eating and was holding his hands to the flames to warm them when he happened to glance to the north and a tingle shot down his spine. He was on his feet before he realized it and moved away from the fire so he could see better.

"What's got you so excited?" Vogel asked, joining him.

Boyd pointed.

Far off, a pinpoint of light flickered. It could only be one thing. Another campfire.

"The outlaws," Vogel said.

"To be so close . . . ," Boyd said.

The cowboys joined them, and Lefty let out a whoop. "They're not that far ahead. About five miles, I reckon, although it's hard to judge in the dark."

"We'll catch up to them tomorrow," Sherm Bonner predicted.

Later, Boyd turned in, feeling more confident than he had felt in days that the end was near. He lay on his back, his hands behind his head, and thought about Cecelia.

He wondered if she was thinking about him.

Boyd wasn't all that worried about her being harmed. Calloway had promised she wouldn't be, and Boyd believed Calloway would keep his word.

It bothered him a little that the outlaw was keeping his promise, and he had broken the one he made. But he'd never intended to keep it. He'd lied when he said he'd take the posse back to town. And while lying, by and large, was wrong, there were times when it was justified.

Boyd heard it said once that a lie told for a good cause wasn't a lie at all. Like when a doctor told a patient that the medicine the patient was to take tasted just fine to get him to take it, when in fact the medicine was god-awful bitter. Or when someone lied about another's looks to spare that person's feelings. Those weren't lies so much as twisting the truth so the other person would feel good. His reason had been nobler than that. He'd lied so he could save a woman's life.

Boyd chuckled to himself. He'd never thought of himself as "noble" before. And if he was to be completely honest, he needed to admit that saving Cecelia was only part of the reason he'd lied. The other part wasn't nearly as "noble."

He wanted the outlaws dead.

Cecelia Wilson lay on her side with a blanket to her chin, her eyes closed as if in sleep when actually she was wide-awake. Nearby, the fire crackled. It had burned low but cast enough light that when she cracked her eyelids, she saw Ira Toomis start to nod off.

The outlaws had divided the night into shifts for keeping watch. Cestus had the first, the Attica the Kid the second. Now it was Toomis's turn. By a clock it would be well past midnight, and the tired outlaw was trying mightily to stay awake. He jerked his head up, shook it, and yawned.

Cecelia clasped her hands and prayed that he would fall asleep. She might never have a better chance to escape. The outlaws had made a mistake, and she intended to take advantage of it.

Her wrists were bound but not her legs.

Bert Varrow had tied her after their supper, and he hadn't bothered with her ankles. Maybe Varrow figured she wouldn't try anything with them so deep into the wilds. Or maybe he was just being nice.

Cecelia turned her head enough to see Harvey Dale. He appeared to be asleep, and unlike her, he was bound hand and foot.

Ira Toomis muttered something.

Shifting, Cecelia waited. She'd spied a fist-sized rock between her and the fire that would suit her purpose. All she needed was for Toomis to doze off.

Cecelia refused to be the bait that lured Boyd and the posse into an ambush. She would escape to warn them, come what may.

Off in the mountains a wolf howled, a long, wavering lament that echoed off the high peaks. The wolf sounded lonesome, a feeling Cecelia shared. She missed Boyd. With

Sam gone, he was all she had left in the world. Her parents were dead. Her first husband and her never had children. Lord knows, they'd tried, but the doctor said it wasn't meant to be.

That was one of her greatest regrets. She'd always yearned for kids. Always imagined how wonderful it would be to be a mother and lavish affection and care on a passel of young ones.

It was a shame life didn't always work out the way a person wanted. Hopes and aspirations were dashed like so many eggs on the cruel rocks of reality. Her hope of children had been dashed, but she'd be damned if she'd let her hope for Boyd and her be dashed as well.

Cecelia had been alone for more than a decade. Alone in the sense of not having a man to share her dreams and aspirations, or to help keep her warm at night. She missed that.

Now along came Boyd Cooper. A handsome figure of a man, in her eyes anyway. He wasn't the most educated gentleman she'd ever met, and his taste in clothes wasn't refined, but that was all right. She wasn't refined either. She wasn't one of those fancy ladies who always had to wear the latest fashions and be driven around in carriages. She was down-to-earth, and so was he. A perfect match, some might say.

Cecelia would like to stop being alone. She enjoyed companionship. Enjoyed having someone to talk to. Someone to rub her back late at night, and the other thing. That might be scandalous to think, but women had urges the same as men. Women were just more discreet.

Enrapt in her reflection, Cecelia was taken aback to suddenly realize that Ira Toomis had slumped over and was snoring lightly. He'd finally succumbed.

Elated, Cecelia sat up and cast her blanket off. She must move quickly. Sliding to the rock, she hefted it. She would only get the one blow. She must make it count.

Toomis mumbled something.

Cecelia checked on the others. Calloway and the Attica Kid had their backs to her. Neither had moved in over an hour. Mad Dog was snoring louder than Toomis. Bert Varrow had his blanket clear up over his head, and he hadn't moved in a long time either.

As slow as a turtle, Cecelia crept up behind Toomis. She raised the rock high, took a deep breath, and smashed it down where Toomis's head met his neck.

She was deathly afraid he would cry out, but he sprawled to the ground like a poleaxed ox and was still.

Cecelia couldn't get over how easy that had been. Setting the rock down, she helped herself to Toomis's belt knife. It made short shrift of the rope binding her. She snatched hold of Toomis's revolver and sidled over to Harvey Dale, placing each foot with care.

A hand enfolded her ankle, and Cecelia nearly cried out. But it was only Harvey Dale, letting her know he was awake. Quickly she slashed the rope around his ankles, then did the same for his wrists.

Dale gestured, indicating he wanted the revolver, and Cecelia gave it to him. She had very little experience with firearms. He was undoubtedly a better shot.

Crooking a finger, Dale moved toward the horses.

Cecelia nodded and followed. It was going better than she'd dared hope. So long as none of the outlaws woke up, she and Dale should get clean away.

The horses were dozing. A few pricked their ears and a couple looked over, but none gave alarm. Why should they, when they were used to Dale and her?

Working swiftly, the scout untied his animal and turned to another. They both froze when Mad Dog Hanks rolled over. But in a bit he rolled away from them and commenced snoring again.

Cecelia couldn't wait to get out of there. She grabbed the reins that Dale thrust at her and moved around to the side of the horse to mount. It didn't have a saddle, but that was all right. She could ride bareback. Farm girls rode bareback all the time. Gripping the mane, she was about to climb on when a hand touched her shoulder and made her jump.

"Didn't mean to spook you" Dale whispered.

"We should go," Cecelia whispered back.

"Stay close to me. If we get separated, head south. It's that way." Dale pointed.

"We should really go."

"I'll get you to Coop and you'll be safe." Dale held a hand down low and cupped it. "Want me to give you a boost?"

"No. *Please*. Let's leave while we still can."

"All right. Calm down. We're as good as gone." Dale smiled and moved around her horse toward his own. He suddenly stopped dead.

"God no," Cecelia breathed.

The Attica Kid stood between the scout and his horse. The Kid was smiling, which was rare for him, his right hand at his side, brushing his holster. "Goin' somewhere, you two?"

"Hell," Harvey Dale said.

"Drop the six-shooter, old man," the Kid said, "and you and the lady go to your blankets and have a seat."

Dale looked down. He was holding the revolver close against his leg, the barrel pointed at the ground. "I don't believe I will."

"Harvey, don't," Cecelia said.

"Listen to her, you old fool," the Attica Kid said. "You can cock that iron and point it and I'll still drop you before you can shoot."

"That's twice you've called me old," Dale said.

"You are," the Kid said, his smile widening. He was mocking the scout, taunting him. "I'd have gunned you already except that Cestus wants you alive. So be smart and shed the six-gun and live a little longer."

Dale looked over at Cecelia. "I'm sorry, ma'am. I was careless. I should have kept an eye on all of them."

"Don't do it," Cecelia begged. "You have nothing to prove."

"Except to myself."

"Old man," the Attica Kid said, stressing each word. "Listen to the lady. I have no hankerin' to kill you. It'd be like killin' an infant. You're not worth the bother."

Harvey Dale drew himself up to his full height. "Could be, I get off a shot. Could be, I wound you, or worse. That would make it worth it."

"Harvey, please," Cecelia said, tears in her eyes.

Two hands flicked, but only one shot boomed.

Chapter 31

Boyd and his men ate a quick breakfast of coffee and corn bread. Divett had brought the bread, courtesy of his wife, who had grabbed it from their cupboard as he was rushing out to join the posse.

Boyd wanted to head straight out at the crack of dawn, but Divett and Titus complained they were hungry, and after thinking about it, he decided that they all needed something in their bellies. They had a long day ahead that might end in a clash with the outlaws.

Now, as he dipped a piece of corn bread in his coffee and bit off the end, he overheard part of a question Divett asked Lefty. "What was that?"

The accountant coughed. "I asked him if he heard a shot last night. About the middle of the night."

"I said I didn't," Lefty said.

"Did you?" Boyd asked Divett.

"I might have. I remember waking up and thinking I'd heard one. I lay there awhile listening for more, but there weren't any. It was awful windy. So maybe it was a dream, or I only imagined it."

"I didn't hear any," Sherm Bonner said.

"Me either," Vogel said with his mouth crammed with corn bread.

Boyd hoped the accountant was mistaken. It had to have been the outlaws. No one else was in that neck of the mountains. The wind would have carried the blast a considerable way. Maybe a roving bear or a hungry mountain lion had come close to the outlaw camp, drawn by the horses. If it had been hostiles, he figured there would have been more than one.

"Today is the day," Lefty said eagerly. "We'll catch up to those varmints at last."

"We hope," Vogel said, taking another huge bite.

"Don't jinx it," the puncher said.

"I'm being practical," Vogel replied. "You said yourself they're five miles or more ahead of us. That's a lot of ground to make up."

"We can do it with Dale markin' the trees for us," Lefty said confidently.

"We hope," Vogel said again.

Sherm Bonner drained his cup and set it down. "It's a shame we don't have Dale's spyglass. It would come in handy."

The important thing, Boyd reflected, was that Dale had one. The old scout was their ace in the hole. With him to mark the way, the Calloway Gang was as good as caught.

Apparently the prospect of swapping lead was weighing on Divett. He coughed nervously, then said, "I've never shot anyone before."

"Me either," young Titus said.

Lefty chuckled. "There's a first time for everything."

"But to shoot another human being," Divett said. "The Book says 'Thou shalt not kill.'"

"Tell that to all the people the outlaws have murdered," Boyd said. "Tell it to Hugo Mitchell. Tell it to Sam Wilson. Tell it to those three men Mad Dog Hanks shot in cold blood. Tell it to those who died gurglin' blood so the Attica Kid could carve a new notch on his six-shooter."

"Does he really do that?" Titus asked. "Like folks say?"

"I haven't seen his pistol up close yet," Boyd said. But he hoped to before the day was out, clutched in the Kid's lifeless hand.

"Mr. Reems, the butcher, will have a fit, me being going so long," Titus mentioned. "We have a shipment of beef coming in today that needs to be carved up for sale."

"He didn't mind, you joining the posse?" Divett asked.

"No, sir," Titus said.

"My wife did. She said I had no business traipsing off into the wilds after a pack of two-legged wolves."

Boyd agreed but held his tongue.

"I told her it was the right thing to do. That a woman had been taken, and that it was an affront to decency and all good-hearted men everywhere."

"Goodness, you have a way with words," Titus said.

Divett blushed. "I read a lot,"

"I never learned how," Lefty said. "Can't write neither, except to make my mark." He drew an X in the air.

"Here we are, talking marks, when we have outlaws to catch," Vogel said.

Boyd didn't mind letting them relax a little. It would help calm them for what lay ahead.

"We catch these hombres," Lefty said, "we'll be the talk of the territory."

"I can do without that, thank you very much," Divett said.

"Why?" Lefty said.

"Who wants to be famous?"

"Not me," Sherm Bonner said. "All I care about are cows."

"Thanks, pard," Lefty said drily.

"I wouldn't mind," Titus said, grinning. "If they write about us in the newspaper, I'll cut out the clipping and send it to my mother. She'll be proud of me for helping that lady and doing what was right."

"Don't get ahead of yourself, boy," Lefty cautioned. "To become famous you have to stay alive."

"I'm not a boy," Titus said indignantly, "and I intend to."

Boyd decided it was time to break up their fun. "Finish up, and let's be on our way. It's light enough now that we can see the marks Dale makes."

"We sure don't want to miss any," Lefty said.

Vogel looked over at Boyd. "I trust you plan to use me to good effect." He patted the Maynard in his lap. "With this, I mean."

"If we can pick them off from a distance without any harm comin' to Miss Wilson, you're the man I'll rely on," Boyd assured him.

"I once brought an elk down at five hundred yards," Vogel reminded him.

"That's fine shootin'," Lefty replied. "Only I bet that elk wasn't shootin' back or huntin' cover."

"I can drop one or two of the outlaws before they do," Vogel said.

"In that case," Lefty said, "make sure it's the Attica Kid and Mad Dog Hanks. They're the dangerous ones. Am I right, Marshal?"

"You're right," Boyd agreed. Without the gun hand and the rabid killer, the outlaws would be considerably weakened.

"Ira Toomis has shot a couple of men," Sherm Bonner mentioned.

"True. But he's no gun hand," Lefty said. "It's the Kid who worries me the most. They say he's as fast as anything."

"At long range I'll match my rifle against his pistol any day," Vogel said.

"That's the way to do in an hombre like him," Lefty said. "From a safe distance."

Boyd emptied his cup, and stood. "When I said to finish up, I meant it. It's time to get this done."

"Or die tryin'," Lefty said, and chuckled.

"That wasn't even a little bit funny," Divett said.

"I wasn't tryin' to be," Lefty said. "Look around you, mister. Come tonight, some of these faces might not be here."

"What a terrible thing to say," Divett said. "I prefer to look at the bright side of things. Come tonight, we could all of us still be alive."

"Keep dreamin'," Lefty said.

Cecelia Wilson was overcome by sorrow. She'd liked Harvey Dale. The old scout had put his life in peril on her account, and always treated her with courtesy. And now he was dead, a bullet between his eyes, thanks to a vicious young killer.

She was astride Dale's horse, her wrists tied once again, riding in single file with the rest. They had placed her between Cestus Calloway and the Attica Kid, and now she glanced back at the Kid and let her spite show.

"Quit doin' that, lady," the Kid said. "It annoys me."

Cestus Calloway wheeled his horse around so it was beside hers. "You should listen, ma'am. You don't want to make the Kid mad."

"I'm not afraid of him," Cecelia said.

"You should be," Cestus said. "Rilin' him could get you shot, and I'd rather you stayed alive awhile yet."

"As bait for the marshal," Cecelia said resentfully.

"You're sure in a mood today."

"What do you expect? I saw a friend gunned down right before my eyes. Harvey Dale gave his life for mine. I'll never forget his sacrifice as long as I live."

"It was a fair fight," Cestus said. "The Kid gave him his chance, but he didn't take it."

"Fair, my foot," Cecelia said. "Your friend is a professional shootist, I believe the term is. Mr. Dale didn't stand a prayer against him and you know it."

Behind her the Attica Kid said, "Keep bitchin' about it, lady, and I'll make it a point to drill that marshal of yours personally."

"See?" Cestus said to her.

Just then hooves drummed a short way back in the forest, and Ira Toomis trotted into view and came past Bert Varrow, Mad Dog, and the Kid. "I left a couple more marks like you wanted."

"Good," Cestus said. "We still haven't found the perfect spot yet."

It was late in the morning. They had been on the go since daybreak, and Cecelia was tired and sore. She noticed Toomis glaring at her and said, "Something the matter?"

"As if you don't know," Toomis growled. "My head still hurts from the wallop you gave me with that rock."

"I'm sorry," Cecelia said even though she wasn't sorry in the least. "It had to be done."

Toomis turned to Calloway. "When it comes time to do her, I want it to be me. Not you or any of the others."

"I haven't made up my mind about that," Cestus said. "I gave my word she wouldn't be harmed."

"To a man who broke his word to you," Toomis said. "Your word to him no longer counts." He reached back and gingerly touched his head where Cecelia had struck him. "I've got a goose egg and keep gettin' dizzy and it's her doin'. She's mine, and I won't take no for an answer."

"You will if Cestus says so," the Attica Kid said.

"Not this time," Toomis said. "Not even if you back him. This bitch hurt me. She has it comin', from me and no one else."

"I'll keep that in mind if and when the times comes," Cestus said.

Toomis glowered at Cecelia, sniffed in hate and contempt, and reined around to fall into line.

"You've made an enemy there, ma'am," Calloway said, and moved ahead of her again.

Cecelia grew despondent. She used to think she had more spunk than a lot of women, but she was wrong. She felt completely drained. She wanted to lie down and curl into a ball and not move for hours on end.

Normally the scenery would interest her. It was spectacular. Miles-high peaks rose in majestic array against the backdrop of an azure sky. Tiers of timber-covered slopes stretched for as far as the eye could see, the green of the pines mixed with the different green of the firs and the shimmering belts of aspens. A bald eagle winged on the air currents, and to the west, high on a cliff, spots of white might be mountain sheep.

Cecelia sighed. No, the scenery held no fascination for her today. All she could think of now was Boyd and the men with him, men who were coming to her aid and might end up like Harvey Dale. She would do anything to keep that from happening.

But what could she do, a lone woman against five outlaws?

The answer that leaped into her mind shocked her.

Cecelia told herself no, that it was ridiculous for her to even contemplate doing it. But the more she thought about it, the more appeal the idea held. So what if she was female? A woman could do anything a man could do. And so what if she was unarmed? A rock had worked once, and would work again. And rocks were all over.

Clearing her throat, Cecelia asked, "Will you be calling a stop soon, Mr. Calloway?"

"Not for a while yet, ma'am. Why?"

"I could use a rest. I didn't sleep well last night."

"Whose fault is that?"

Cecelia didn't press the issue. It might make him suspicious. They would stop, eventually, and she would put her plan into effect.

Suddenly she wasn't despondent anymore. She felt a rush of hope, and energy. She would stand up for herself, even if it got her killed. She owed that much to Harvey Dale and to Sam.

Boyd's image floated before her, but she refused to let that dissuade her. As much as she cared for him, as much as she looked forward to possibly becoming Mrs. Cecelia Cooper one day, this was more important. For her self-respect, if nothing else.

"There's a clearin' up ahead," Cestus Calloway called out. "We'll stop and rest the horses a bit."

Good, Cecelia thought. Turning in her saddle, she smiled in delight at the Attica Kid.

"Why are you lookin' at me that way, lady?"

Cecelia didn't answer. She couldn't come right out and tell him that she was going to kill him.

Chapter 32

Boyd squatted and poked at the charred remains of the outlaws' campfire with a stick. Not so much as a wisp of smoke rose. Casting the stick aside, he straightened. "They got an earlier start than we did," he guessed.

The rest of the posse were still on their mounts. All except Vogel, who was moving about the clearing, examining the ground.

"We're still not far behind," Lefty said. "We keep on hard, we'll catch them by nightfall."

Divett licked his lips and swallowed.

Boyd was about to climb back on the chestnut when the blacksmith called his name. Vogel was on a knee, touching his fingertips to something. "What is it?" he asked, going over.

"Blood."

Boyd remembered that the accountant thought he'd heard a shot, and went over.

Red drops had spattered the grass, dozens of tiny drops that no one would have noticed unless, like Vogel, they were looking for sign.

"Notice anything?" Vogel asked.

"Besides the blood?" Boyd wasn't sure what the blacksmith meant.

"The grass," Vogel said. "Clumps have been pulled out and then the dirt smoothed over."

Now that the blacksmith mentioned it, Boyd realized there were more than half a dozen fist-sized patches where grass had been removed. "What the hell?"

"See how these are clumped together?" Vogel said, indicating a spot where the most grass had been pulled. "What do you want to bet they had more blood on them?"

Boyd stood and took a step back, and a pattern came into focus. The tiny drops he'd first seen were the periphery of the spray. Most of the blood must have splattered where most of the grass was missing. "I'll be damned."

Vogel looked up. "Someone was shot."

A sinking feeling came over Boyd. The outlaws wouldn't shoot themselves. That left one possibility. "Cecelia," he said breathlessly.

"We shouldn't jump to conclusions," Vogel said. "But . . ." He didn't finish. Rising, he gazed about the clearing. "Whoever it was, I doubt they took the body with them."

"You think they buried it?" Boyd said skeptically. Digging a grave, as hard as the ground was, would take an hour or more.

"No," Vogel said. "What would you have done if you were them?"

"Drag the body into the woods and cover it," Boyd reckoned.

"That would be my guess."

Boyd followed the blacksmith to the trees and then along the tree line.

"I don't see any drag marks yet," Vogel said.

"Maybe they carried it."

Over on his horse, Lefty called out, "What's goin' on, Marshal? What are you two up to?"

It was Vogel who answered, "Someone was shot. We're trying to figure out what happened to the body."

The cowboys and the townsmen dismounted and joined

the search. It was Sherm Bonner, who was scouring the ground on the south side of the clearing, near where they had entered it, who hollered, "Lookee here. I found some blood."

Everyone hurried over.

The blood wasn't much, a handful of drops in a straight line. Drops that led into the forest.

"It must have been dripping and they didn't notice or they'd have pulled out the grass," Vogel said. Bending, he pointed. "There's a boot heel. And here's another. They're different. Two of them were carrying whoever they shot."

"But who would they . . . ?" Lefty began, and glanced sharply at Boyd. "Oh Lordy. I hope not."

"Hush, you lunkhead," Sherm said.

Vogel entered the trees with Boyd a few steps behind. Boyd dreaded what they might find. If his fear came true, it proved that Cestus Calloway's word wasn't worth a pile of horse manure. Calloway hadn't kept Cecelia alive, as he'd promised.

"Here's another footprint," Vogel said, "and some brush they broke walking through."

"They took the body a ways," Lefty said.

"So we wouldn't find it," Sherm said.

"Should we have left our horses untended?" Divett asked nervously. "I'd hate to be stranded afoot."

Boyd put an end to the grisly images of a murdered Cecelia that had been filling his head. "Go back and keep watch over them," he directed.

"Glad to, Marshal," the accountant said, and scampered away as if the ghost of whoever had been shot was after him.

"Should I go with him?" Titus asked.

"If you want to." Boyd didn't care. He was only interested in one thing.

"I reckon I'll stay with you. I want to see."

Vogel went around a blue spruce and drew up short. "We found it," he declared.

Limbs, leaves, and brush had been piled in a mound six feet long and three feet wide.

"This wouldn't have taken them long, all of them working together," Vogel said. "They did it quick and lit a shuck."

Boyd tried not to think of who lay under the pile. "Let me," he said, and moving past the blacksmith, he knelt and scooped at the piled. He didn't have to scoop more than a few times before he exposed an arm.

"Oh hell," Sherm Bonner said.

"That's a man's hand," Lefty said, "not a gal's."

"The man's shirt," Vogel said. "It's buckskin."

It couldn't be, Boyd told himself, and yet it was. He scooped faster, exposing a shoulder and part of the dead man's chest.

"Is that who I think it is?" young Titus said in confusion.

Boyd grabbed a handful of leaves and threw them to one side. In doing so, his fingers scraped cold flesh.

A face stared blankly skyward, the eyes glazed, a bullet hole at the top of the bridge of the nose.

"Harvey Dale!" Lefty exclaimed.

"How can this be?" Titus said. "Did he get careless and they caught him?"

"Dale was too smart to let that happen," Lefty said.

Boyd held up a hand. "Quiet, both of you. I need to think." He removed more of the brush and sat back on his bootheels, pondering. Dale had been shot in the clearing. That much was obvious. He must have been staying close to the outlaws for Cecelia's sake, and somehow or other they got hold of him. "It could be," he said, sharing his thoughts out loud, "that Harve tried to sneak in and free Miss Wilson."

"That must be it," Vogel agreed. "He waited until he figured the outlaws were asleep, but one of them wasn't and shot him."

"Makes sense to me," Lefty said.

"What doesn't make sense," Sherm Bonner said, "is why

they went to all this bother with the body. Why didn't they leave it where he fell?"

"To rub our noses in it?" Lefty said. "Good point, pard."

Boyd had no answer to that.

"Do we leave him like this or plant him ourselves?" Lefty wanted to know.

As much as Boyd would like to give Dale a decent burial, there was Cecelia to think of. "We've lost too much time as it is. For now we leave him. We'll come back later and do it right." The others helped him cover the face and chest and arm, and together they hustled to the clearing.

In his eagerness to make up for the delay, Boyd brought the chestnut to a trot. He hadn't gone more than a quarter of a mile when, on climbing a short slope to a shelf, he drew rein in bewilderment.

The rest of the posse came up on either side of him, and it was safe to say they were as astounded as he was.

"How can this be?" Lefty said.

"It can't," Vogel said.

Yet there it was, for all of them to see: an arrow carved in a tree.

The outlaws weren't paying much attention to her, which suited Cecelia just fine. Her bound hands in front of her, she pretended to be idly walking about to stretch her legs while all the time searching for a rock that would suit her purpose.

Ira Toomis was over by the horses. Now and then he glared at her to remind her he was still mad about the knot on his head.

Cestus Calloway, the Attica Kid, and Mad Dog Hanks were huddled out of earshot, talking in low tones.

Bert Varrow had gone off into the woods and not returned yet.

Cecelia was conscious of running out of time. They had stopped minutes ago, and Calloway wouldn't stay there much longer. His rests were always short.

She had to find a rock, and quickly.

So far Cecelia had only seen small flat rocks and small round ones, neither of which would do. She needed a long one, with a sharp point. About to turn toward the trees, she stopped. Sticking out of the ground in front of her might be the answer to her prayer. Several inches of stone, tapered to a tip, jutted from the soil.

Stepping up to it so it was between her legs, she stooped and fiddled with the laces to one of her embroidered boots. She had been wearing them instead of her work boots because she'd hoped Boyd would come calling and wanted to look her best.

Toomis glared at her, and looked away. None of the others paid her any mind, and there was still no sign of Bert Varrow.

Cecelia gripped the rock and tried to move it. It didn't budge. She tried harder and succeeded in loosening it a little. Encouraged, she gripped it with both hands, careful not to cut her fingers. Pushing and tugging as hard as she could, she loosened it even more.

Cecelia pried at the dirt with her fingernails, scraping enough away that she could tell that two or three more inches of rock were embedded in the earth. It was exactly what she needed.

Swiping at a bang that fell over her yes, Cecelia strained. The rock moved more than ever but still wasn't loose enough to pull out.

"What the hell are you doin'?"

Her heart leaping into her throat, Cecelia looked up. Ira Toomis had come over and was regarding her suspiciously. "Nothing much," she said. "Adjusting my shoe."

"Liar."

"I'll thank you to leave me be," Cecelia said.

"Move away from there," Toomis ordered her.

"I will not."

"I want to see what you're up to. Stand up and step back or I'll move you myself."

"You're not to lay a finger on me," Cecelia blustered.

"Or what? You'll scream?" Toomis stepped up, placed his hand on her shoulder, and shoved.

Cecelia was thrown off balance. She fell onto her back but contrived to lower her legs so her dress hid the rock. "How dare you!"

The other outlaws had seen and were rising. Cestus Calloway wasted no time in striding over and demanding to know, "What's goin' on? Why are you pushin' her, Ira?"

"She's a lyin' sack," Toomis said. "She's up to somethin' and she won't say what it is."

"Miss Wilson?" Cestus said.

"I have no idea what he's talking about," Cecelia said. "He's been out to get me since I hit him with that rock."

"Move your legs," Toomis said.

"I beg your pardon?"

"You heard me, bitch. Move your legs." Toomis drew his six-shooter and pointed it at her.

Cecelia turned to Calloway. "Are you going to let him treat me this way? It's despicable. Or aren't you the gentleman you claimed to be?"

"I never claimed any such thing," Cestus said.

"Have her move her legs," Toomis said.

"What for?"

"Have her do it, damn it," Toomis said. "I don't ask a lot. You can at least do this, and we'll both see."

"Move your legs," Cestus said.

"I refuse," Cecelia replied.

"Lady, you don't move them, I'll by God pistol-whip you," Toomis warned her. "Let's see how uppity you are when you're swallowin' your teeth."

"Please, ma'am. Do as he says."

"No, I say."

Bending, Cestus reached for her ankles.

"Don't touch me," Cecelia said, and pumping her elbows and legs, she slid back far enough that he couldn't.

"Well, look at that," Toomis said. He took a short step and kicked the rock. "She was tryin' to pull this out of the ground."

Cestus Calloway made a clucking sound and wagged a finger at her. "Last night, and now this. What am I to do with you?"

Ira Toomis bared his teeth in a sneer. "I have an idea," he said, and raised his revolver. "Give her to me."

Chapter 33

To say that Boyd and the posse were stunned didn't describe it by half. They sat their saddles and stared at the mark in the tree and then at one another and at the mark again.

Lefty broke their shock with "This doesn't make no sense."

"The scout is dead," Sherm Bonner said. "He can't have made that mark."

Boyd gigged the chestnut over and ran his fingers along the arrow. It certainly looked like those that Dale had made, but so did all of the ones they'd come across.

"I'm not the only one who is confused, then?" Divett asked. "How can a dead man leave sign for us?"

"He can't," Vogel said. "But that's not the real question." He regarded them gravely. "The real question is, how long has this been going on?"

Boyd gave a start. If Harve hadn't done this one, then he hadn't done others for how far back? "It depends on when they got their hands on him. If it was at the clearing, then this is the first mark they've faked."

"What if they caught him before the clearin'?" Sherm Bonner said.

Lefty nodded. "What if it was as far back as the cave? Or

even before that? They could have been leavin' marks for miles and miles."

Divett fidgeted in his saddle. "I'm more confused than ever. Can someone explain to me why they would do that? Leave marks for us to follow them? They certainly don't want us to catch them."

"Maybe they do," Vogel said, staring meaningfully at Boyd. "Maybe they've been stringing us along until they're ready to turn the tables."

"Meaning?" young Titus said.

"An ambush," Lefty said. "They'll draw us off into the wilds until they're ready, and then bushwhack us."

"Clever," Sherm said.

"My word," Divett declared. "Then we've been duped all along? We've been at their mercy and not known it?"

"Not yet, we're not," Vogel said.

Boyd reined the chestnut around to face them. "We were lucky to catch on before it was too late. If we hadn't found Dale's body . . ." He didn't like to think of the probable outcome: all of them dead, and Cecelia with no hope whatsoever of being rescued.

"What do we do? Turn back?" Divett asked.

"Be serious, pencil pusher," Lefty said.

"I am," Divett responded. "What does it matter if we know the marks are fake or not? We still have to follow them, and they'll still lie in wait and ambush us. We'd be fools to carry on."

"We'd be weak sisters not to," Sherm Bonner said.

"Exactly right, pard," Lefty said. "The hunters became the hunted, but now the hunters can do the huntin' again."

"Huh?" Divett said.

Boyd agreed with Lefty. "Now that we know, we can use it against them. We'll push on, for Miss Wilson's sake if nothin' else, but we'll be more careful than ever."

"How do we keep from riding into their ambush?" Divett wanted to know. "They could jump us at any time."

Boyd scratched his chin. "One of us will have to ride ahead and keep his eyes peeled. He spots the trap, he rides back and warns us."

"What if he doesn't spot it? What if they kill him and lie in wait for the rest of us?"

"That's a chance we'll have to take."

"I'm not sure I want to," the accountant said. "When I agreed to join the posse, I didn't anticipate anything like this. I never imagined we'd be playing cat and mouse with these fellows."

"You can't predict life," Lefty said.

"I beg to differ," Divett said. "You can at least apply logic, and this isn't logical. Not at all. We continue on and some of us are bound to die."

"Maybe all of us," Lefty said.

"Was that supposed to be funny? I don't find the prospect the least bit amusing. In fact—"

Boyd was tired of him. "Enough. I've told you before. You're welcome to head back any time you want, and anyone else who wants to go with you is welcome to tag along. But I'm not givin' up. Those bastards have Cecelia. They've killed my friends. I'll go on alone if I have to, but I'm going."

"You're not alone, Marshal," Lefty said.

"No, you're not," Sherm Bonner said.

Vogel nodded grimly.

Young Titus appeared uncertain. He glanced at Divett, and at the arrow. "I never counted on anything like this either. But there's a lady at stake, and for me, that's what matters. No one should ever harm a female. Not ever. That's as wrong as wrong can be. I have a ma and I have sisters, and they'd want me to keep going."

"Well, then," Divett said bleakly, "if all of you are continuing on, I must as well."

"You don't sound very happy about it," Lefty said.

"I'll do my part. Never fear."

Boyd would just as soon that the accountant did go back.

He was their weak link, and they could do just as well without him. "None of us will hold it against you if you turn around."

"No, I say."

"Then no more bellyachin'," Boyd said. "From here on out, keep your gloom and doom to yourself. We have enough on our minds."

"Calling our enterprise folly isn't necessarily gloom."

Lefty threw back his head and cackled. "Mister, if we were fightin' those outlaws with words, you'd win by your lonesome."

"Huh?" Divett said again.

"Now that that's settled," Vogel said, "how do we decide who rides ahead? Flip a coin? Take turns? Or do you want a volunteer?"

"Turns would be fairest," Lefty said. "I don't mind if the rest of you don't, but I reckon it's up to the law dog."

"Turns it will be," Boyd said, "except for Mr. Divett and Mr. Titus."

"Excuse me?" Divett said.

"I want to help too," Titus said.

Boyd pointed at the accountant. "You're no good in these woods. You make too much noise, and you've hardly ever used that revolver of yours." He pointed at the butcher's apprentice. "You're still green behind the ears. You'd do better than he would, but the four of us can do even better, so Lefty, Bonner, Vogel, and me will take the turns."

"Count your blessin's, boy," Lefty said.

"I'm a man," Titus said, "and I don't like being treated as if I'm not."

"Listen to the marshal, son," Vogel said. "He's been a lawman for years and knows what he's doing. Me, I hunt all the time. These cowhands are always out riding the range. They're used to the outdoors, and can sense things you wouldn't. It's smart that it's the four of us, and not an insult to you."

"It feels like an insult," Titus said, "but when you put it that way, I guess I shouldn't be upset."

"Now that that's settled, I'll take the first turn," Boyd said. "Keep followin' the signs." He started to rein around, and paused. "And if you hear shots, come on damn quick."

Cecelia had never been so humiliated in her life. She was tied wrists and ankles, both, and belly-down over the back of Ira Toomis's horse. He kept looking down at her, and chuckling. Worst of all, whenever it struck his fancy, he reached back and smacked her posterior.

He did it again just now, and laughed. "That's a nice fanny you've got, lady, for an old gal."

"You're despicable," Cecelia said.

"Because I like fannies? Hell, most folks do. Well, men at least. I don't know what you ladies look for in a man, whether it's our behinds or somethin' else."

"I don't ever look at a man's behind," Cecelia said indignantly.

"Really? Me, that's all I look at when I go to a sportin' house. All those pretty gals in tight dresses sashayin' around with their fannies stickin' out. I tell you, I just about drool."

"You're not only despicable, you're crude."

"If crude is likin' fannies, then I'm crude as hell."

"Enough about fannies. I'd rather talk about something else. Or better yet, not talk to you at all."

"Keep puttin' on airs," Toomis said. "It will make it easier when the time comes."

"The time for what?" Cecelia asked, although she knew full well.

Toomis smirked and didn't answer.

Resting her cheek against the horse, Cecelia closed her eyes. It had been bad before, but this was worlds worse. As a punishment, Cestus Calloway had handed her over to Toomis and told him to look after her until they stopped for the night.

Toomis took to it with glee. He'd thrown her over his horse instead of letting her ride, and had been fondling her to his heart's content. The man was wicked through and through.

"I hope Cestus lets me keep you after we're done with that posse," Toomis remarked. "You could be sort of my pet," he said, and chuckled.

"I'm no one's dog, thank you very much."

"Or better yet, we could take turns with you. You have a fine figure for a gal your age."

"If my hands were free and I had a gun, I'd shoot you."

"After that rap you gave me on my noggin', I believe you," Toomis said. "My head still hurts."

"I'll give you another rap when I'm able," Cecelia said.

"You won't be. We went easy on you before, but not anymore. You spoiled it for yourself by helpin' that scout. And your lover spoiled it more by breakin' his word to Cestus."

"Boyd does what he has to. He probably felt it was necessary to save me from your clutches."

"All it did was make Cestus mad. He's a peaceable fella and doesn't get mad often, but he's mad now, and that's good."

Despite herself, Cecelia asked, "Good how?"

"Cestus doesn't like to hurt folks. All that robbin' we did, you ever hear of us shootin' anybody? No, you didn't. Because Cestus wouldn't let us. But now his dander is up and he's out for blood."

"Why not just leave me and ride on by yourselves? The posse won't pursue you once they have me."

"You'd like that, wouldn't you? But they'd just send you back to town with one or two of them and the rest will keep after us until they run us into the ground or we buck them out in gore."

"You kill them and you'll hang. You know that, don't you?"

"Lady, I've been on the wrong side of the law since who

flung the chunk. I have stole and I have killed, enough that I could be hanged six times over. Givin' the law more cause doesn't bother me any."

Cecelia lapsed into silence. The swaying motion of the horse, and the smell, made her think of her childhood. Her father had given her a pony for her tenth birthday and she'd spent every spare moment riding and grooming and feeding it.

It got so that one time her mother teased her that she smelled like the pony.

Her legs were beginning to cramp. She shifted to try to relieve the pain, but it didn't help. The rope around her ankles was too tight.

"Won't you please let me ride?"

"No," Toomis said.

"I'm hurting."

"Good."

"Are you so hard-hearted that you would let another human being suffer?"

Toomis laughed. "What do you think?"

"Has anyone ever told you that you're almost as vile as Mad Dog Hanks?" Cecelia said.

"If that was an insult it was a poor one."

Cecelia fell silent again. She was wasting her breath. These men were truly heartless. Even Calloway, who pretended to be different but deep down he wasn't.

Ira Toomis drew rein next to a tall pine and took a clasp knife from his pocket and opened it.

"Another mark?" Cecelia said.

"What else?"

"You're wasting your time. They won't ride into your gun sights. Boyd is too smart to be ambushed."

"Keep tellin' yourself that, lady." Toomis jabbed the tip of the blade into the bark and went to work.

Cecelia thought about smacking the horse with her arms to make it spook, but what good would that do? She might be pitched off, and Toomis would finish making the mark anyway.

"When it comes to smart, there's no one as clever as Cestus," Toomis informed her. "He's a fox, that man is. It's why we've stuck with him so long."

"That's nice," Cecelia said.

Toomis twisted around, and sneered. "You won't think that when you see your lover leakin' blood like a sieve."

Chapter 34

Boyd rode at a walk. As much as he yearned to gallop to Cecelia's rescue, now that he knew the outlaws might be lying in wait somewhere ahead, extreme caution was called for.

He couldn't get Harvey Dale out of his head. He missed the old scout. Dale had been reliable, the one person he could count on. More so than Mitch, whose only true fault had been that he was new to the job. More experience would have molded Mitch into a fine lawman.

The chestnut cleared a rise, and there was another arrow. It pointed to the northwest this time.

Boyd went past without stopping. The outlaws appeared to be heading for the Divide. Either they intended to cross over to the other side, or they had a more sinister purpose.

Boyd couldn't see the outlaws crossing over. They'd always operated on this side of the Rockies. The higher they went, though, the fewer trees there would be, allowing plenty of places for an ambush.

An hour went by, and then two. The strain of staying alert, of never knowing when a rifle might thunder and a slug sear his body, began to tell. He was tired and on edge.

Boyd supposed he should wait for the others and let

someone else take a turn at riding point. But thinking about Cecelia goaded him on. He would give anything for a glimpse of her, just to know she hadn't been harmed.

The trees thinned and came to an end at the base of a steep slope covered with talus.

Boyd wasn't about to risk the chestnut breaking a leg. He scoured the talus but saw no evidence the outlaws had dared to climb it either. Reining right, he came on several clear tracks. The outlaws had gone around as he was doing.

The slope was almost half a mile across. Aspens bordered it, their leaves shaking in the breeze. A pair of ravens took flight, the rhythmic beat of their wings unnaturally loud in the rarified air.

His hand on his Colt, Boyd entered the aspens. It was an unlikely spot for an ambush; there was too much cover for him to use. The outlaws would spring their surprise out in the open where they could pick him or anyone else off as easy as pie.

A couple of black-tailed does bounded off, their trails raised like flags.

More proof the outlaws weren't nearby.

Another arrow had been carved into a large aspen at the end of the stand. It too pointed northwest.

The slopes became steeper, and rockier. Alpine growth replaced the timber. Once, in the distance, a bull elk stared at him without fear.

Boyd decided to stop. The chestnut could use the rest. He came to a boulder field and drew rein at the bottom after scouring the boulders for movement or any other hint the outlaws were lying in wait.

A swig from his canteen quenched his thirst for the moment. Opening a saddlebag, he helped himself to a piece of jerky. A flat boulder gave him a place to roost, and he sat and chewed and scanned the heights.

Boyd smothered a yawn and wished he had some coffee. He could use a cup or three.

Turning his attention to the lower slopes, Boyd sought sign of the posse. He figured they weren't far behind unless by some fluke they'd lost the sign. He was so intent on spotting them that when the chestnut nickered, he didn't look to see why. Only when he heard the unmistakable click of a gun hammer did he jerk around, and freeze.

"Howdy, law dog," the Attica Kid said. He had come out from behind a boulder not ten feet away, his Lightning level at his waist.

Boyd almost went for his revolver. Only the fact that he'd be shot before he touched it stopped him.

"You made this plumb easy," the Attica Kid said. "For a tin star you're not much."

Boyd was incensed at how handily he'd been taken. He considered throwing himself off the flat boulder and scrambling to another but knew he wouldn't make it.

"Whatever you're thinkin'," the Attica Kid said, "don't."

Boyd glanced at other boulders. "Where are your pards? And where's Miss Wilson?"

"I should think you'd be wantin' to know why you're still alive. I could have splattered your brains."

"Like you did Harvey Dales's?"

"That old scout? How did you guess? Yes, that was my work."

"And now you've been waitin' here for me," Boyd said.

The Kid's mouth quirked. "You're awful slow between the ears. Cestus saw you comin' from a mile back. He's got the spyglass, the one that used to belong to the old scout."

Boyd had forgotten all about it in the shock of finding Harve's body.

"We could have picked you off, but Cestus wants you breathin', which is why you're sittin' there with that dumb look on your face." The Kid extended the Lightning. "I want you to shed your gun belt, real slow."

Boyd started to move his hand.

"Slow means slow. No sudden moves," the Kid warned.

"You never answered me about Miss Wilson," Boyd said as he imitated molasses. "Have you harmed her?"

"Toomis has been spankin' your sweetheart's rump a lot, but I wouldn't call that harm."

"Spankin' . . . ?" Boyd said, and grew hot with fury. "Calloway let him lay a hand on her?"

"Don't you dare," the Attica Kid said. "You're a fine one to talk. You gave your word to him, remember? You sittin' there proves how much that's worth."

Boyd's gun belt made a *thunk* as it struck the flat boulder. He hiked his hands and went to stand.

"No!" the Kid barked. "What do you think you're doin'? I'll say when you can get up."

"I want to see her."

The Attica Kid walked over and reached down without taking his eyes, or his Lighting, off Boyd. He helped himself to Boyd's gun belt, stepped back, and slung it over his shoulder.

"Didn't you hear me?"

"What *you* want doesn't count," the Attica Kid said. "You're ours now. You've stepped in it and that's no lie."

Boyd simmered in frustration. Things had gone to hell so fast he could scarcely believe it. "The posse isn't far behind me," he tried. "You shoot, and they'll hear and come on fast."

"You're a terrible liar," the Attica Kid said. "Cestus told me your boys are a good ways behind you. That spyglass sure does come in handy."

Boyd wouldn't give two bits for his chances if he let the outlaws take him prisoner. He glanced at his chestnut, at the Winchester in the saddle scabbard.

"You must be hankerin' to get yourself shot," the Attica Kid said. "Go ahead and try. I'll wing you in the leg so Cestus can do as he wants with you, but I can't promise you won't bleed to death."

With considerable effort, Boyd willed himself not to try.

"That's it," the Attica Kid said. "Keep a level head and you'll last a little longer." Stepping to one side, he glanced up the mountain and hollered, "I've got him corralled. Come on down."

Figures appeared at the top of the slope, leading their horses. Cestus Calloway waved to the Attica Kid, climbed onto his animal, and headed down.

Boyd remembered the farmhouse, and the death of his friend. "Tell me somethin'. Was it you who shot Sam Wilson?"

"That farmer?" the Attica Kid said. "What if it was?"

"He was a good man."

"Now he's a dead man," the Kid replied. "What did bein' good get him except an early grave?"

"He'd still be alive if not for you."

"Well, boo-hoo-hoo," the Kid said. "We all bite the dust sooner or later. It's nothin' to get in a tizzy about."

"When your time comes, I hope it hurts like hell."

The Attica Kid shook his head. "Not me, mister. I'll go out shootin'. It'll be quick and not much pain."

"No one knows when or how," Boyd said. "If there's any justice in this world, you'll be gut-shot like Cockeye."

"You're commencin' to annoy me," the Kid said. "You're takin' all this much too personal."

"You murdered my best friend. How else do you think I'm goin' to take it?"

"However you do, you'd best keep it to yourself. I am tired of your guff."

Boyd didn't provoke him further. He was more interested in the line of riders, particularly the last one. It shocked him to see Cecelia draped over Ira Toomis's horse as if she were a sack of flour. She was looking down at him, but he couldn't see her face all that well for the hair hanging over it. He smiled and gave a little wave.

"How sweet," the Attica Kid said. "Why not blow the old gal a kiss while you're at it?"

"Go to hell."

"Careful," the Kid said.

Cestus Calloway was beaming like a patent medicine man who had just sold out his stock. "I told you it would work," he crowed as he brought his horse to a halt.

"That you did," the Attica Kid said.

Mad Dog Hanks brought his animal past Calloway's and placed his hand on his six-shooter. "Can I shoot the son of a bitch?"

"You can not," Cestus said. Swinging a leg up and over his saddle horn, he slid down.

"He threw me in his jail," Mad Dog said. "I owe him."

"You killed his deputy," Cestus said. "I'd call that even."

"You're always spoilin' my fun," Mad Dog complained.

"I didn't say you couldn't shoot him later," Cestus replied. "I just said you can't shoot him now. We need him for the next part of my plan."

Boyd barely heard them. He was focused on Cecelia. Only one eye showed through her hair, and it glistened. She reached out with her bound hands as if to touch him. He heard her say his name, softly.

Ira Toomis laughed. "Look at this. It must be true love, the way she's carryin' on."

"Leave her be," Bert Varrow said.

Clucking to his horse, Toomis brought it to within an arm's reach of the flat boulder. "Here's your sack of female, law dog." Bending down, he smirked. "The two of you can hold hands and make cow eyes at each other."

Boyd was off the boulder before he knew what he was doing. He leaped and seized Toomis by the shirt and together they spilled to the ground. Someone shouted and Cecelia called his name, but he couldn't hear them for the roaring in his ears. His blood was on fire. He punched Toomis in the face, twice, then gripped the outlaw's wrist to prevent him from drawing. Toomis cursed and tried to push away. Boyd hit him again and again, aware that Toomis was punching him too, but he didn't feel the blows.

Then hands were on him, and Boyd was hauled to his feet. His arms were gripped by Mad Dog on his right and Bert Varrow on his left. Boyd would have struggled except that Varrow pressed a pistol against his ribs.

Bellowing in rage, Ira Toomis pushed to his feet and clawed his revolver from its holster. "I'll kill you for that!"

"No!" Cestus Calloway shouted, stepping between them. "We need him."

"You saw what he did?" Toomis was so enraged he shook. "I'll be damned if you'll stop me."

"You'll be dead if you don't," the Attica Kid said.

Toomis swiped at blood trickling from his mouth. "Don't prod me, Kid," he said, but he shoved his revolver back into his holster, then jabbed Calloway in the chest. "I'm tellin' you now, Cestus. When the time comes, he's mine and mine alone."

"Like hell," Mad Dog Hanks said.

"I mean it, Mad Dog," Toomis said. "I won't back down, not even for you."

"Boys, boys," Cestus said, smiling. "You're like two cats squabblin' over a mouse. There's enough of him for both of you." Turning, he brushed dirt from Boyd's shirt and chuckled. "That was mighty dumb, Cooper. You could have been killed, and then where would your gal be?"

Boyd glared at Toomis.

"If they let you go, will you behave?" Cestus asked.

"Please, Boyd," Cecelia said, raising her head. "Don't provoke them further. For my sake."

"I think I'm goin' to cry," Mad Dog said.

Boyd felt some of the rage drain out of him. "I'll behave," he said, "so long as you keep Toomis away from her."

"What did Ira do?" Cestus said.

It was the Attica Kid who answered him. "That might have been my doin'. I told him how Toomis was fondlin' her."

"Well, no wonder." Cestus nodded at Mad Dog and Varrow, and they released Boyd and stepped back. "Ira, you simmer down. And, Marshal, you'll let us tie your hands. Then I'm takin' the two of you a little higher and settin' things up. There are some fish down below I aim to hook, and you two are my worms."

Chapter 35

It was clever, the trap Cestus Calloway set. Damn clever.

Boyd admitted that to himself as he sat in a small clearing with a crackling fire in front of him. On the other side of the fire sat Cecelia.

The outlaws had hauled them above the boulder field to a bench mostly bare of vegetation. Above it grew thick brush but few trees. The outlaws had gathered enough brush and limbs for a fire that would put off a lot of smoke. They had bound Boyd's ankles as they had already bound Cecelia's, and made the pair of them sit. Then Cestus Calloway, the Attica Kid, Mad Dog Hanks, and Ira Toomis had gone up into the brush and hidden themselves while Bert Varrow took their horses far enough off that the posse wouldn't spot them. Varrow was to stay with their animals until the slaughter was over.

That was how Mad Dog Hanks referred to it. "I can't wait to start the slaughter," he'd mentioned with a grin, then hefted his rifle and gone up into the brush with the others.

"Your poor posse," Cecelia now said. "They'll be shot to pieces, and it's all my fault."

"You don't see me sittin' here?" Boyd said.

"You're part of the bait, as Calloway called it," Cecelia

said, "but none of you would be in this predicament if the outlaws hadn't taken me captive."

"Put the blame where it belongs. On them."

Cecelia gazed at where the shelf fell away into the boulder field below. "How soon before they show up?"

"I can't predict." Boyd didn't think it would be long. Vogel and the others would spot the smoke and use caution until they reached the top and saw Cecelia and him. He could shout to warn them, but Cestus had made it clear that if he so much as opened his mouth when the posse appeared, Mad Dog would put a slug in Cecelia's head.

"I have somethin' to ask of you," Boyd said to her.

"Anything," Cecelia answered, her eyes silently saying a world more than that single word.

"I have to do what I can to warn my men," Boyd said. "When I tell you to, drop onto your side with your back to the brush and curl up to make yourself as small a target as you can." Mad Dog wouldn't be able to see her head, let alone shoot it.

"I know what you're thinking," Cecelia said. "I don't mind taking a bullet to save the others. I truly don't."

"Has anyone ever told you that you're as fine a woman as ever drew breath?"

"Not lately, no."

They both smiled.

"Look at us," Cecelia said. "There's about to be a bloodbath and we're making light of it."

"We're doin' no such thing," Boyd said. "When a fella is courtin' a gal, he flatters her a lot. It's just natural."

"You're trying to put me at ease, aren't you? To keep me calm for when the shooting commences."

"Is that what I'm doin'?" For the tenth or eleventh time, Boyd tested the ropes around his wrists. He strained. He tugged. He twisted his wrists.

"Are they loosening?"

"Not a lick."

Cecelia bowed her head, and her hair fell over her face. "Oh, Boyd. I'm so sorry. If the men with you die, I'll never forgive myself. Yes, I know I'm not to blame. But still."

The ring of metal on rock, from down below, brought Boyd's head up. "Did you hear that?"

"No. What?"

"I think they're comin'." Boyd glanced at the brush. The outlaws were so well concealed he didn't see any of them.

Again a hoof struck rock, and there could be no doubt.

"Oh, Lord," Cecelia said, "please preserve us."

Boyd reckoned that the outlaws had heard too. They would be watching for the posse to come up over the shelf. They wouldn't be watching him. Or so he prayed as he shifted so his back was to the brush, then placed his wrists directly in the flames.

"Boyd, no!"

"Shhh," Boyd said, and had to grit his teeth as waves of agony washed over him. The heat was so intense he wanted to scream. He clenched his fists to try to spare his fingers.

"You could cripple yourself."

Boyd smelled burning rope, and burning flesh. He moved his hands a little so they weren't quite in the flames but the rope was. His shirt caught fire, but it couldn't be helped. Strands of the rope blackened and parted and he exerted all his strength to try to break it.

More hooves thudded. The posse was taking its time, climbing warily.

Boyd dreaded the moment they'd come over the rim. That was when the shooting would start. He needed to be free by then. But he didn't know how much more he could take. The pain was so bad he smothered a groan. More of the rope parted, but his forearms were blistered. They hurt terribly.

"Boyd!" Cecelia whispered. "Ira Toomis is watching you!"

Sure enough, Toomis had popped his head out from behind a scrub and was staring suspiciously down at him.

Boyd stared back with as calm an expression as he could manage, and after a bit Toomis dropped from sight again.

"Do you think he suspects?"

Boyd couldn't answer. He didn't trust himself to utter a sound. He tried one more time to break the rope, and gasped with delight when it worked. His hands were free. Quickly he pressed his forearms to his lap to smother the small flames licking at his shirt.

"Are you all right?" Cecelia asked.

Boyd grunted.

"You're terribly burned."

Boyd wished she wouldn't remind him. He could move his fingers, though, and set to work on the rope around his ankles. The knots were tight, but he had strong fingernails.

"They're taking forever," Cecelia remarked.

That was good, Boyd told himself. It bought him the time he needed. He pried so hard he nearly tore a nail off, but a knot loosened.

"I saw some brush move where Calloway went to ground."

Boyd was only interested in the rope. *Come on! Come on!* he thought, and pried harder.

The loudest *clink* yet of a horseshoe on stone preceded a nicker.

"What on earth?" Cecelia said.

The last knot came undone just as Boyd looked up.

A horse had come over the crest. Vogel's, only the blacksmith wasn't on it. A few seconds more, and a second and third animal appeared. They too were riderless.

"What does it mean?" Cecelia said.

Damned if Boyd knew. His posse had sent the horses up alone? It made no sense. Or did it? He watched, and a hatless head appeared. Vogel's. The blacksmith ducked down again. It happened so fast the outlaws might not have seen him.

"Boyd?"

"I'm goin' to grab you and make a run for it."

"You'll be shot."

"Not if my men cover me," Boyd said, coiling his legs under him.

"It's too risky. Please don't."

"Are you my woman or not?"

Cecelia looked at him in surprise. "I am."

"Then we work together and do this. Be ready." Boyd turned his head just enough to scan the brush without being obvious. None of the outlaws had shown themselves. Taking a deep breath, he exploded into motion. In a bound he reached Cecelia and scooped her into his arms. The pain was tremendous, but he shut it out and raced for the edge of the shelf. He stayed doubled over, although it was difficult to do with Cecelia in his arms. She helped by pressing close to his chest to give him better balance.

Guns boomed behind him.

Boyd winced at a searing pang in his left leg. Stumbling, he almost fell. Then the heads and shoulders of the posse members rose over the rim, all with rifles, and they opened up on the outlaws, firing as rapidly as they could work their weapons.

Boyd weaved, or attempted to. His left leg wasn't working as it should. He had been hit in the thigh, and the leg was throbbing.

"Run, Marshal, run!" Lefty hollered.

Boyd did, for dear life. A slug plucked at his shirt; another nicked his hat. Then he was at the slope and threw himself over it. His bootheels hit hard. Before he could dig them in and stop, his momentum, and Cecelia's weight, pitched him forward. A boulder filled his vision, and for a moment he feared he would smash headfirst into it. But iron fingers clamped hold of his upper arm and he was yanked to a stop inches from disaster.

"Got you," Vogel said.

The big blacksmith lowered them to the ground. "Easy. You nearly bashed your brains out."

Cecelia wriggled free and Vogel helped her to sit up. "We're alive!" she said in amazement.

Rifles still thundered. The posse and the outlaws were swapping lead fast and furious.

"I need to help the others," Vogel said. Jamming the Maynard to his shoulder, he flattened himself and joined in.

Boyd wasted no time in freeing Cecelia. Her knots were as tight as his had been, and resisted.

"I see a couple of 'em!" Lefty bawled. "They're scamperin' away!"

The shooting gradually died. By the time Boyd finished with Cecelia, the last shot had been fired. His ears rang in the abrupt silence. He turned, and swore.

Divett lay sprawled on his back with his arms out, his right eye and part of his forehead blasted away. For all his carping, the accountant had died game.

Vogel was examining a wound in his right arm. The slug appeared to have gone clean through.

"Nice to see you again, Marshal," Sherm Bonner said. "You and your lady friend."

Lefty, grinning, was reloading his rifle.

Young Titus gaped aghast at Divett.

"Calloway thought he had you dead to rights," Boyd said to Vogel. "That you'd ride on up and be picked off."

"I snuck ahead of the others on foot," Vogel said while using two fingers to enlarge the bullet hole in his shirt to expose the wound. "When I saw you two sitting there, I got suspicious. It seemed strange that your horse wasn't anywhere around. Strange too that there wasn't a pot of coffee or food on the fire. Why else make one in the middle of the day?"

"Good thinkin'," Boyd said.

"When the others came up, we gave the horses a slap on their rumps to see what would happen," Vogel continued, "and here you are, safe and sound."

"Sort of," Boyd said, bending to inspect his leg.

"That poor man isn't so sound," Cecelia said, staring sadly at Divett.

Lefty was peering over the top. "I only saw the two ske-daddle. How many were up there?"

"Four," Boyd said.

"Did we get the other two?"

"Only one way to find out," Sherm Bonner said.

"Not yet," Boyd said. "I need a gun. They relieved me of mine."

"You're welcome to my rifle," Sherm said, holding it out. When Boyd took it, Bonner drew his Colt. "I'm partial to my pistol anyway."

"Wait," Cecelia said, and pointed at Boyd's leg. "You've been hit. You're bleeding. We should see how bad it is."

"No time for that," Boyd said. He wanted it over with. He wanted the outlaws dead, and to take Cecelia home.

"You should make time, Marshal," Vogel advised. "I saw you limping. As slow as you are, they'll drop you, easy."

Reluctantly Boyd loosened his belt enough to slide his hand down in his pants. The wound was about five inches long and a quarter inch deep, and the bleeding had pretty much stopped. "I'll live," he announced, and hitched his pants up. "Vogel, you stay with Miss Wilson. The rest of us will tend to this."

"Not on your life. Have the boy guard her," the black-smith said. "I've come this far. I'm in for the finish."

Boyd shrugged. "Titus?"

"I heard him, sir."

Cecelia reached out and clasped Boyd's hand. "I can't thank you enough. All of you."

"It's not over yet," Boyd said. He squeezed her fingers, then dropped flat and crawled to the rim. With extreme care he raised his head high enough to see over. The fire had almost gone out, and there wasn't a trace of the outlaws.

"It could be a trick," Lefty said. "It could be they're waitin' to drop us as soon as we show ourselves."

"Let's find out," Boyd said.

Chapter 36

Boyd looked at the others. "Ready?" When they nodded, he rose and burst toward the brush-covered slope. On his right came the cowboys, on his left the blacksmith.

They weren't halfway when a rifle cracked. Lefty cried out and pitched to his knees. Instantly Sherm Bonner had hold of him and hauled him along.

Vogel fired on the run, his heavy-caliber Maynard booming like thunder.

Boyd didn't see anyone to shoot at. He reached the vegetation and hunkered. This high up, the growth consisted mostly of stunted trees, dwarf shrubs, sedges, and high grass. Many of the trees and shrubs had been bent and twisted by the relentless wind, creating a tangle.

Vogel was covering them with his Maynard. "I think I hit one. I'm not sure who it was."

Lefty had a hand to his side and groaned. "Of all the dumb luck."

"Hush, you baby." Sherm Bonner unbuttoned his friend's shirt partway and raised it to peer under. Recoiling as if he'd been slapped, he blurted, "No."

"Got me good, didn't they?" Lefty said. He was his usual self, grinning at the world and everyone in it, but there was nothing usual about the dark blood that trickled from a corner of his mouth. "I think I'm lung-shot, pard," he said, and coughed violently.

Sherm looked at Boyd in appeal, but there was nothing Boyd could do.

"Shouldn't have shown ourselves, I reckon," Lefty said. "But we had it to do." He clutched Bonner's arm and pulled him lower. "Get word to my folks. Let my pa know I died game."

"Damn it," Sherm said.

"Don't start blubberin'," Lefty said as more dark blood oozed. "You never once gave me cause to be ashamed of you. Don't start now."

"Pard . . ."

"Who's the infant?" Lefty rejoined, and started to laugh. Another coughing fit struck him, and he quaked from his hat to his boots. Looking at Sherm, his chin smeared with blood, he chuckled and said, "Ain't this a hell of a note?"

And with that, he died.

Boyd grew hard inside. Another life to chalk up to the outlaws, another life they must pay for.

Sherm Bonner had gone rigid and his face had become like rock.

"I liked that cowpoke," Vogel said quietly. "He was a good man at heart."

"He sure was," Sherm said softly, "and he was my pard." Suddenly he rose and hurtled into the brush, disappearing around a bent tree.

"Wait!" Boyd cried, too late.

"That cowboy is going to get himself killed," Vogel said.

"Stay here," Boyd said, and ran after Bonner. He scurried around the bent tree, but Bonner wasn't there. He darted to a patch of scrub, but Bonner wasn't there. He heard boots pound and plunged on through. Bonner was just going past another tree. Boyd swallowed a yell that would give him away, and sprinted to catch up. He heard a shot, and then he was past the tree and two men were to his left, separated by a dozen feet.

Mad Dog Hanks, sneering in defiance, was propped against a log, a red stain on his shirt. He had fired his rifle, and was working the lever to feed another cartridge into the chamber.

Sherm Bonner fanned the hammer of his Colt three times, too swiftly for the eye to follow.

Smashed back, Mad Dog let out a screech of rage. He gamely tried to raise his rifle.

"No, you don't." Sherm Bonner took aim and shot Hanks in the head. "That was for my pard, you son of a bitch."

Keeping low, Boyd went over. "That was reckless."

"I'm goin' to kill every one of the varmints," Sherm informed him while reloading.

"You're not in this alone," Boyd said, helping himself to Mad Dog's six-shooter, "and you're to do as I say."

"They shot Lefty," Sherm said. "I do as I please."

This was the last thing Boyd needed. But there was no time to argue. "We'll separate and look around. Lefty saw two of them running off, so there has to be another here somewhere, breathin' or not."

"I find him and he's breathin', he won't be for long."

As it turned out, Boyd found the body. A limp hand poking out of high grass drew him to it.

Ira Toomis lay on his belly, part of his head blown away. It had to be Vogel's handiwork, and that Maynard of his. Brains, hair, and parts of Toomis's hat were splattered all over.

Sherm Bonner came up, and frowned. "One less for me."

"There's still the other three," Boyd said.

"What are we waitin' for?" Turning on a heel, Sherm started back.

Boyd would have liked to take the bodies down, but the gun hand was on the prod and nothing he said or did would change that. He hurried after him, saying, "We do this my way, remember?"

Bonner didn't respond.

As they emerged from the growth, Vogel rose and acted surprised when the cowboy strode past without even looking at him. "I take it his dander is up?"

"Higher than the mountains," Boyd said.

"What are you going to do?"

"Stick with him and hope for the best."

Bonner was already in the saddle and heading out when Boyd reached Cecelia and Titus. The younger man looked relieved when Boyd instructed him to stay with her.

"Why can't I go with you?" Cecelia asked.

"You know better." Boyd limped to the chestnut and grabbed the reins. He was loath to leave her, but it had to be done. "We should be back before dark," he said with more hope than confidence. "If we're not, find a spot to make a fire where it can't be seen." Wincing at his hurt leg, he swung on and straightened. "If we're not back by daybreak, take Miss Winslow to Alpine."

"I sure will, Marshal," the young man said.

"Don't let her talk you out of it," Boyd cautioned. "If we're not back, it will mean the outlaws have won and might be comin' for you."

Titus swallowed. "Don't you worry. I won't let anything happen to your sweetheart."

"Boyd," Cecelia said, and reached out a hand.

"Take care," Boyd said, and got out of there.

Vogel came alongside and didn't say a word. Together they trotted to overtake Sherm Bonner, who was holding to a fast walk. The cowboy barely glanced over.

Bonner was intent on one thing and one thing only

"This doesn't bode well," Vogel said to Boyd.

The footprints were plain in the dust. Two of the outlaws had been running flat out. They'd gone around a bend to where Varrow waited with their horses and the three had fanned the breeze. Not north or northwest as Boyd reckoned they might, but due east, down the mountain.

Sherm Bonner used his spurs and rode at a breakneck pace, quickly pulling ahead. He didn't seem to care how steep the slopes were, or that a misstep could result in a broken leg for his horse, and a bad spill.

"Damn, that puncher can handle a horse," Vogel said in admiration.

Boyd was more interested in not breaking his neck. He was no slouch in a saddle, but he couldn't compare to the cowhand, who rode as if he and his horse were one. He was kept busy reining aside from obstacles and ducking to avoid low limbs. He had to lean back when a particularly sheer slope threatened to pitch him from his animal.

It was the type of riding only a madman would do, or someone hell-bent on vengeance.

Boyd could only hope Bonner was following the outlaws' trail, because he'd lost all sight of any sign. He glanced ahead whenever he could but didn't catch sight of Calloway and the others.

Slope after slope fell behind them. The trees changed from firs and aspens to pines and spruce. There was less undergrowth, which made it easier, but it also let Bonner ride faster.

Boyd didn't know how the cowboy did it. He was about to shout to Bonner to slow up when, behind him, Vogel yelled something that Boyd's didn't catch. He risked a glance over his shoulder and Vogel pointed down the mountain.

A quarter mile below, three riders were crossing a meadow. Even at that distance Boyd recognized them: Cestus Calloway, the Attica Kid, and Bert Varrow.

The Kid appeared to be bent over his saddle.

Sherm Bonner saw them too and let out with a sharp yip, like a hunting dog that had spied the buck it was after.

Boyd was about to shout for the cowboy to wait for Vogel and him, when he swept around a wide spruce and without warning a deadfall barred his way. Reining sharply to avoid crashing into it, he lost even more ground to Bonner.

The last slope came to an end. Before Boyd stretched the meadow, Sherm was already three-fourths of the way across.

Boyd lashed his reins, but it was hopeless. He'd never catch up.

At the far end, a rifle banged. Simultaneous with the blast, Bonner swung onto the side of his horse, Comanche-fashion, and then swung up again and used his spurs.

It was superb horsemanship, a feat Boyd couldn't duplicate in a hundred years. Drawing the revolver, he brought the chestnut to a full gallop. He glanced back again but didn't see Vogel.

Sherm Bonner suddenly veered and did his trick. A pistol cracked, but somehow Bonner and his mount made it into the forest.

A bolt of alarm jolted Boyd. He was out in the open and rushing headlong into the outlaws' guns. He reined wide in the opposite direction from Bonner. A revolver belched lead and smoke, enabling him to spot the silhouette of the shooter, and he responded in kind.

Then the trees closed around him, and Boyd drew rein and vaulted down.

Pistols popped like fireworks. Sherm Bonner and the outlaws were swapping slugs.

Boyd started to rush to Bonner's aid, and off in the greenery something moved. Boyd dived flat as a revolver cracked. He swore he heard the thwack of the slug coring a tree above him.

The shooting suddenly stopped.

Boyd crept past several small pines and went prone. An unnatural stillness gripped the wilds. The birds and other animals had gone quiet. It was as if the world were holding its breath, awaiting the outcome.

THE LAW AND THE LAWLESS

Shaking the silly notion from his head, Boyd snaked to a log, crawled around one end, and made for a boulder. He reached it, rose onto a knee, and went to go around.

A hand holding a cocked six-gun was thrust at him, pointed at his chest.

Boyd froze.

"Got you, law dog," Bert Varrow said, and stepped out from the other side of the boulder. Varrow's derby and suit were caked with dust and smudged.

"You shoot me," Boyd said, "you'll be a wanted man."

"I already am," Varrow said, "and no one will ever know." Tilting his head, he went on. "I'm sorry about this. I'm not a killer. But it has to be done so we can get away."

Boyd wouldn't die meekly. Not after all that had happened. He coiled to spring aside.

"Anything you want me to tell that nice gal of yours if I see her?" Bert Varrow asked. Not in mockery. He was being sincere.

"You're makin' a mistake," was all Boyd could think of to say.

"Wouldn't surprise me any," Bert Varrow said. "I've made heaps of them." He extended his arm. "Good-bye."

A rifle boomed, and the left side of Varrow's head seemed to collapse in on itself even as the other side showered the boulder and the ground with gore.

Boyd jumped back.

With pieces of his brain oozing from the exit wound, Bert Varrow melted into a pile.

Boyd looked over his shoulder. Back near the meadow, Vogel pumped his Maynard in the air, pleased at the shot he'd made. He was on foot, and ran toward Boyd.

Boyd moved too, hunting for Sherm Bonner and the last two outlaws. A dozen strides brought him to the bank of a small stream. Not twenty feet from away, on the same side, stood Sherm Bonner. Across from the cowboy, on the other bank, was the Attica Kid, a bloodstain barely noticeable on the front of his black shirt. Farther off, his hands on his hips, stood Cestus Calloway.

"Well, look who it is," Cestus said, and laughed.

"What in the . . . ?" Boyd blurted. Neither Sherm nor the Kid held a six-shooter. Each had replaced his revolver in his holster.

"You're just in time, Marshal," Cestus said. "These two are fixin' to settle somethin'."

"Sherm, don't," Boyd said.

"Stay out of this, you hear? It's between the Kid and me."

"The Kid wants it this way," Cestus said. "He says he has somethin' to prove before he cashes in his chips."

"Quit talkin'," the Attica Kid barked, his gaze locked on Bonner.

Boyd debated what to do. By rights he should shoot the Kid, Bonner's wishes be damned.

"I hear tell you're a hellion with your shootin' iron," the Kid taunted the cowboy. "Folks say the same about me. I reckon I'll put you to the test."

"Whenever you're ready," Sherm said.

"Law dog, clap your hands," the Attica Kid said.

"I will not," Boyd replied.

"I will," Cestus offered cheerfully, and without any hesitation, he brought his palms together with a sharp slap.

At the sound, two Colts blurred. The Attica Kid's boomed first. The slug spun Sherm Bonner completely around. He held on to his Colt, though, and the instant he turned, he fanned it twice as fast as anything.

The Attica Kid was jarred onto his heels. Tottering, he looked down at the new holes in his shirt. "Well, hell," he said. "I beat him." His eyes rolled up into his head and he dropped where he stood.

Bonner was falling too, his hand pressed to his shoulder.

Boyd had taken his eyes off Cestus Calloway, and the

outlaw leader had jerked his pistol and was pointing it. Boyd fired just as Calloway did. Calloway stumbled, and Boyd fired again. Calloway went to his knees, and Boyd fired a third time.

"It's just not my day," Cestus Calloway declared, and died with a grin on his face.

The undergrowth crackled and out burst Vogel, wheezing like the bellows in his blacksmith shop. "I came as quick as I could. My horse broke a leg." He looked at the bodies. "Is it over?"

"I reckon so," Boyd said.

Epilogue

Sherm Bonner recovered and was riding range at the Circle T inside of a month. Eventually he became foreman. He married and went off to Montana and started a ranch of his own. He never again drew his Colt on another human being.

Vogel went back to blacksmithing. When people asked about his experiences with the posse, he'd heft his big hammer and suggest they talk about something else.

One week to the day after the posse returned to Alpine, Marshal Boyd Cooper and Cecelia Wilson were wed at a small ceremony at the Wilson Farm. The parson wanted to perform the rite at his church, but Cecelia insisted it be the farmhouse, in memory of Sam.

Within a year, the town dried up. The mines weren't producing. A lot of the townsfolk packed their bags and moved to St. Elmo, a new town where the mines were.

Boyd was out of a job. He considered applying at one of the Kansas cow towns or up in Dakota Territory, but Cecelia had a better idea. She'd heard all sorts of wonderful things about San Francisco. The climate was pleasant, the people were friendly, and businesses were booming. She talked Boyd into trying his hand at running a mercantile. Against his better judgment, he agreed, and became the proud owner of his very own store.

Several years passed, and one evening, as they sat on their porch in their rocking chairs, Cecelia asked Boyd if he missed being a lawman.

Boyd was gazing out over the bay and watching gulls on the wing. He thought about it and looked at her and shook his head. "Not a bit."

"That's good to hear. It would upset me considerably if you got a hankering to pin on a badge again."

"Law work is for younger men."

"You're hardly old."

"Why, thank you, my dear," Boyd said. "If you care to join me in the parlor, I'll show you that you're right."

Cecelia blushed, and laughed. "Why, Mr. Cooper. That was naughty of you."

"But I didn't hear you say no."

"And you never will." Rising from her chair, Cecelia grinned and held out her hand. "Why are you still sitting there?"

"Oh my," Boyd said.

Read on for an excerpt from

BROTHER'S KEEPER

A Ralph Compton Novel by David Robbins.
Available from Signet in paperback and e-book.

Thalis Christie knew he was in trouble moments after he opened his eyes. Dawn was about to break, and he lay there debating whether to get up or wait a few minutes.

That was when something brushed against his leg.

Thal nearly jumped out of his skin. There shouldn't be anything under the tarpaulin and blanket that covered him— except him. It didn't help matters that before he'd turned in, he'd stripped off every stitch of clothing.

Thal was on his side, with just his head poking out of his bed. Goose bumps erupted as the thing that had crawled in with him slithered onto his shin. *Snake,* his mind screamed, and it was all he could do not to scramble out. He didn't move for two reasons. The first was that he would rather die than let the other Crescent H punchers see him naked. The second reason mattered more. The snake might be a rattler. If he moved his leg, the thing might bite.

No one else was up yet except the cook, Old Pete, who was over at the chuck wagon fixing breakfast. A few of the hands were snoring. His pard, Ned Leslie, was closest to him, and snoring the loudest.

"Ned!" Thal whispered.

Ned went on sounding like a bear in hibernation.

Thal tensed as the snake inched up his leg. It was the

creepiest feeling. Worse than that time a black widow spider had crawled up his arm in the woodshed. At least he could see the spider.

His mouth was so dry Thal had to try twice to say a little louder, "Ned, consarn you. Wake up."

Another puncher muttered and rolled over, smacking his lips.

Thal swiveled his eyes from side to side, seeking anyone else who might be awake.

The snake reached his knee.

Thal blamed himself for his predicament. He shouldn't have used the tarp, as hot as it was. But thunderheads had been rumbling noisily in the distance when he turned in, and he hadn't cared to be soaked. It never did rain, though. The storm had passed them by.

Because of the heat, Thal had left a gap for air to circulate. That was how the snake had gotten in with him.

Of all the ways for a man to meet his Maker, Thal reflected, being bit in his bed was downright dumb. He'd be the laughingstock of the hereafter.

He saw the tarp bulge slightly as the serpent inched up his thigh, and he broke out in a cold sweat.

To the east the sky had brightened and the stars were fading. Others would wake up soon. The first puncher who did, Thal would ask for help. He didn't know what anyone could do, but there had to be something.

Luck was with him, for just then Ned Leslie slowly rose onto his elbows and sleepily gazed around. Ned's hat was off, and his usually slick black hair stuck out at all angles. He yawned and gave his head a slight shake, then saw Thal staring at him. "Mornin', ugly."

"I need help," Thal whispered.

"What's that, pard?" Ned said, scratching himself. "Didn't your ma ever teach you not to mumble? You'll have to speak up."

"I need help," Thal whispered a little louder.

"You sure do," Ned said, his green eyes twinkling. "That filly over to the Mossy Horn Saloon wouldn't warm to you nohow the last time we were there. And Lordy, how you tried."

Thal smothered a few choice cusswords. Ned had been needling him about his attempt at romance for weeks now. "Snake," he whispered.

"Shake?" Ned said, and sat up. "You got cottonmouth or somethin'? I don't see how you could, seein' as how we haven't had a lick of liquor for days." He ran a hand over his hair to smooth it down. "Maybe more whiskey would have helped you with that filly. Get a gal drunk enough and she'll do just about anything."

"Snake," Thal said.

Ned didn't seem to hear him. "The problem with that is, by the time the gal is drunk, you are too. Some of those doves hold red-eye like it's water. The last time a gal and me got drunk together, I woke up in an outhouse with no idea how I got there or what happened to her. So gettin' drunk ain't no guarantee you'll get lucky."

"Ned, snake, damn you."

"What's that, Thalis?" Ned jammed his hat on. "You're actin' awful peculiar. Quit whisperin'. My ears haven't quite woke up yet, although the rest of me has."

Thal took a gamble. He said out loud, "There's a snake in my beddin', you lunkhead."

"You don't say?" Ned said calmly.

Thal could have hit him. The reptile had reached his hip and was posed along his unmentionables. He shuddered to think of the thing's fangs sinking into his private parts.

"That's what you get for bundlin' in all that canvas in the summer," Ned was saying. "Snakes like hot spots and the inside of your beddin' must be an oven."

"Ned," Thal said, "I'm unshucked."

Ned started to laugh, and caught himself. "You're buck naked?" he said, and then did laugh. "Well, ain't this a pickle?"

"It could be a rattler."

"Has it rattled yet?"

"Not that I've heard."

"That's good," Ned said. "They usually only bite when they're riled, and they usually rattle before they bite. So long as it doesn't, you should be all right."

"Ned, for the love of heaven."

"Oh, all right." Ned cast his blanket off. He had gone to sleep with his shirt and pants on. He'd taken off his boots, though, and now he commenced to pull one on.

Much too slowly, for Thal's liking. "Any chance you could hurry it up? Bein' snakebit ain't nothin' to sneeze at."

"Maybe it's not the heat," Ned said, tugging harder. "Maybe it's how you smell."

"What?"

"You and your baths," Ned said. "Always goin' on about how you like to smell clean when we go to town so the gals will fancy you more. But bein' clean didn't help with that dove, did it? And after you sat in that river water for pretty near ten minutes, scrubbin' yourself raw. I don't see why you bother. You probably gave the fish fits."

Thal couldn't believe his pard was ribbing him, yet again, about his fondness for baths. Not at a time like this. "If I get bit and die, I'm comin' back to haunt you."

"That's the spirit," Ned said, reaching for his other boot.

"I mean it. I'll come back and make you take baths just to get even."

Ned paused. "Can a ghost do that? Make somebody do somethin' they don't want to do? If so, you can keep your darn baths. Twice a year was good enough for my pa and twice a year is good enough for me. That's why wash pans were invented. Our face and our hair are all that counts. Who cares about the rest of us? No one can see how dirty we are if we have our clothes on."

Thal felt a feathery touch on his thigh. The snake's tongue, he reckoned. "Ned, honest to God."

"Don't be bringin' the Almighty into this. It's not His fault He gave you a brain and you don't use it."

The snake was on the move again. Thal felt it creep past his hip, climbing higher.

Ned stood and stomped each foot a couple of times. "There. I'm all together. Or pretty near." Bending, he scooped up his gun belt and proceeded to strap on his six-shooter. When he was done, he patted his Colt. "I'm not Jesse Lee, but I reckon I can hit a snake in a bedroll."

"Like blazes you will," Thal said. "You're liable to hit me." Neither of them was much shakes with a revolver. They only ever used their six-guns, ironically enough, for snakes and such.

"I know what made it crawl in with you," Ned said, and snapped his fingers. "It's not the heat or your smell. It's that yellow hair of yours. I bet the snake mistook it for the sun and you for a flat rock."

"You're not even a little bit funny." Thal was whispering again. The snake had reached his chest. He nearly shuddered.

"Some folks might not think so," Ned said. "But I like to start my day with a grin. It puts me in a good mood for whatever comes after."

"The snake," Thal whispered.

"Oh, Thalis," Ned said with an exaggerated sigh. "The way you harp on the little things. It's not as if you've got a bear in there. That filly doesn't know how lucky she is that she didn't let you lead her to the altar. You'd have harped her to death with all your gripin.'"

"I swear," Thal said. The snake was almost to his shoulder. Peering down in, he imagined he saw the tips of its forked tongue.

This whole time, others had been waking up and rising. A pair of them ambled over. Like Thal and Ned, they were pards. Unlike Thal and Ned, who were both in their twenties, one of the pair was past forty and the other was the youngest hand in the outfit.

Jesse Lee Hardesty was seventeen. He hailed from North Carolina, and was Southern through and through. He liked to wear a gray shirt as a kind of tribute to his pa, who had lost an arm in the War Between the States. His shirt matched his gray eyes. His bandanna was red. Another splash of color decorated his hip. Where the rest of the punchers got by with an ordinary Colt, Jesse Lee's sported ivory handles and nickel plating. He was uncommonly quick on the draw, and accurate. Around the campfire at night, he loved to hear stories about shootists. Some of the more seasoned punchers worried that if the boy wasn't careful, he'd turn into one himself.

Crawford Soames was one of those worriers. He'd been Jesse Lee's pard for going on a year. A lot of the men figured that Crawford had taken Jesse Lee under his wing to keep him out of trouble.

"What's goin' on?" Crawford now asked Ned Leslie. "Why is your pard still in bed? Is he sick?"

"Thal has come down with a case of snake," Ned said with mock gravity.

"He's done what, now?" Jesse Lee drawled.

"A snake has crawled in with him," Crawford had realized. "That happens from time to time. I remember Charley Logan, over to the Bar H. A snake crawled in with him one time and bit him when he rolled on top of it. Lucky for him it was a copperhead and not a rattler. Copperhead bites don't always kill, but he was in misery for months."

Thal was about to burst with exasperation. "Are you three goin' to stand there jawin' or are you goin' to help me?"

"Someone flip that tarp off," Jesse Lee said, placing his right hand on his ivory-handled Colt. "I bet I can shoot the sidewinder before it bites him."

"Sidewinders are desert rattlers," Ned said. "Southwest Texas is a lot of things, but it's not no desert."

"Most likely the snake's a diamondback," Crawford said. "Timber rattlers like trees and we're not near any woods."

"We have diamondbacks in North Carolina," Jesse Lee said. "Folks say they're the most dangerous there is."

"They are," Crawford said.

The snake reached Thal's shoulder. Now he definitely could see its tongue darting out and in. "I hope you all die," he said.

"We'd better do somethin'," Ned said. "I don't want to have to break in a new pard." He came over to the tarp. "I'll grab this side. Craw, you take the other. When I count to three, we'll flip it off and Jesse Lee can try and shoot the serpent before it can strike."

"Try?" Jesse Lee said.

"Hold on," Thal said, breaking out in even more sweat. "There's got to be a better way."

"What would you have us do?" Ned said. "Ask it 'pretty please' to not bite you, and come out and leave you be?"

Jesse Lee chuckled. "Wouldn't that be somethin'? A snake with manners."

"The things you come up with," Crawford said.

"Let's hear your plan," Ned said to Thal. "Do you have a trick for lurin' the reptile out?"

Thal was about to say that all he cared about was not being bitten when the snake's snout appeared at the edge of the tarp. Eyes with vertical slits peered back at him with what he took to be malignant purpose. He recollected his grandma telling him once that snakes were evil, that they were Satan's progeny on earth, as she'd put it, constant re-minders of the fact that Satan had disguised himself as a snake to cause the Fall. "It's right here," he whispered.

"Here where?" Ned said.

The rattlesnake slithered into the open.

Thal nearly cried out. It was indeed a diamondback. Over three feet long and as thick as his wrist, the snake glided by within inches of his face.

As if it had become aware of the others, the rattler sud-denly streaked toward a patch of high grass.

Just like that, Jesse Lee's Colt was in his hand. He fired once, from the hip, and the snake's head exploded. The body stopped cold, writhed spasmodically, and was still.

Shouts came from different quarters, cowhands demanding to know what was going on.

"Just a rattler!" Ned hollered, and smiling, he squatted and tapped Thal on the head. "Are you fixin' to lie abed all day? Or did you wet yourself and you need a towel?"

"What I need," Thal said, "is a new pard."